John Buchan was born in 1875 in Perth, the son of a minister. Childhood holidays were spent in the Borders, for which he had a great love. His passion for the Scottish countryside is reflected in his writing. He was educated at Glasgow University and Brasenose College, Oxford, where he was President of the Union.

Called to the Bar in 1901, he became Lord Milner's assistant private secretary in South Africa. In 1907 he was a publisher with Nelson's. In World War I he was a *Times* correspondent at the Front, an officer in the Intelligence Corps and adviser to the War Cabinet. He was elected Conservative MP in one of the Scottish Universities' seats in 1927 and was created Baron Tweedsmuir in 1935. From 1935 until his death in 1940 he was Governor General of Canada.

Buchan is most famous for his adventure stories. High in romance, these are peopled by a large cast of characters, of which Richard Hannay is his best known. Hannay appears in *The Thirty-nine Steps*. Alfred Hitchcock adapted it for the screen. A TV series featured actor Robert Powell as Richard Hannay.

TITLES BY THE SAME AUTHOR
ALL PUBLISHED BY HOUSE OF STRATUS

FICTION

THE BLANKET OF THE DARK
✓ CASTLE GAY
THE COURTS OF THE MORNING
THE DANCING FLOOR
✓ THE FREE FISHERS
THE GAP IN THE CURTAIN
✓ GREENMANTLE
GREY WEATHER
THE HALF-HEARTED
✓ HUNTINGTOWER
✓ THE ISLAND OF SHEEP
✓ JOHN BURNET OF BARNS
THE LONG TRAVERSE
A LOST LADY OF OLD YEARS
MIDWINTER
THE PATH OF THE KING
THE POWER-HOUSE
✓ PRESTER JOHN
A PRINCE OF THE CAPTIVITY
THE RUNAGATES CLUB
SALUTE TO ADVENTURERS
THE SCHOLAR GIPSIES
SICK HEART RIVER
✓ THE THIRTY-NINE STEPS
✓ THE THREE HOSTAGES
THE WATCHER BY THE THRESHOLD
WITCH WOOD

NON-FICTION

AUGUSTUS
THE CLEARING HOUSE
GORDON AT KHARTOUM
JULIUS CAESAR
THE KING'S GRACE
THE MASSACRE OF GLENCOE
✓ MONTROSE
✓ OLIVER CROMWELL
SIR WALTER RALEIGH
✓ SIR WALTER SCOTT

✓ MR. STANDFAST
✓ JOHN MACNAB

JOHN BUCHAN

THE HOUSE OF THE FOUR WINDS

HOUSE OF
STRATUS

This edition published in 2001 by House of Stratus, an imprint of Stratus Books Ltd, 21 Beeching Park, Kelly Bray, Cornwall, PL17 8QS, UK.

www.houseofstratus.com

Typeset, printed and bound by House of Stratus.

A catalogue record for this book is available from the British Library and the Library of Congress.

ISBN 1-84232-772-0

CONTENTS

THE HOUSE OF THE
FOUR WINDS

Casa dei Quattro Venti,
fumida prua del Vascello protesa
nella tempesta.

D'ANNUNZIO

NOTE

The earlier doings of some of the personages in this tale will be found recorded in *Huntingtower* and *Castle Gay*.

J B

PROLOGUE

Great events, says the philosophic historian, spring only from great causes, though the immediate occasion may be small; but I think his law must have exceptions. Of the not inconsiderable events which I am about to chronicle, the occasion was trivial, and I find it hard to detect the majestic agency behind them. What world force, for example, ordained that Mr Dickson McCunn should slip into the Tod's Hole in his little salmon-river on a bleak night in April; and, without changing his clothes, should thereafter make a tour of inspection of his young lambs? His action was the proximate cause of this tale, but I can see no profounder explanation of it than the inherent perversity of man.

The performance had immediate consequences for Mr McCunn. He awoke next morning with a stiff neck, an aching left shoulder, and a pain in the small of his back – he who never in his life before had had a touch of rheumatism. A vigorous rubbing with embrocation failed to relieve him, and, since he was accustomed to robust health, he found it intolerable to hobble about with a thing like a toothache in several parts of his body. Dr Murdoch was sent for from Auchenlochan, and for a fortnight Mr McCunn had to endure mustard plasters and mustard baths, to swallow various medicines, and to submit to a rigorous diet. The pains declined, but he found himself to his disgust in a low state of general health, easily tired, liable to sudden cramps, and with a poor appetite for his meals. After three weeks of this condition he lost his temper. Summer was beginning, and he reflected that, being now sixty-three years of age, he had only a limited number of summers left to him. His gorge rose at the thought of dragging his wing through the coming delectable months – long-lighted June, the hot July noons with the corncrakes busy in the hay, the days on August hills, red with heather and musical with bees. He curbed his distaste for medical science, and departed to Edinburgh to consult a specialist.

That specialist gave him a purifying time. He tested his blood and his blood pressure, kneaded every part of his frame, and for the better part of a week kept him under observation. At the end he professed himself clear in the general but perplexed in the particular.

'You've never been ill in your life?' he said. 'Well, that is just your trouble. You're an uncommonly strong man – heart, lungs, circulation, digestion, all in first-class order. But it stands to reason that you must have secreted poisons in your body, and you have never got them out. The best prescription for a fit old age is a bad illness in middle life, or, better still, a major operation. It drains off some of the middle-age humours. Well, you haven't had that luck, so you've been a powder magazine with some nasty explosives waiting for the spark. Your tomfool escapade in the Stinchar provided the spark, and here you are – a healthy man mysteriously gone sick. You've got to be pretty careful, Mr McCunn. It depends on how you behave in the next few months whether you will be able to fish for salmon on your eightieth birthday, or be doddering round with two sticks and a shawl on your seventieth.'

Mr McCunn was scared, penitent and utterly docile. He professed himself ready for the extremest measures, including the drawing of every tooth in his head.

The specialist smiled. 'I don't recommend anything so drastic. What you want first of all is an exact diagnosis. I can assess your general condition, but I can't put my finger on the precise mischief. That needs a technique which we haven't developed sufficiently in this country. Next, you must have treatment, but treatment is a comparatively simple affair if you first get the right diagnosis. So I am going to send you to Germany.'

Mr McCunn wailed. Banishment from his beloved Blaweary was a bitter pill.

'Yes, to Germany. To quite a pretty place called Rosensee, in Saxon Switzerland. There's a *Kurhaus* there run by a man called Christoph. You never heard his name, of course – few people have – but he is a therapeutic genius of the first order. You can take my word for that. I've known him again and again pull people out of their graves. His main subject is nerves, but he is good for everything that is difficult and mysterious, for in my opinion he is the greatest diagnoser in the world... By the way, you live in Carrick? Well, I sent one of your neighbours to Rosensee last year – Sir Archibald Roylance – he was having trouble with a damaged leg – and now he walks nearly as well as you and me. It seems there was a misplaced sinew which everybody else had overlooked... Dr Christoph will see you three times a day, stare at you like an owl, ask you a thousand questions and make no comment for at least a fortnight. Then he will deliver judgment, and you may take it that it will be right. After that the treatment is a simple matter. In a week or two you will be got up in green shorts and a Tyrolese hat and an alpenstock and a rope round your middle, climbing the little rocks of those parts... Yes, I think I can promise you that you'll be fit and ready for the autumn salmon.'

Mr McCunn, trained to know a competent man when he saw him, accepted the consultant's prescription, and rooms were taken for him at the Rosensee *Kurhaus*. His wife did not accompany him for three reasons: first, she had a profound distaste for foreign countries and regarded Germany as still a hostile State; second, she could not believe that rheumatism, which was an hereditary ailment in her own family, need be taken seriously, so she felt no real anxiety about his health; third, he forbade her. She proposed to stay at Blaweary till the end of

June, and then to await her husband's return at a Rothesay hydropathic. So early in the month Mr McCunn a little disconsolately left these shores. He took with him as body-servant and companion one Peter Wappit, who at Blaweary was gamekeeper, forester and general handyman. Peter, having fought in France with the Scots Fusiliers, and having been two years a prisoner in Germany, was believed by his master to be an adept at foreign tongues.

Nor was there any profound reason in the nature of things why Lord Rhynns, a well-preserved gentleman of sixty-seven, should have tumbled into a ditch that spring at Vallescure and broken his left leg. He was an active man and a careful, but his mind had been busy with the Newmarket entries, so that he missed a step, rolled some yards down a steep slope of rock and bracken, and came to rest with a leg doubled unpleasantly under him. The limb was well set, but neuritis followed, with disastrous consequences to the Rhynns' *ménage*. For his wife, whose profession was a gentle invalidism, found herself compelled to see to household affairs, and as a result was on the verge of a nervous breakdown. The family moved from watering place to watering place, seeking a cure for his lordship's affliction, till at the mountain village of Unnutz Lady Rhynns could bear it no longer. A telegram was despatched to their only child requiring her instant attendance upon distressed parents.

This was a serious blow to Miss Alison Westwater, who had been making very different plans for the summer. She was then in London, living with her Aunt Harriet, who two years before had espoused Mr Thomas Carlyle Craw, the newspaper magnate. It was the Craws' purpose to go north after Ascot to the Westwater house, Castle Gay, in the Canonry, of which Mr Craw had a long lease, and Alison, for whom a very little of London sufficed, had exulted in the prospect. Now she saw before her some dismal weeks – or months – in an alien land, in the company of a valetudinarian mother and a presumably irascible

father. Her dreams of Scotland, to which she was passionately
attached, of salmon in the Callowa and trout in the hill lochs and
bright days among the heather, had to be replaced by a dreary
vista of baking foreign roads, garish foreign hotels, tarnished
pine woods, tidy clothes and all the things which her soul
abominated.

There was perhaps more of a cosmic motive in the
determination that summer of the doings of Mr Dougal
Crombie and Sir Archibald Roylance, for in their cases we touch
the fringe of high politics. Dougal was now a force, almost the
force, in the Craw Press. The general manager, Mr Archibald
Bamff, was growing old, he had taken to himself a wife, and his
fancy toyed pleasantly with retirement to some country
hermitage. So in the past year Dougal had been gradually taking
over his work, and, since he had the complete confidence of Mr
Craw, and the esteem of Mr Craw's masterful wife, he found
himself in his early twenties charged with much weighty and
troublesome business. He was a power behind the throne, and
the more potent because few suspected his presence. Only one or
two people – a Cabinet minister, an occasional financial magnate,
a few highly placed Government officials – realised the authority
that was wielded by this sombre and downright young man.
Early in June he set out on an extensive Continental trip, the
avowed purpose of which was to look into certain papermaking
concerns which Mr Craw had acquired after the war. But his
main object was not disclosed, for it was deeply secret. Mr Craw
had long interested himself in the republic of Evallonia, his
sympathies being with those who sought to restore the ancient
monarchy. Now it appeared that the affairs of that country were
approaching a crisis, and it was Dougal's mission to spy out the
land.

As for Sir Archibald Roylance, he had been saddled with an
honourable but distasteful duty. He had been the better part of
two years in the House of Commons, and had already made a
modest mark. He spoke infrequently and always on matters

which he knew something about – the air, agriculture, foreign affairs – and his concise and well-informed speeches were welcomed amid the common verbiage of debate. He had become parliamentary private secretary to the Under-Secretary for Foreign Affairs, who had been at school with him. That summer the usual Disarmament Conference was dragging its slow length along; it became necessary for Mr Despenser, the Under-Secretary, to go to Geneva, and Sir Archie was ordered to accompany him. He received the mandate with little pleasure. The session that summer would end early, and he wanted to get to Crask, for he had been defrauded of his Easter holiday in the Highlands. Geneva he believed might last for months and he detested the place, which, as Lord Lamancha had once said, was full of the ghosts of mouldy old jurisconsults, and the living presence of cosmopolitan bores. But his spirits had improved when he discovered that he might take Janet with him.

'We'll find a chance of slipping away,' he told his wife. 'One merit of these beastly conferences is that they are always adjourning. We'll hop it into eastern Europe or some other fruity place. Hang it all, now that I've got the use of both legs, I don't see why we shouldn't climb a mountain or two. Dick Hannay's yarns have made me rather keen to try that game.'

Certain of these transmigrations played havoc with the plans of Mr John Galt, of St Mark's College, Cambridge, who, having just attained a second class in his tripos and having so concluded his university career, felt himself entitled to an adequate holiday. He had intended to make his headquarters at Blaweary, which was the only home he had ever known, and thence to invade the Canonry, fishing its lochs and sleeping in its heather. But Blaweary would presently be shut up in Mr McCunn's absence, and if Alison Westwater was not at Castle Gay, the Canonry lost all its charm. Still, he must have some air and exercise. The summer term had been busy and stuffy, and to a Rugby player there were few attractions in punts among lilied backwaters. He would probably have to go alone to the Canonry, but his fancy had begun to toy with another scheme – a walking tour in south-eastern France or among the Jura foothills, where new sights and smells and sounds would relieve his loneliness. It was characteristic of him that he never thought of finding a male companion; for the last two years Alison had been for him the only companion in the world.

On the 13th of June he was still undecided, but that night his thoughts were narrowed to a happy orbit. For Alison was dining with him before her journey abroad, and together they were going on to a party which the Lamanchas were giving to the delegates to an international conference then in session in London. For one evening at least the world was about to give him all he desired.

It was a warm night, but the great room at Maurice's was cool with fans and sunblinds, though every table was occupied. From their corner, at the foot of the shallow staircase which is the main entrance, they had an excellent view of the company. There seemed to be a great many uniforms about, and a dazzling array of orders, no doubt in view of the Lamancha function. It was easy to talk, for at Maurice's there is no band till supper time.

'You shouldn't have brought me here, Jaikie,' said Alison. 'It's too extravagant. And you're giving me far too good a dinner.'

'It's a celebration,' was the answer. 'I've done with Cambridge.'

'Are you sorry?'

'No. I liked it, for I like most things, but I don't want to linger over them.'

The girl laughed merrily, and a smile slowly crept into Jaikie's face.

'You're quite right,' he said. 'That was a priggish thing to say, but it's true, all the same.'

'I know. I never met anyone who wasted so little time in regrets. I wish I were like you, for I want anything I like to go on for ever. Cambridge must have slipped off you like water off a duck's back. What did you get out of it?'

'Peace to grow up. I've very nearly grown up now. I have discovered most of the things I can do and the things I can't. I know the things I like and the things I don't.'

Alison knitted her brows. 'That's not much good. So do I. The thing to find out is, what you can do best and what you like most. You told me a year ago that that was what you were after. Have you decided?'

'No,' was the glum answer. 'I think I have collected the material, so to speak, but I haven't sorted it out. I was looking to you to help me this summer in the Canonry, and now you're bolting to Italy or somewhere.'

'Not Italy, my dear. A spot called Unnutz in the Tirol. You're not very good at geography.'

'Mayn't I come too?'

'No, you mayn't. You'd simply loathe it. A landscape like a picture postcard. Tennis and bumble-puppy golf and promenades, all in smart clothes. Infinite boring evenings when I have to play picquet with Papa or talk hotel French to Mamma's friends. Besides, my family wouldn't understand you. You haven't been properly presented to them, and Unnutz is not the place for that. You wouldn't be at your best there.'

Two people passed on the way to their table, a tall young man with a lean ruddy face, and a pretty young woman, whose hair was nearly as bright a thing as Alison's. The young woman stopped.

'My dear Allie,' she cried, 'I haven't seen you for ages. Archie, it's Cousin Allie. They tell me you're being dragged abroad, the same as us. What's your penitentiary? Ours is Geneva.'

'Mine's a place in the Tirol. Any chance of our meeting?'

'There might be. Archie has a notion of dashing about, for apparently an international conference is mostly adjournments. He's so spry on his legs since Dr Christoph took him in hand that he rather fancies himself as a mountaineer. What's your address?'

The lady scribbled it down in a notebook which she took from her bag, nodded gaily, and followed her husband and a waiter to their own table. Alison looked after them.

'That's the nicest couple on earth. She was Janet Raden, a sort of cousin of mine. Her husband, Archie Roylance...'

Jaikie interrupted.

'Great Scot! Is that Sir Archibald Roylance? I once knew him pretty well – for one day. I've told you about the Gorbals Diehards and Huntingtower. He was the ally we enlisted – lived at a place called the Mains of Garple. Ask Mr McCunn about him. I've often wondered when I should see him again, for I felt pretty certain I would – some day. He hasn't changed much.'

'He can't change. Sir Archie is the most imperishable thing God ever created. He'll be a wild boy till he's ninety. Even with Janet to steady him I consider him dangerous, especially now that he has no longer a game leg... Hullo, Jaikie. We're digging into the past tonight. Look who's over there.'

She nodded towards a very brilliant table where some twenty people were dining, most of them in uniform. Among them was a fair young man in ordinary evening dress, without any decorations. He suddenly turned his face, recognised Alison, and, with a word of apology to the others, left his seat and came towards her. When she rose and curtsied, Jaikie had a sudden recollection.

'It is Miss Westwater, is it not?' said the young man, bowing over her hand. 'My adorable preserver! I have not forgotten Prince Charlie and the Solway sands.'

He turned to Jaikie.

'And the Moltke of the campaign, too! What is the name? Wait a minute. I have it – Jaikie. What fun to see you again! Are you two by any happy chance espoused?'

'Not yet,' said Alison. 'What are you doing in England, sir?'

'Holidaying. I cannot think why all the world does not holiday in England. It is the only really peaceful and pleasant place.'

'How true, sir! I have to go abroad tomorrow, and I feel like an exile.'

'Then why do you go?'

'I am summoned by neglected parents. To Unnutz, in the Tirol.'

The young man's pleasant face grew suddenly grave.

'Unnutz. Above the Waldersee, in the Firnthal?'

'The same. Do you know it, sir?'

'I know it. I do not think it is a very good place for a holiday – not this summer. But if it becomes unpleasant you can return home, for you English are always free to travel. But I should be careful in Unnutz, my dear Miss Westwater, and I should take Mr Jaikie with you as a protector.'

He shook hands and departed smiling, but he left on the two the impression of an unexpected solemnity.

'What do you suppose is worrying Prince John?' Alison asked. 'The affairs of Evallonia. You remember at Castle Gay we thought the Republic would blow up any moment and that a month or two would see Prince John on the throne. That's two years ago and nothing has happened. Dougal is out there now looking into the situation. He may ginger them up.'

'What makes him so solemn about Unnutz? By all accounts it's the ordinary gimcrack little foreign watering place. He talked of it as if it were a sort of Chicago slum.'

'He is a wise man, for he said you should take me with you.'

They had reached the stage of coffee and cigarettes, and were now more free to watch their neighbours. It was a decorous assembly, in accordance with the tradition of Maurice's, and the only gaiety seemed to be among the womenkind of Prince John's party. The Prince's own face was very clear in the light of an overhanging lamp, and both Alison and Jaikie found themselves watching it – its slight heaviness in repose, its quick vivacity when interested, the smile which drew half its charm from a most attractive wrinkling around the eyes.

'It is the face of a prince,' said Alison, 'but not of a king – at any rate, not the kind of king that wins a throne. There's no dynamite in it.'

'What sort of face do you give makers of revolutions?' Jaikie asked.

The girl swung round and regarded him steadily.

'Your sort,' she said. 'You look so meek and good that everybody loves you. And wise, wise like an old terrier. And yet, in the two years I have known you, you have filled up your time with the craziest things. First' – she counted on her fingers – 'you went off to Baffin Island to trade old rifles for walrus ivory.'

Jaikie grinned. 'I made seventy-three pounds clear: I call that a success.'

'Then you walked from Cambridge to Oxford within a day and a night.'

'That was a failure. I was lame for a fortnight and couldn't play in the Welsh match.'

'You went twice as a deckhand on a Grimsby trawler – first to Bear Island and then to the Whales' Back. I don't know where these places are, but they sound beastly.'

'They were. I was sick most of the time.'

'Last and worst, it was only your exams and my prayers that kept you from trying to circumnavigate Britain in a sailing canoe, when you would certainly have been drowned. What do you mean by it, Jaikie? It looks as if you were as neurotic as a Bloomsbury intellectual, though in a different way. Why this restlessness?'

'I wasn't restless. I did it all quite calmly, on purpose.' Into Jaikie's small face there had come an innocent seriousness.

'You see,' he went on, 'when I was a small boy I was rather a hardy citizen. I've told you about that. Then Mr McCunn civilised me, which I badly needed. But I didn't want it to soften me. We are living in a roughish world today, and it is going to get rougher, and I don't want to think that there is any experience to which I can't face up. I've been trying to keep myself tough. You see what I mean, Alison?'

'I see. It's rather like painting the lily, you know. I wish I were going to the Canonry, for there's a lot of things I want to have out with you. Promise to keep quiet till I come back.'

The Lamanchas' party was so large and crowded that Alison and Jaikie found it easy to compass solitude. Once out of the current that sucked through the drawing-rooms towards the supper-room there were quiet nooks to be discovered in the big house. One such they found in an alcove, where the upper staircase ascended from the first floor, and where, at a safe distance, they could watch the procession of guests. Alison pointed out various celebrities to the interested Jaikie, and a number of relations with whom she had no desire to have closer contact. But on one of the latter she condescended to details. He was a very tall man, whose clothes, even in that well-dressed assembly, were conspicuous for their elegance. He had a neatly trimmed blond beard, and hair worn a little longer than the fashion and as wavy as a smart woman's coiffure. They only saw his profile as he ascended the stairs, and his back as he disappeared into the main drawing-room.

'There's another cousin of mine,' said the girl, 'the queerest in all our clan. His name is Randal Glynde, and he has been everything in his time from cowpuncher to film star, not to mention diplomat, and various sorts of soldier, and somebody's private secretary. The family doesn't approve of him, for they never know what he'll do next, but he was very nice to me when I was a little girl, and I used to have a tremendous *culte* for him.'

Jaikie was not listening, for he felt very depressed. This was his last hour with Alison for months, and the light had suddenly gone out of his landscape. He had never been lonely in his life before he met her, having at the worst found good company in himself; but now he longed for a companion, and out of the many millions of the world's inhabitants there was only one that he wanted.

'I can't go to Scotland,' he said. 'Blaweary is impossible, and if I went into the Canonry with you not there I'd howl.'

'Poor Jaikie!' Alison laid a hand upon his. 'But it's only another bit of the toughening you're so fond of. I promise to write to you a great deal, and it won't be long till the autumn. You won't be half as lonely as I.'

'I wish I thought that,' said Jaikie, brightening a little. 'I like being alone, but I don't like being lonely. I think I'll go abroad too.'

'Why don't you join Mr McCunn?'

'He won't let me. He's doing a cure and is forbidden company.'

'Or Dougal?'

'He wouldn't have me either. He thinks he's on some silly kind of secret service, and he's as mysterious about it as a sick owl. But I might go for a tramp somewhere. My finances will just run to it.'

'Hullo, here's Ran,' said Alison. The tall man with the fair beard had drifted towards them, and was now looking down on the girl. On a closer view he appeared to be nearer forty than thirty. Jaikie noticed that he had Alison's piercing blue eyes, with the same dancing light in them. There and then, being accustomed to rapid judgments, he felt well disposed towards the tall stranger.

'Alison dear.' Mr Glynde put his hand on the girl's head. 'I hear that your father has at last achieved gout.'

'No. It's neuritis, which makes him much angrier. He would accept gout as a family legacy, but he dislikes unexpected visitations. I go out to him tomorrow.'

'Unnutz, isn't it? A dreary little place. I fear you won't enjoy it, my dear.'

'Where have you come from, Ran? We last heard of you in Russia.'

'I have been in many places since Russia.' Mr Glynde's voice had an odd quality in it, as if he were gently communing with himself. 'After a time in deep water I come up to breathe, and then go down again.'

'You've chosen very smart clothes to breathe in.'

'I always try to suit my clothes to my company. It is the only way to be inconspicuous.'

'Have you been writing any more poetry?'

'Not a word in English, but I have written some rather charming things in mediaeval Latin. I'll send you them. It is the best tongue for a vagabond.'

Alison introduced Jaikie.

'Here's another of your totem, Cousin Ran. You can't corrupt him, for he is quite as mad as you.'

Mr Glynde smiled pleasantly as he shook hands, and Jaikie had an impression that his eyes were the most intelligent that he had ever seen, eyes which took in everything, and saw very deep, and had a mind behind them that did not forget. He felt too that something in his own face pleased the other, for there was friendliness behind the inquisition.

'He has just finished Cambridge, and finds himself at a loose end. He is hesitating between Scotland and a tramp on the Continent. What do you advise?'

'When you are young these decisions may be fateful things. I have always trusted to the spin of a coin. I carry with me a Greek stater which has made most of my decisions for me. What about tossing for it?'

He took from the pocket of his white waistcoat a small gold coin and handed it to Jaikie.

'It's a lucky coin,' he said. 'At least it has brought me infinite amusement. Try it.'

Jaikie had a sudden queer feeling that the occasion had become rather solemn, almost sacramental. 'Heads Scotland, tails abroad,' he said and tossed. It fell tails.

'Behold,' said Mr Glynde, 'your mind is made up for you. You will wander along in the white dust and drink country wine and doze in the woods, knowing that the unseen Powers are with you. Where, by the way, did you think of going? You have no preference? You have been very little abroad? How fortunate to have all Europe spread out for your choice. But I should not go too far east, Mr Galt. Keep to the comfortable west if you want peace. If you go too far east this summer, you may find that the spin of my little stater has been rather too fateful.'

As Jaikie put Alison into a taxi, he observed Mr Glynde leaving the house on foot with a companion. He had a glimpse of that companion's face, and saw that it was Prince John of Evallonia.

CHAPTER 1

The Man with the Elephant

The inn at Kremisch, the Stag with the Two Heads, has an upper room so bowed with age that it leans drunkenly over the village street. It is a bare place, which must be chilly in winter, for the old casement has many chinks in it, and the china stove does not look efficient, and the rough beechen table, marked by many beer mugs, and the seats of beechwood and hide are scarcely luxurious. But on this summer night to one who had been tramping all day on roads deep in white dust under a merciless sun it seemed a haven of ease. Jaikie had eaten an admirable supper on a corner of the table, a supper of cold ham, an omelet, hot toasted rye-cakes and a seductive cheese. He had drunk wine tapped from a barrel and cold as water from a mountain spring, and had concluded with coffee and cream in a blue cup as large as a basin. Now he could light his pipe and watch the green dusk deepen behind the onion spire of the village church.

The milestones in his journey had been the wines. Jaikie was no connoisseur, and indeed as a rule preferred beer, but the vintage of a place seemed to give him the place's flavour and wines made a diary of his pilgrimage. His legs bore him from valley to valley, but he drank himself from atmosphere to atmosphere. He had begun among strong burgundies which needed water to make a thirst-quenching drink, and continued through the thin wines of the hills to the coarse red stuff of south

1

Germany and a dozen forgotten little local products. In one upland place he had found a drink like the grey wine of Anjou, in another a sweet thing like Madeira, and in another a fiery sherry. Each night at the end of his tramp he concocted a long drink, and he stuck manfully to the juice of the grape; so, having a delicate palate and a good memory, he had now behind him a map of his track picked out in honest liquors.

Each was associated with some vision of sun-drenched landscape. He had been a month on the tramp, but he seemed to have walked through continents. As he half dozed at the open window, it was pleasant to let his fancy run back along the road. It had led him through vineyards grey at the fringes with dust, through baking beet-fields and drowsy cornlands and solemn forests; up into wooded hills and flowery meadows, and once or twice almost into the jaws of the great mountains; through every kind of human settlement, from hamlets which were only larger farms to brisk burghs clustered round opulent town houses or castles as old as Charlemagne; by every kind of stream – unfordable great rivers, and milky mountain torrents, and reedy lowland waters, and clear brooks slipping through mint and watercress. He had walked and walked, seeking to travel and not to arrive, and making no plans except that his face was always to the sunrise. He was very dimly aware at any moment of his whereabouts, for his sole map was a sketchy thing out of a Continental Bradshaw.

But he had walked himself into contentment. At the start he had been restless and lonely. He wished that he could have brought Woolworth, now languishing at Blaweary, but he could not condemn that long-suffering terrier to months of quarantine. He wrote disconsolate letters to Alison in his vile handwriting, and received from her at various *postes-restantes* replies which revealed the dullness of her own life at Unnutz. She had nothing to write about, and it was never her habit to spoil good paper with trivial reflections. There was a time at the start when Jaikie's mind had been filled with exasperating little cares, so that he turned a blank face to the world he was traversing. His future – what was he to do now that he was done with Cambridge? Alison – his need of her grew more desperate every day, but what could he offer her worthy of her acceptance? Only his small dingy self, he concluded, with nothing to his credit except a second-class degree, some repute at Rugby football, and the slenderest of bank balances. It seemed the most preposterous affair of a moth and a star.

But youth and the sun and wide spaces played their old healing part. He began to rise whistling from his bed in a pinewood or in a cheap country inn, with a sense that the earth was very spacious and curious. The strong aromatic sunlight drugged him into cheerfulness. The humours of the road were spread before him. He had learned to talk French fairly well, but his German was scanty; nevertheless, he had the British soldier's gift of establishing friendship on a meagre linguistic basis, and he slipped inside the life of sundry little communities. His passion for new landscapes made every day's march a romance, and, having a love of the human comedy, he found each night's lodging an entertainment. He understood that he was looking at things in a new perspective. What had seemed a dull track between high walls was now expanding into open country.

Especially he thought happily about Alison. He did not think of her as a bored young woman with peevish parents in a dull health resort, but as he knew her in the Canonry, an audacious ally in any venture, staunch as the hills, kind as a west wind. So far as she was concerned, prudential thoughts about the future were an insult. She was there waiting for him as soon as he could climb to her high level. He encountered no delicacy of scene or weather but he longed to have her beside him to enjoy it. He treasured up scraps of wayside humour for her amusement, and even some shy meditations which some day he would confide to her. They did not go into his letters, which became daily scrappier – but these letters now concluded with what for Jaikie were almost the messages of a lover.

He was in a calmer mood, too, about himself. Had he been more worldly-wise he might have reflected that some day he must be a rich man. Dickson McCunn had no chick nor child nor near relation, and he and Dougal were virtually his adopted sons. Dougal was already on the road to wealth and fame, and Dickson would see that Jaikie was well provided for. But characteristically he never thought of that probability. He had his own way to make with no man's aid, and he was only waiting to discover the proper starting point. But a pleasing lethargy possessed him. This delectable summer world was not the place for making plans. So far he was content with what he had done. Dickson had drawn him out of the depths into the normal light of day, and it had been his business to accustom his eyes to it. He was aware that, without Cambridge, he would have always been a little shy and suspicious of the life of a class into which he had not been born; now he knew it for what it was worth, and could look at it without prejudice but also without glamour. 'Brother to a beggar, and fellow to a king' – what was Dougal's phrase? Jaikie was no theorist, but he had a working philosophy, with the notion at the back of his head that human nature was much the same everywhere, and that one might dig out of the unlikeliest places surprising virtues. He considered that he had been lucky enough to have the right kind of education for the practice of this creed.

But it was no philosopher who sat with his knees hunched on the window seat, but a drowsy and rather excited boy. His travels had given him more than content, for in these last days a faint but delicious excitement had been creeping into his mind. He was not very certain of his exact whereabouts on the map, but he knew that he had crossed the border of the humdrum world and was in a land of enchantments. There was nothing in the ritual of his days to justify this; his legs like compasses were measuring out the same number of miles; the environment was the same, the slow kindly peasants, the wheel of country life, the same bright mornings and cool evenings, the same plain meals voraciously eaten, and hard beds in which he fell instantly asleep. He could speak little of the language, and he did not know one soul within a hundred miles. He was the humblest of pilgrims, and the lowness of his funds would presently compel his return. Nevertheless, he was ridiculously expectant. He laughed at himself, but he could not banish the mood. He was awaiting something – or something was awaiting him.

The apple-green twilight deepened into emerald, and then into a velvet darkness, for the moon would rise late, and a haze obscured the stars. Long ago the last child had been hunted from the street into bed. Long ago the last villagers had left the seat under the vine trellis where they had been having their evening sederunt. Long ago the oxen had been brought into the byres and the goats driven in from the hillside. A wood-wagon had broken down by the bridge, and the blacksmith had been hammering at its axle, but his job was finished, and a spark of a lamp beaconed the derelict cart. Otherwise there was no light in earth or heaven, and no sound except the faraway drone of a waterfall in the high woods and an occasional stirring of beasts in byre or stable. Kremisch was in the deep sleep of those who labour hard, bed early, and rise with the dawn. Jaikie grew drowsy. He shook out his pipe, drew a long breath of the cool night air, and rose to take the lamp from the table and ascend to his bedroom.

Suddenly a voice spoke. It came from the outer air at about the level of the window, And it asked in German for a match.

Balaam was not more startled by the sudden loquacity of his ass than was Jaikie by this aerial summons. It shook him out of his sleepiness and made him nearly drop the lamp. 'God bless my soul,' he said – his chief ejaculation, which he had acquired from Mr McCunn.

'He will,' said the voice, 'if you'll give me a light for my cigarette.'

The spirit apparently spoke English, and Jaikie, reassured, held the lamp to the darkness of the open casement. There was a face there, suspended in the air, a face with cheeks the colour of a dry beech leaf and a ragged yellow beard. It was a friendly face, and in the mouth was an unlit cigarette.

'What are you standing on?' Jaikie asked, for it occurred to him that this must be a man on stilts. He had heard of these as a custom in malarial foreign places.

'To be accurate, I am sitting,' was the answer. 'Sitting on an elephant, if you must know. An agreeable female whom I call Aurunculeia. Out of Catullus, you remember. Almost his best poem.'

Jaikie lit a match, but the speaker waved it aside. 'I think, if you don't mind,' he said, 'I'll come in and join you for a minute. One doesn't often meet an Englishman in these parts, and Aurunculeia has no vulgar passion for haste. As you have no doubt guessed, she and I are part of a circus – an integral and vital part – what you might call the *primum mobile*. But we were detained by a little accident. I was asleep, and we strayed from the road and did havoc in a field of marrows, which made some unpleasantness. So our lovely companions have faded and gone ahead to savour the fleshpots of Tarta, while we follow at our leisure. You have never ridden on an elephant? If you go slow enough, believe me it is the very poetry of motion, for you are part, as it were, of a cosmic process. How does it go? "Moved round in earth's diurnal course, With rocks and stones and trees."'

A word was spoken in a lower tone, there was the sound of the shuffling of heavy feet, and a man stepped lightly on to the window-sill and through the casement. His first act was to turn up the wick of the lamp on the table, and light his cigarette at its funnel.

Jaikie found himself gazing at a figure which might have been the Pied Piper. It was very tall and very ragged. It wore an old tunic of horizon-blue from which most of the buttons had gone, a scarlet cummerbund, and flapping cotton trousers which had once been white. It had no hat, and besides its clothes, its only other belonging was a long silver-mounted porcupine quill, which may have been used for the encouragement of Aurunculeia.

The scarecrow looked at Jaikie and saw something there which amused him, for he set his arms akimbo and laughed heartily. 'How nature creeps up to art!' he cried. 'Had this been an episode in a novel, it would have been condemned for its manifest improbability. There was an impish propulsive power about my little gold stater.'

He took a small coin from his pocket and regarded it affectionately. Then he asked a question which brought Jaikie out of his chair. 'Have you any news of Cousin Alison, Mr Galt?'

Slowly, to Jaikie's startled sight, the features of the scarecrow became the lineaments of the exquisite Mr Randal Glynde. The neat hair was now shaggy and very dusty, the beard was untrimmed, and every semblance of respectability had gone from his garments. But the long lean wrists were the same, the long slim fingers, and the penetrating blue eyes.

Mr Glynde replaced the stater in some corner of his person, and beamed upon Jaikie. He stretched an arm and grasped the jug of wine of which Jaikie had drunk about half, took a long pull at it, and set it down with a wry face.

'Vinegar,' he said. 'I had forgotten that the Flosgebirge wine sours in an hour. Do not trouble yourself, Mr Galt, for I have long ago supped. We were talking about Cousin Alison, for whom I understand you have a kindness. So have I. So gracious is my memory of her that I have been reciting verses in her honour in the only tongue in which a goddess should be hymned.

Alison, bella puella candida,
Quae bene superas lac et lilium
Album, quae simul rosam rubidam
Aut expolitum ebur Indicum,

Pande, puella, pande capillulos
Flavos, lucentes ut aurum nitidum

What puzzles me is whether that is partly my own or wholly John the Silentiar's. I had been reading John the Silentiar, but the book was stolen from me, so I cannot verify… No, I will not sleep here. I must sleep at Tarta, though it will be broad daylight before I shut my eyes. Tatius, my manager, is a worthy man, but he is to Meleager my clown as acid to a raw wound, and without me to calm them they will be presently rubbing each other's noses in the mud.'

'Are you a circus proprietor?' Jaikie asked.

Mr Glynde nodded pleasantly.

'In me you see the sole proprietor of the epochal, the encyclopaedic, the grandiose Cirque Doré of Aristide Lebrun. The epithets are not mine, but those of the late Aristide, who these three years has been reposing in full evening dress in the cemetery of Montléry. I purchased the thing from his widow, stock-in-trade, goodwill and all – even the gentle Aurunculeia. I have travelled with it from the Pyrenees to the Carpathians and from the Harz to the Apennines. Some day, who knows, I will widen these limits and go from the Sierra-Nevada to the Urals, and from the Jotunheim to Parnassus. Geography has always intoxicated me.'

'I understand the fun of travelling,' said Jaikie, 'but isn't a circus rather heavy baggage to lug after you?'

'Ah, no. You do not realise the power of him who carries with him a little world of merriment, which can be linked to that substratum of merriment which is found in every human species. No fumbling for him – he finds the common touch at once. He must suit himself of course to various tastes. Clowning in one place, horse-tricks in a second, the sweet Aurunculeia in a third. The hills have different fancies from the valleys, and the valleys from the plains. The Cirque Doré is small, but I flatter myself it is select. We have as fine white barbs as ever came out of Africa, and Meleager my clown has the common denominator of comedy at which all Europe can laugh. No women. Too temperamental and troublesome. My people quarrel in every known tongue, but, being males, it is summer lightning... Ah, Mr Galt, I cannot explain to you the intoxication of shifting camp weekly, not from town to town, but from one little human cosmos to another. I have the key which unlocks all doors, and can steal into the world at the back of men's minds, about which they do not speak to their politicians and scarcely even to their priests.

'I have power, too,' Mr Glynde went on; 'for I appeal to something old and deep in man's nature. Before this I have wrecked a promising insurrection through the superior charm of my circus over an *émeute* in a market-place. I have protected mayors and burgomasters from broken heads, and maybe from cut throats, by my mild distractions. And I have learned many things that are hidden from diplomats and eager journalists. I, the entertainer, the *fils de joie*, I am becoming an expert, if I may say so modestly, on the public opinion of Europe – or rather on that incoherent soul which is greater than opinion.'

'Well, and what do you make of it?' Jaikie asked. He was fascinated by his visitor, the more so as he was a link with Alison, but sleep was descending upon him like an armed man, and he asked the conventional question without any great desire to hear the answer.

'Bad,' said Mr Glynde. 'Or, since a moral judgment is unnecessary, shall I say odd? We are now in the midst of the retarded liquidation of the war. I do not mean debts and currencies and economic fabrics, but something much more vital – the thoughts of men. The democracies have lost confidence. So long as they believed in themselves they could make shift with constitutions and parliaments and dull republics. But once let them lose confidence, and they are like children in the dark, reaching out for the grasp of a strong hand. That way lies the dictator. It might be the monarch if we bred the right kind of king... Also there is something more dangerous still, a stirring of youth, disappointed, aggrieved youth, which has never known the discipline of war. Imaginative and incalculable youth, which clamours for the moon and may not be content till it has damaged most of the street lamps.

'But you nod,' said Mr Glynde rising. 'I weary you. You must to bed and I to Tarta. I must not presume upon the celestial patience of Aurunculeia.'

Jaikie rose too and found the tall man's hand on his shoulder. He observed sleepily that his visitor's face, now clear in the lamplight, had changed, the smile had gone from it, and the eyes were cool and rather grave. Also the slight artifice of his speech, which recalled an affected Cambridge don of his acquaintance, was suddenly dropped.

'I gave you certain advice,' said Mr Glynde, 'when you spun my stater in London. I told you that if you wanted peace you should stick to the west. You are pretty far east, Mr Galt, so I assume that a quiet life is not your first object. You have been walking blindly and happily for weeks waiting for what the days brought forth. Have you any very clear notion where you have got to?'

'I'm rather vague, for I have a rotten map. But I know that I've come to the end of my money. Tomorrow I must turn about and make for home. I mean to get to Munich and travel back by the cheapest way.'

'Three and a quarter miles from Kremisch the road to Tarta drops into a defile among pine trees. At the top there are two blockhouses, one on each side of the highway. If you walked that way armed guards would emerge from the huts and demand your passport. Also they would make an inquisition into your baggage more peremptory than most customs officers. That is the frontier of Evallonia.'

Jaikie's sleepiness left him. 'Evallonia!' he cried. 'I had no notion I was so near it.'

'You have read of Evallonia in the English press?'

'Yes, and I have heard a lot about it. I've met Evallonians too – all sorts.' He counted on his fingers. 'Nine – ten, including Prince John.'

'Prince John! Ah, you saw him at Lady Lamancha's party.'

'I saw him two years before that in Scotland, and had a good deal to do with him. With the others, too. I can tell you who they were, for I'm not likely to forget them. There were six Republicans – Mastrovin, Dedekind, Rosenbaum, Ricci, Calaman, and one whose name I never knew – a round-faced fellow in spectacles. There were three Monarchists – Count Casimir Muresco, Doctor Jagon and Prince Odalchini.'

The tall man carefully closed the window, and sat down again. When he spoke it was in a low voice.

'You know some very celebrated people. I think I can place you, Mr Galt. You are called Jaikie, are you not, by your friends? Two years ago you performed a very notable exploit, which resulted in the saving of several honest men and the confounding of some who were not so honest. That story is famous in certain circles. I have laughed over it often, not dreaming that one day I should meet the hero.'

Jaikie shifted nervously, for praise made him unhappy. 'Oh, I didn't do anything much. It was principally Alison. But what has gone wrong with Evallonia? I've been expecting ever since to hear that the Monarchists had kicked out Mastrovin and his lot, but the whole thing seems to have fizzled.'

Mr Glynde was regarding him with steady eyes, which even in the dim light seemed very bright.

'It has not fizzled, but Evallonia at this moment is in a critical state. It is no place for a quiet life, but then I do not think that is what you like... Mr Galt, will you forgive me if I ask you a personal question? Have you any duty which requires your immediate return home?'

'None. But I've finished my money. I have just about enough to get me back.'

'Money is nothing – that can be arranged. I would ask another question. Have you any strong interest in Evallonian affairs?'

'No. But some of my friends have – Mr Craw, the newspaper man, for example, and Dougal Crombie, his chief manager.'

Mr Glynde brooded. 'You know Mr Craw and Mr Crombie? Of course you would. But you have no prepossession in the matter? Except an inclination to back your friends' view?'

'Yes. I thought Prince John a decent fellow, and I liked the queer old Monarchist chaps. Also I greatly disliked Mastrovin and his crowd. They tried to bully me.'

The other smiled. 'That I am sure was a bad blunder on their part.' He was silent for a minute, and then he laid a hand on Jaikie's knee. 'Mr Galt,' he said solemnly, 'if you continued your walking tour tomorrow eastward down the wooded glen, and passed the frontier – I presume your passport is in order? – you would enter a strange country. How strange I have no time to tell you, but I will say this – it is at the crisis of its destiny and any hour may see a triumph or a tragedy. I believe that you might be of some use in averting tragedy. You are a young man, and, I fancy, not indisposed to adventure. If you go home you will be out of danger in that happy cosseted world of England. If you go on, you will certainly find danger, but you may also find wonderful things for which danger is a cheap price. How do you feel about it?'

Jaikie felt many things. Now he knew why all day he had had that curious sense of expectation. There was a queer little flutter at his heart.

'I don't know,' he said. 'It's all rather sudden. I should want to hear more about it.'

'You shall. You shall hear everything before you take any step which is irrevocable. If you will make one day's march into Evallonia, I will arrange that the whole situation is put honestly before you... But no! I have a conscience. I can foretell what you will decide, and I have no right even to bring you within the possibility of that decision, for it will mean danger – it may even mean death. You are too young to gamble with.'

'I think,' said Jaikie, 'I should like to put my nose inside Evallonia just to say I'd been there. You say I can come back if I don't like it. Where's that little coin of yours? It sent me out here, and it may as well decide what I do next.'

'Sportsman,' said Mr Glynde. He produced the stater and handed it to Jaikie, who spun it – 'Heads go on, tails go home.' But owing to the dim light, or perhaps to sleepy eyes, he missed his catch, and the coin rolled on the floor. He took the lamp to look for it, and behold it was wedged upright in a crack in the board – neither heads nor tails.

Mr Glynde laughed merrily. 'Apparently the immortal Gods will have no part in this affair. I don't blame them, for Evallonia is a nasty handful. The omens on the whole point to home. Goodnight, Mr Galt. We shall no doubt meet in England.'

'I'll sleep on it,' said Jaikie. 'If I decide to go on a little farther, what do I do?'

'You will reach Tarta by midday, and just beyond the bridge you will see a gipsy-looking fellow, short but very square, with whiskers and earrings and a white hat with 'Cirque Doré' embroidered on it in scarlet. That is Luigi, my chief fiddler. You will ask him the way to the Cirque, and he will reply in French, which I think you understand, that he knows a better restaurant. After that you will be in his charge. Only I beg of you to keep your mind unbiased by what I have said, and let sleep give you your decision. Like Cromwell I am a believer in Providences, and since that wretched stater won't play the game, you must wait for some other celestial guidance.'

He opened the casement, spoke a word in an unknown tongue, and a heavy body stirred in the dust below. Then he stepped lightly into the velvet darkness, and there followed a heaving and shuffling which presently died away. When a minute later the moon topped the hill, the little street was an empty silver alley.

13

CHAPTER 2

The House of the Four Winds

The night brought no inspiration to Jaikie, for his head was no sooner on his chaff-filled pillow than he seemed to be awake in broad daylight. But the morning decided him. There had been an early shower, the dust was laid in the streets, and every cobble of the sidewalk glistened. From the hills blew a light wind, bearing a rooty fragrance of pine and moss and bracken. A delicious smell of hot coffee and new bread ascended from below; cats were taking their early airing; the vintner opposite, who had a face like a sun, was having a slow argument with the shoemaker; a pretty girl with a basket on her arm was making eyes at a young forester in velveteen breeches and buckskin leggings; a promising dogfight was in progress near the bridge, watched by several excited boys; the sky above had the soft haze which promises a broiling day.

Jaikie felt hungry both for food and enterprise. The morning's freshness was like a draught of spring water, and every sense was quick and perceptive. He craned his head out of the window, and looked back along the way he had come the night before. It showed a dull straight vista between trees. He looked eastward, and there, beyond the end of the village, the world dropped away, and he was looking at the blue heavens and a most appetising crook in the road, which seemed to hesitate, like a timid swimmer, before plunging downwards. There could be no question about it. On this divinest of mornings he refused dully to retrace his steps. He would descend for one day into Evallonia.

He breakfasted on fried eggs and brook trout, paid a diminutive bill, buckled on his knapsack, and before ten o'clock had left Kremisch behind him. The road was all that it had promised. It wound through an upland meadow with a strong blue-grey stream to keep it company, and every now and then afforded delectable glimpses of remote and shining plains. The hills shouldered it friendlily, hills with wide green rides among the firs and sometimes a bald nose of granite. Jaikie had started out with his mind chiefly on Randal Glynde, that suddenly-discovered link with Alison. Evallonia and its affairs did not interest him, or Mr Glynde's mysterious summons to adventure. His meditations during recent weeks had been so much on his own land and the opportunities which it might offer to a deserving young man that he was not greatly concerned with the doings of foreigners, even though some of them were his acquaintances. But he was strongly interested in Mr Glynde. He had never met anybody quite like him, so cheerful and secure in his absurdities. The meeting with him had rolled from Jaikie's back many of the cares of life. The solemnity with which he had proposed a visit to Evallonia seemed in the retrospect to be out of the picture and therefore negligible. Mr Glynde was an apostle of fantasy and his seriousness was itself a comedy. The memory of him harmonised perfectly with this morning world, which with every hundred yards was unveiling a new pageant of delight.

Presently he forgot even Mr Glynde in the drama of the roadside. There was a pool in the stream, ultramarine over silver sand, with a very big trout in it – not less than three pounds in weight. There was a bird which looked like a dipper, but was not a dipper. There was a hawk in the sky, a long-winged falcon of a kind he had never seen before. And on a boulder was perched – rarity of rarities – an unmistakable black redstart... And then the glen seemed to lurch forward and become a defile, down which the stream dropped in a necklace of white cascades. At the edge was a group of low buildings, and out of them came two men carrying rifles.

Jaikie looked with respect at the first Evallonians he had seen on their native heath. They were small men with a great breadth of shoulder, and broad good-humoured countenances – a typical compound, he thought, of Slav and Teuton. But their manner belied their faces, for they were almost truculent, as if they had been soured by heavy and unwelcome duties. They examined everything in his pack and his pockets, they studied his passport with profound suspicion, and they interrogated him closely in German, which he followed with difficulty. Several times they withdrew to consult together; once they retired into the blockhouse, apparently to look up some book of regulations. It was the better part of an hour before they allowed him to pass. Then something ingenuous in Jaikie's face made them repent of their doubts. They grimaced and shook hands with him, and shouted *Grüss Gott* till he had turned a corner.

'Evallonia is a nervous country,' thought Jaikie. 'Lucky I had nothing contraband on me, or I should be bankrupt.'

After that the defile opened into a horseshoe valley, with a few miles ahead the spires of a little town. He saw the loop of a river, of which the stream he had followed must be a tributary. On the north side was something which he took for a hill, but which closer inspection revealed to be a dwelling. It stood high and menacing, with the town huddled up to it, built of some dark stone which borrowed no colour from the bright morning. On three sides it seemed to be bounded by an immense park, for he saw great spaces of turf and woodland which contrasted with the chessboard tillage of other parts of the plain.

A peasant was carrying hay from a roadside meadow. Jaikie pointed to the place and asked its name.

The man nodded. 'Yes, Tarta.'

'And the castle?'

At first the man puzzled; then he smiled. He pronounced a string of uncouth vocables. Then in halting German: 'It is the great Schloss. I have given you its name. It means the House of the Four Winds.'

As Jaikie drew nearer the town he saw the reason why it was so called. Tarta stood in the mouth of a horseshoe and three glens debouched upon it, his own from the west and two other sword-cuts from the north and south. It was clear that the castle must be a very temple of Aeolus. From three points of the compass the winds would whistle down the mountain gullies, and on the east there was no shelter from the devilments bred in the Asian steppes.

Before noon he was close to the confines of the little town. His stream had ceased to be a mountain torrent, and had expanded into broad lagoons, and just ahead was its junction with the river. Over the latter there was a high-backed bridge flanked by guardhouses, and beyond a jumble of masonry which promised narrow old-world streets. The castle, seen at closer range, was more impressive than ever. It hung over the town like a thundercloud, but a thundercloud from which the lightnings had fled, for it had a sad air of desolation. No flag flew from its turrets, no smoke issued from its many chimneys, the few windows in the great black sides which rose above the streets were like blind eyes. Yet its lifelessness made a strong appeal to Jaikie's fancy. This bustling little burgh under the shadow of a mediaeval relic was like a living thing tied to a corpse. But was it really a corpse? He guessed at its vast bulk stretching northward into its wild park. It might have turned a cold shoulder on Tarta and yet within its secret demesne be furiously alive. Meantime it belied its name, for not a breath of wind stirred in the sultry noon. Somewhere beyond the bridge must be Luigi, the chief fiddler of the Cirque Doré. He hoped that Luigi would take him where he could get a drink.

He was to get the drink, but not from Luigi's hands. On the other side of the bridge farthest from the town the road passed through a piece of rough parkland, perhaps the common pasturage of the mediaeval township. Here a considerable crowd had gathered, and Jaikie pressed forward to discover the reason of it. Down the road from Tarta a company of young men was marching, with the obvious intention of making camp in the park; indeed, certain forerunners had already set up a grove of little shelter-tents. They were remarkable young men, for they carried themselves with disciplined shoulders, and yet with the free swing from the hips of the mountaineer. Few of them were tall, but their leanness gave the impression of a good average height, and they certainly looked amazingly hard and fit. Jaikie, accustomed to judge physique on the Rugby field, was impressed by their light-foot walk and their easy carriage. They were not in the least like the Wandervögel whom he had met on many German roads, comfortable sunburnt folk out for a holiday. These lads were in serious training, and they had some purpose other than amusement.

As they passed, the men in the crowd saluted by raising the left hand and the women waved their handkerchiefs. In the rear rode a young man, a splendid figure on a well-bred flea-bitten roan. The rank and file wore shorts and green shirts open at the neck, but the horseman had breeches and boots and a belted green tunic, while a long hunting knife swung at his middle. He was a tall fellow with thick fair hair, a square face and dark eyebrows – a face with which Jaikie was familiar in very different surroundings.

Jaikie, in the front row of the crowd, was so overcome with amazement that his left hand remained unraised and he could only stare. The horseman caught sight of him, and he too registered surprise, from which he instantly recovered. He spoke a word to the ranks; a man fell out, and beckoned Jaikie to follow. The other spectators fell back from him as from a leper, and he and his warder followed the horse's tail into the open space, where the rest were drawing up in front of the tents.

Then the horseman turned to him.

'Salute,' he said.

Jaikie's arm shot up obediently.

The leader cast an eye over the ranks, and bade them stand easy and then fall out. He dismounted, flinging his bridle to an orderly. 'Follow me,' he said to Jaikie in English, and led him to a spot on the river bank, where a larger tent had been set up. Two lads were busy there with kit and these he dismissed. Then he turned to Jaikie with a broad grin. 'What on earth are you doing here?' he asked.

'Give me a drink first, Ashic,' was the answer.

The young man dived into the tent and produced a bottle of white wine, a bottle of a local mineral water, and two tumblers. The two clinked glasses. Then he gave Jaikie a cigarette. 'Now,' he said, 'what's your story?'

'I have been across half Europe,' said Jaikie. 'I must have tramped about five hundred miles. My money's done, and I go home tomorrow, but I thought I'd have a look inside Evallonia first. But what are *you* doing, Ashie? Is it Boy Scouts or a revolution?'

The other smiled and did not at once reply. That was a mannerism, which the University of Cambridge had taught him, for when Count Paul Jovian (he had half a dozen other Christian names which we may neglect) entered St Mark's he had been too loquacious. He and a cousin had shared lodgings, and at first they were not popular. They had an unpleasant trick of being easily insulted, talking about duels, and consequently getting their ears boxed. When they migrated within the College walls, the dislike of the cousin had endured, but Count Paul began to make friends. Finally came a night when the cousin's trousers were removed and used to decorate the roof, as public evidence of dislike, while Paul was unmolested. That occasion gave him his nickname, for he was christened Asher by a piously brought-up contemporary, the tribe of Asher having, according to the Book of Judges, 'abode in its breaches'. 'Ashie' he had remained from that day.

Jaikie had begun by disliking him, he was so noisy and strange and flamboyant. But Count Paul had a remarkable gift of adapting himself to novel conditions. Presently his exuberance quietened down, he became more sparing in speech, he developed a sense of humour and laboured to acquire the idiom of their little society. In his second year he was indistinguishable from the ordinary English undergraduate. He had a pretty turn of speed, but it was found impossible to teach him the Rugby game; at boxing too he was a complete duffer; but he was a brilliant fencer, and he knew all that was to be known about a horse. Indeed, it was in connection with horses that Jaikie first came to like him. A groom from a livery stable lost his temper with a hireling, who was badly bitted and in a fractious temper. The Count's treatment of the case rejoiced Jaikie's heart. He shot the man into the gutter, eased the bit, and quieted the animal with a curious affectionate gentleness. After that the two became friends, in spite of the fact that the Count's taste for horses and hunting took him into a rather different set. They played together in a cricket eleven of novices called the 'Cads of all Nations', who for a week of one long vacation toured the Midlands, and were soundly beaten by every village team.

There was a tough hardihood about the man which made Jaikie invite him more than once to be his companion in some of his more risky enterprises – invitations regretfully refused, for some business always took Ashie home. That home Jaikie knew to be in Eastern Europe, but he had not associated him with Evallonia. There was also an extreme innocence. He wanted to learn everything about England, and took Jaikie as his mentor, believing that in him he had found the greatest common measure of the British people. Whether he learned much may be doubted, for Jaikie was too little of a dogmatist to be a good instructor. But they slipped into a close friendship, and rubbed the corners off each other's minds.

'I know what I'm doing,' said Ashie at last; 'but I am not quite sure where it will finish. But that's a long story. You're a little devil, Jaikie, to come here at the tag-end of your holiday. If you had come a month ago we might have had all sorts of fun.'

He had relapsed into the manner of the undergraduate, but there was something in him now which made it a little absurd. For the figure opposite Jaikie was not the agreeable and irresponsible companion he had known. Ashie looked desperately foreign, without a hint of Cambridge and England; bigger too, more mature, and rather formidable. The thick dark eyebrows in combination with the fair hair had hitherto given his appearance a touch of comedy; now the same brows bent above the grey eyes had something in them martial and commanding. Rob Roy was more of a man on his native heath than on the causeways of Glasgow.

'If you can arrange to stay here for a little,' said Ashie, 'I promise to show you life.'

'Thank you very much, but I can't. I must be off home tomorrow – a week's tramping, and then the train.'

'Give me three weeks.'

'I'm sorry, but I can't.' Jaikie found it hard to sort out his feelings, but he was clear that he did not want to dally in Evallonia.

Ashie's voice became almost magisterial.

'What are you doing here today?' he asked.

'I'm lunching with a friend and going back to Kremisch in the evening.'

'Who's your friend?'

'I'm not quite sure of his name.' Jaikie's caution told him that Mr Glynde might have many *aliases*. 'He's in a circus.'

Ashie laughed – almost in the old light-hearted way. 'Just the kind of friend you'd have. The Cirque Doré? I saw some of the mountebanks in the streets... You won't accept my invitation? I can promise you the most stirring time in your life.'

'I wish I could, but – well, it's no use, I can't.'

'Then we must part, for I have a lot to do.'

'You haven't told me what you're doing.'

'No. Some day I will – in England, if I ever come back to England.'

He called one of his scouts, to whom he said something in a strange tongue. The latter saluted and waited for Jaikie to follow him. Ashie gave him a perfunctory handshake – 'Goodbye. Good luck to you'; and entered his tent.

The boy led Jaikie beyond the encampment, and, with a salute and a long stare, left him at the entrance to the bridge. A clock on a steeple told him that it was a quarter past twelve, pretty much the time that Mr Glynde had appointed. The bridge was almost empty, for the sightseers who had followed Ashie's outfit had trickled back to their midday meals. Jaikie spent a few minutes looking over the parapet at the broad waters of the river. This must be the Rave, the famous stream which sixty miles on flowed through the capital city of Melina. He watched its strong current sweep past the walls of the great Schloss, which there dropped sheer into it, before in a wide circuit it formed the western boundary of the castle park. What an impregnable fortress, he thought, must have been this House of the Four Winds in the days before artillery, and how it must have lorded it over the little burgh under its skirts!

There was a gatehouse on the Tarta side of the bridge, an ancient crumbling thing bright with advertisements of the Cirque Doré. Beyond it a narrow street wound under the blank wall of the castle, ending in a square in which the chief building was a baroque town house. From where Jaikie stood this town house had an odd apologetic air, a squat thing dwarfed by the Schloss like a dachshund beside a mastiff. The day was very warm, and he crossed over from the glare of one side of the street to the shadow of the other. The place was almost empty, most of the citizens being doubtless engaged with food behind shuttered windows. Jaikie was getting hungry, and so far he had looked in vain for Mr Glynde's Luigi. But as he moved towards the central square a man came out of an entry, and, stopping suddenly to light a cigarette, almost collided with him. Jaikie saw a white cap and scarlet lettering, and had a glimpse of gold earrings and a hairy face. He remembered his instructions.

'Can you show me the way to the Cirque Doré?' he asked.

The man grinned. 'I will lead you to a better restaurant,' he said in French with a villainous accent. He held out his hand and shook Jaikie's warmly, as if he had found a long-lost friend. Then he gripped him by the arm and poured forth a torrent of not very intelligible praise of the excellence of the cuisine to which he was guiding him.

Jaikie found himself hustled up the street and pulled inside a little dark shop, which appeared to be a combination of a bird fancier's and a greengrocer's. There was nobody there, so they passed through it into a court strewn with decaying vegetables and through a rickety door into a lane, also deserted. After that they seemed to thread mazes of mean streets at a pace which made the sweat break on Jaikie's forehead, till they found themselves at the other end of the town, where it ebbed away into shacks and market gardens.

'I am very hungry,' said Jaikie, who saw his hopes of luncheon disappearing.

'The Signor must have patience,' was the answer. 'He has still a little journey before him, but at the end of it he will have honest food.'

Luigi was an adept at under statement. He seemed to wish to escape notice, which was easy at this stagnant hour of the day. Whenever anyone appeared he became still as a graven image, with an arresting hand on Jaikie's arm. They chose such cover as was available, and any track they met they crossed circumspectly. The market gardens gave place to vineyards, which were not easy to thread, and then to wide fields of ripe barley, hot as the Sahara. Jaikie was in good training, but this circus-man Luigi, though he looked plump and soft, was also in no way distressed, never slackening pace and never panting. By and by they entered a wood of saplings which gave them a slender shade. At the far end of it was a tall palisade of chestnut stakes, lichened and silvery with age. 'Up with you,' said Luigi, and gave Jaikie a back which enabled him to grasp the top and swing himself over. To his annoyance the Italian followed him unaided, supple as a monkey.

'Rest and smoke,' he said. 'There is now no reason for hurry except the emptiness of your stomach.'

They rested for ten minutes. Behind them was the palisade they had crossed, and in front of them glades of turf, and wildernesses of fern and undergrowth, and groves of tall trees. It was like the New Forest, only on a bigger scale.

'It is a noble place,' said Luigi, waving his cigarette. 'From here it is seven miles to Zutpha, where is a railway. Tarta in old days was only, so to say, the farmyard behind the castle. From Zutpha the guests of the princes of this house were driven in great coaches with outriders. Now there are few guests, and instead of a coach-and-eight a Ford car. It is the way of the world.'

When they resumed their journey it was at an easier pace. They bore to their left, and presently came in view of what had once been a formal garden on a grandiose scale. Runnels had been led from the river, and there was a multitude of stone bridges and classic statuary and rococo summer houses. Now the statues were blotched with age, the bridges were crumbling, and the streams were matted beds of rushes. Beyond, rising from a flight of terraces, could be seen the huge northern façade of the castle, as blank as the side it showed to Tarta. It had been altered and faced with a white stone a century ago, but the comparative modernity of this part made its desolation more conspicuous than that of the older Gothic wings. What should have been gay with flowers and sunblinds stood up in the sunlight as grim as a deserted factory; and that, thought Jaikie, is grimmer than any other kind of ruin.

Luigi did not take him up the flights of empty terraces. Beyond the formal garden he turned along a weedy path which flanked a little lake. On one side was the Cyclopean masonry of the terrace wall, and, where it bent at an angle, cloaked by a vast magnolia, they came suddenly upon a little paved court shaded by a trellis. It was cool, and it was heavily scented, for on one side was a thicket of lemon verbena. A table had been set for luncheon, and at it sat two men, waited on by a footman in knee breeches and a faded old coat of blue and silver.

'You are not five minutes behind time,' said the elder of the two. 'Anton,' he addressed the servant, 'take the other gentleman indoors and see to his refreshment.' ...To Jaikie he held out his hand. 'We have met before, Mr Galt. I have the honour to welcome you to my poor house. Mr Glynde I think you already know.'

'You expected me?' Jaikie asked in some surprise.

'I was pretty certain you would come,' said Mr Glynde.

Jaikie saw before him that Prince Odalchini whom two years ago he had known as one of the tenants of the Canonry shooting of Knockraw. The Prince's hair was a little greyer, his well-bred face a little thinner, and his eyes a little darker round the rims. But in the last burned the same fire of a gentle fanaticism. He was exquisitely dressed in a suit of white linen with a tailed coat, and shirt and collar of turquoise-blue silk – blue and white being the Odalchini liveries. Mr Randal Glynde had shed the fantastic garments of the previous night, but he had not returned to the modishness of his English clothes; he wore an ill-cut suit of some thin grey stuff that made him look like a *commis voyageur* in a smallish way of business, and to this part he had arranged his hair and beard to conform. To his outfit a Guards tie gave a touch of startling colour.

'We will not talk till we have eaten,' said the Prince. 'Mr Galt must have picked up an appetite between here and Kremisch.'

Jaikie had one of the most satisfying meals of his career. There was an omelet, a dish of trout, and such peaches as he had never tasted before. He had acquired a fresh thirst during his journey with Luigi, and this was assuaged by a white wine which seemed to be itself scented with lemon verbena, a wine in slim bottles beaded with the dew of the ice cellar. He was given a cup of coffee made by the Prince's own hands, and a long fat cigarette of a brand which the Prince had specially made for him in Cairo.

'Luigi spoke the truth,' said Mr Glynde smiling, 'when he said that he would conduct you to a better restaurant.'

The footman withdrew and silence fell. Bees wandered among the heliotrope and verbena and pots of sapphire agapanthus, and even that shady place felt the hot breath of the summer noon. Sleep would undoubtedly have overtaken Jaikie and Mr Glynde, but for the vigour of Prince Odalchini, who seemed, like a salamander, to draw life and sustenance from the heat. His high-pitched, rather emotional voice kept his auditors wakeful. 'I will explain to you,' he told Jaikie, 'what you cannot know or have only heard in a perversion. I take up the history of Evallonia after Prince John sailed from your Scotch loch.'

He took a long time over his exposition, and as he went on Jaikie found his interest slowly awakening. The cup of the abominations of the Republican Government had apparently long ago been filled. Evallonia was ready to spew them out, but unfortunately the Monarchists were not quite ready to take their place. This time it was not trouble with other Powers or with the League of Nations. Revolutions had become so much the fashion in Europe that they were taken as inevitable, whether their purpose was republic, monarchy, or dictatorship. The world was too weary to argue about the merits of constitutional types, and the nations were too cumbered with perplexed economics to have any desire to meddle in the domestic affairs of their neighbours. Aforetime the Monarchists had feared the intervention of the Powers or some finding of the League, and therefore they had sought the mediation of British opinion. Now their troubles were of a wholly different kind.

Prince Odalchini explained. Communism was for the moment a dead cause in Evallonia, and Mastrovin and his friends had as much chance of founding a Soviet republic as of plucking down the moon. Mastrovin indeed dared not show himself in public, and the present administration of his friends staggered along, corrupt, incompetent, deeply unpopular. It would collapse at the slightest pressure. But after that?

'Everywhere in the world,' said the Prince, 'there is now an uprising of youth. It does not know what it seeks. It did not know the hardships of war. But it demands of life some hope and horizon, and it is determined to have the ordering of things in its hands. It is conscious of its ignorance and lack of discipline, so it seeks to inform and discipline itself, and therein lies its danger.'

'Ricci,' he went on. 'You remember him in the Canonry? – a youngish man like a horse-dealer. At that time he was a close ally of the Republican Government, but eighteen months ago he became estranged from it – he and Count Jovian, who was not with the others in Scotland. Well, Ricci had an American wife of enormous wealth, and with the aid of her money he set out to stir up our youth. He had an ally in the Jovian I have mentioned, who was a futile vain man, like your Justice Shallow in Shakespeare, easily flattered and but little respected, but with a quick brain for intrigue. These two laid the foundations of a body called Juventus, which is now the strongest thing in Evallonia. They themselves were rogues, but they enlisted many honest helpers, and soon, like the man in the *Arabian Nights*, they had raised a jinn which they could not control. Jovian died a year ago – he was always sick – and Ricci is no longer the leader. But the thing itself marches marvellously. It has caught the imagination of our people and fired their pride. Had we an election, the Juventus candidates would undoubtedly sweep the board. As it is, it contains all the best of Evallonian youth, who give up to it their leisure, their ambition and their scanty means. It is in its way a noble thing, for it asks only for sacrifice, and offers no bribes. It is, so to speak, a new Society of Jesus, sworn to utter obedience. But, good or ill, it has most damnably spiked the guns of us Royalists.'

Jaikie asked why.

'Because it is arrogant, and demands that whatever is done for Evallonia it alone shall do it. The present Government must go, and at once, for it is too gross a scandal. If we delay, there will be a blind revolution of the people themselves. You will say – let Juventus restore Prince John. Juventus will do nothing of the kind, since Prince John is not its own candidate. If we restore him, Juventus will become anti-Monarchist. What then will it do? I reply that it does not yet know, but there is a danger that it may set up one of its own people as dictator. That would be tragic, for in the first place Evallonia does not need or desire a dictator, being Monarchist by nature, and in the second place Juventus does not want a dictatorship either. It is Nationalist, but not Fascist. Yet the calamity may happen.'

'Has Juventus any leader who could fill the bill?' Jaikie asked.

The Prince shook his head. 'I do not think so – therefore its action would be only to destroy and obstruct, not to build. Ricci with his wife's millions is now discredited; they have used him and cast him aside. There are some of the very young with power I am told – particularly a son of Jovian's.'

'Is his name Paul?' Jaikie asked, and was told yes.

'I know him,' he said. 'He was at Cambridge with me. I have just seen him, for about two hours ago he stood me a drink.'

The Prince in his surprise upset the coffee pot, and even the sophisticated eyes of Mr Glynde opened a little wider.

'You know Paul Jovian? That is miraculous, Mr Galt. Will you permit me to speak a word in private with Mr Glynde? There are some matters still too secret even for your friendly ears.'

The two withdrew and left Jaikie alone in the alcove among bees and butterflies and lemon verbena. He was a little confused in his mind, for after a solitary month he had suddenly strayed into a place where he seemed to know rather too many people. Embarrassing people, all of whom pressed him to stay longer. He did not much like their country. It was too hot for him, too scented and airless. He was not in the least interested in the domestic affairs of Evallonia, either the cantrips of Ashie or the solemn intrigues of the Prince. It was not his world; that was a cool, bracing upland a thousand miles away, for which he had begun to feel acutely homesick. Alison would soon be back in the Canonry, and he must be there to meet her. He felt that for the moment he was fed up with foreign travel.

The two men returned, and sat down before him with an air of purpose.

'Where did you find Count Paul?' the Prince asked.

'On the Kremisch side of the Tarta bridge. He was going into camp with a detachment of large-sized Boy Scouts.'

'You know him well?'

'Pretty well. We have been friends ever since his first year. I like him – at least I liked him at Cambridge, but here he seems a rather different sort of person. He wanted me to stay on in Evallonia – to stay for three weeks.'

The two exchanged glances.

'So!' said the Prince. 'And your answer?'

'I refused. He didn't seem particularly well pleased.'

'Mr Galt, we also make you that proposal. Will you be my guest here in Evallonia for a little – perhaps for three weeks – perhaps longer? I believe that you can be of incalculable value to an honest cause. I cannot promise success – that is not commanded by mortals – but I can promise you an exciting life.'

'That was what I said to you last night,' said Mr Glynde smiling. 'My little stater would give you no guidance, but the fact that you have ventured into Evallonia encourages me to hope.'

Jaikie at the moment had no desire for excitement. He felt limp and drowsy and oppressed; the Prince's luncheon had been too good, and this scented nook choked him; he wanted to be somewhere where he could breathe fresh air. Evallonia was wholly devoid of attractions.

'I don't think so,' he said. 'I'm tremendously honoured that you should want me, but I shouldn't be any use to you, and I must get home.'

'You are not to be moved?' said Mr Glynde.

Jaikie shook his head. 'I've had enough of the continent of Europe.'

'I understand,' said Mr Glynde. 'I too sometimes feel that satiety, and think I must go home.' He turned to the Prince. 'I doubt if we shall persuade Mr Galt. I wish Casimir were here. Where, by the way, is he?'

The Prince replied with a word which sounded to Jaikie like 'Unnutz,' a word which woke a momentary interest in his lethargic mind.

'What then do you propose to do?' The Prince turned to him.

'Go back to Kremisch tonight, sleep there and set off home tomorrow.'

'What must be must be. But I do not think it wise for you to start yet awhile. Let us go indoors, and I will show you some of the few household gods which poverty has left me.'

Jaikie spent an hour or two pleasantly in the cool chambers of the great house. The place was shabby but not neglected, and there were treasures there which, judiciously placed on the market, might well have restored the Odalchini fortunes. He looked at long lines of forbidding family portraits; at a little room so full of masterpieces that it was a miniature Salle Carrée; at one of the finest collections of armour in the world; and at a wonderful array of sporting trophies, for the Odalchinis had been famous game-shots. He was given tea at a little table in the hall quite in the English fashion. But very soon he became restless. The sun was getting low, and he had a considerable distance to walk before supper.

'You had better go first to the Cirque Doré,' said Mr Glynde. 'There I will meet you, and show you the way out of the town. You have been in dangerous territory, Mr Galt, and must be circumspect in leaving it. No, we cannot go together. I will take a different road and meet you there. Luigi will guide you. You will cross the park by the way you came, and Luigi will be waiting for you outside the pale.'

'I am sorry,' said the Prince. He shook hands with so regretful a face, and his old eyes were so solemn that Jaikie had a moment of compunction. When he left the castle the cool of the evening was beginning, and the twilight scents came freshly and pleasantly to his nostrils. This was a better place than he had thought, and he felt more vigorous and enterprising. He had the faintest twinge of regret about his decision. After all, there was nothing to call him home, for there would be no Dickson McCunn there yet awhile, and no Dougal, and perhaps no Alison. But there would be the Canonry, and he fixed his mind upon its delectable glens as he retraced his path of the morning. One of Jaikie's endowments was an almost perfect instinct for direction, and he struck the high chestnut pale pretty much at the spot where he had first crossed it.

Getting over without Luigi's help was a difficult business, and, Jaikie's energy being wholly employed in the task, he did not trouble to prospect the land... He tumbled over the top and dropped into what seemed to be a crowd of people.

Strong hands gripped him. A cloth was skilfully wound round his face, blinding his eyes and blanketing his voice. Another wrapped his arms to his side, and a third bound his legs. He struggled, but his sense of the physical superiority of his assailants was so great that he soon gave it up; he was like a thin rabbit in the clutch of an enormous gamekeeper. Yet the hands were not unkindly, and his bandages, though effective, were not painful.

He was carried swiftly along for a few minutes and then placed in some kind of car. Somebody sat down beside him. The car was started, and bumped for a little along very rough roads... Then it came to a highway and moved fast... Jaikie had by this time collected his thoughts, and they were wrathful. His first alarm had gone, for he reflected that there was no one likely to mean mischief to him. He was pretty certain what had happened. This was Prince Odalchini's way of detaining an unwilling guest. Well, he would presently have a good deal to say to the Prince and to Mr Glynde.

The car slowed down, and his companion, whoever he was, began with deft hands to undo his bonds. First he loosed his legs. Then, almost with the same movement, he released his arms and drew the bandages from his face. Then he snapped a switch which lit up dimly the interior of the limousine in which the blinds had been drawn.

Jaikie found himself looking at the embarrassed face of Ashie.

CHAPTER 3

Diversions of a Marionette

Miss Alison Westwater dropped with a happy sigh beside a bed of wild strawberries still wet with dew, and proceeded to make a second breakfast. It was still early morning – not quite seven o'clock – but she had been walking ever since half past five, when she had broken her fast on a cup of coffee and a last-night's roll provided by a friendly chambermaid. She had left the highway, which, switchbacking from valley to valley, took the traveller to Italy, and had taken a forest track which after a mile or two among pines came out on an upland meadow, and led to a ridge, the spur of a high mountain, from which the kingdoms of the earth could be surveyed. The sky was not the pale turquoise bowl which in her own country heralded a perfect summer day, but an intense sapphire; the shadows were also blue, and the sunshine where it fell was a blinding essential light without colour, so that the grass looked like snowdrifts. The air had an aromatic freshness which stung the senses, and Alison drew great breaths of it till her throat was as cold as if she had been drinking spring water.

This was her one satisfactory time in the day. The rest of her waking hours were devoted to a routine which seemed void alike of mirth or reason. Her father's neuritis had almost gone, but so had his good humour, and it was a very peevish old gentleman that she accompanied in pottering walks by the lakeside or in aimless motor drives on blinding hot highways. Lord Rhynns was particular about his food, and the hotel cuisine did not please him, so he was in the habit of sampling, without much success, whatever Unnutz produced in the way of café and *konditorei*. He was also particular about his clothes, and since he dressed always in the elder fashion of tight trousers, coloured waistcoat, stiff collar and four-in-hand tie, he was generally warm and correspondingly irascible. Her mother did not appear till after midday, and required a good deal of coddling, for, having been driven out of her accustomed beat, she found herself short of acquaintances and quite unable to plan out her days. One curious consequence was that both, who had habituated themselves to a life of Continental vagrancy, suddenly began to long passionately for home. His lordship remembered that the shooting season would soon begin in the Canonry, and was full of sad reminiscences of the exploits of his youth, while to her ladyship came visions of the cool chambers and the smooth and comforting ritual of Castle Gay.

'I am a marionette,' Alison had written to Jaikie. 'I move at the jerk of a string, and it isn't my parents that pull it. It's this ghastly place, which has invented a regime for the idle middle classes of six nations. I defy even you to break loose from it. I do the same things and make the same remarks and wear the same clothes every day at the proper hour. I'm a marionette and so are the other people – quite nice they are, and well-mannered, and friendly, but as dead as salted herrings. A good old-fashioned bounder would be a welcome change. Or a criminal.'

As she sat on the moss she remembered this sentence – and something else. Unnutz was mainly villas and hotels, but there was an old village as a nucleus – wooden houses built on piles on the lake shore, and one or two narrow twisting streets with pumpkins drying on the shingle roofs. There was a bathing place there very different from the modish thing on the main promenade, a place where you dived in a hut under a canvas curtain into deep green water, and could swim out to some fantastic little rock islets. She had managed once or twice to bathe there, and yesterday afternoon she had slipped off for an hour and had had a long swim by herself. Coming back she had recognised in a corner of the old village the first face of an acquaintance she had met since she came to Unnutz. Not an acquaintance exactly, for he had never seen her. But she remembered well the shaggy leonine head, the heavy brows and the forward thrust of the jaw. She had watched those features two years ago during some agonised minutes in the library of Castle Gay, till Mr Dickson McCunn had adroitly turned melodrama into farce, and she was not likely to forget them. She remembered the name too – Mastrovin, the power behind the Republican Government of Evallonia. Had not Jaikie told her that he was the most dangerous underground force in Europe?

What was this dynamic personage doing in a dull little Tirolese health resort? Was her wish to be granted, and their drab society enlivened by a criminal?

The thought only flitted across her mind, for she had other things to think about. She must make the most of her holiday, for by half past ten she must be back to join her father in his *petit déjeuner* on the hotel verandah. Usually she had the whole hillside to herself, but this morning she had seen a car on the road which led to the high pastures. It had been empty, standing at the foot of one of the tracks which climbed upward through the pines. Someone else had her taste for early mornings in the hills. It had annoyed her to think that her sanctuary was not inviolable. She hoped that the intruder, whoever he or she was, was short in the wind and would not get higher than the wood.

She got up from her lair among the strawberries and wandered across the meadow, where every now and then outcrops of rock stuck grey noses through the flowers. She had a drink out of an ice-cold runnel. She saw a crested lit, a bird which she had never met before, and screwed her single field-glass into her eye to watch its movements. Also she saw a kite high up in the blue, and, having only once in her life met that type of hawk, regarded him with a lively interest. Then she came to a little valley the top of which was a ravine in the high rocks, and the bottom of which was muffled in the woods. There was a woodcutter's cottage here, wonderfully hidden in a cleft, with the pines on three sides and one side open to the hill. Where Alison stood she looked down upon it directly from above, and could observe the beginning of its daily life. She had been here before, and had seen an old woman, who might have come out of Grimm, carrying pails of water from a pool in the stream.

Now instead of the old woman there was a young man, presumably her son. He came slowly from the cottage and moved to the fringe of the trees, where a path began its downhill course. He possessed a watch, for he twice consulted it, as if he were keeping an appointment. His clothes were the ordinary forester's baggy trousers of homespun, heavy, iron-shod boots, and an aged velveteen jacket with silver buttons. He carried himself well, Alison thought, better than most woodmen, who were apt to be round-shouldered and slouching.

A second man came out of the wood – also a tall man, but dressed very differently from the woodcutter, for he wore flannels and a green Homburg hat. 'My motorist,' thought Alison. 'He must know something about the woods, for the way through them to this cottage isn't easy to find.'

The newcomer behaved oddly. He took off his hat. The woodcutter gave him his hand and he bowed over it with extreme respect. Then the woodcutter slipped his arm in his and led him towards the cottage.

Alison in her perch far above put the glass to her eye and got a good view of the stranger. There could be no mistake. Two years ago she had sat opposite him at dinner at Castle Gay and at breakfast at Knockraw. She recognised the fine shape of his head, and the face which would have been classically perfect but for the snub nose. One did not easily forget Count Casimir Muresco.

But who was the other? Noblemen with nine centuries of pedigree behind them do not usually bow over the hands of foresters and uncover their heads. She could not see his face, for it was turned away from her, but before the two entered the cottage she had no doubt about his identity. She was being given the back view of the lawful monarch of Evallonia.

From that moment Alison's boredom vanished like dew in the sun. She realised that she had stumbled upon the fringe of great affairs. What was it that Prince John had said to her at the dinner at Maurice's? That Unnutz was not a very good place for a holiday that summer, that it might be unpleasant, but that, being English, she would always be free to get away. That could only mean that something momentous was going to happen at Unnutz. What was Prince John doing disguised as a woodcutter in this remote and secret hut?... What was Count Casimir, architect of revolutions, doing there so early in the morning? Plots were being hatched thought the girl in a delicious tremor of excitement. The curtain was about to rise on the play, and, unknown to the actors, she had a seat in a box.

And then suddenly she remembered the face she had seen the afternoon before in the lakeside alley. Mastrovin! He was the deadly enemy of Count Casimir and the Prince. He must know, or suspect, that the Prince was in the neighbourhood. Casimir probably knew nothing of Mastrovin's presence. But she, Alison, knew. The thought solemnised her, for such knowledge is as much a burden as a delight.

Her first impulse was to scramble down the hillside to the cottage, break in on the conspirators, and tell them what she knew. But she did not move, for it occurred to her that she might be more useful, and get more fun out of the business, if she remained silent. She waited for ten minutes till the two men appeared again. This time she had a good view of the woodcutter through her glass, and she recognised the comely and rather heavy countenance of Prince John. Casimir took a ceremonious leave and started down the track through the forest. Alison, who knew all the paths, followed him at a higher level. She wanted to discover whether or not his steps had been dogged.

Alison had taught Jaikie many things, and he had repaid her by instructing her in some of his own lore. He had made her almost as artful and silent a tracker as himself, and under his tuition she had brought to a high pitch her own fine natural sense of direction. Like a swift shadow she flitted through the pines, now on bare needle-strewn ground, now among tangles of rock and whortleberry. The route she took was almost parallel to Casimir's, but now and then she had to make a circuit to avoid some rocky dingle, and there were times when she had to cast back or cast ahead to trace him. It was rough going in parts, and since Casimir showed a remarkable turn of speed she had sometimes to slither down steeps and sometimes to run. By and by came glimpses of the valley below, and at last through a thinning of the pines she saw the last twisting of the hill path before it debouched on the highway. Presently she saw the waiting car, and the tracker, being a little ahead of the tracked, sank down among the whortleberries to await events.

Casimir appeared, going warily, with an eye on the white strip of high road. It was still empty, for the Firnthal does not rise early. He reached the car, and examined it carefully, as if he feared that someone might have tampered with it in his absence. Satisfied, he took the driver's seat, backed on to the high road, and set out in the direction of Italy.

Alison observed his doings with only half an eye, for between her and the car she had seen something which demanded attention. She was now some two hundred yards above the road, and the ground immediately below her was occupied by a little rockfall much overgrown with fern and scrub. There was something among the bushes which had not been put there by nature. Her glass showed her that that something was the head of a man. It was a bare head, with grizzled hair and one bald patch at the back, and she knew to whom it belonged. Mastrovin was not in Unnutz for the sake of the excellent sulphur baths or the mountain air.

Alison slipped out of her lair and as noiselessly as she could crawled to her right along the slope of the hill. She struck the path by which Casimir had descended, a path which was, so to speak, the grand trunk road from the hills, and which a little higher forked in several directions. Waiting a moment to get her breath, she made a hasty bouquet of some blue campanulas and sprigs of whortleberry and then sauntered down the path, a little flushed, a little untidy about the hair and wet about the shoes, but on the whole a creditable specimen of early-rising vigorous maidenhood.

Mastrovin, when she came in sight of him, was descending the hill and had already reached the high road. He had covered his head with a green hat, and wore a dark green suit of breeches and Norfolk jacket, just like any other tourist in a mountain country. Alison's whistling caught his ear, and at the foot of the track he stopped to wait for her.

'*Grüss Gott!*' he said, forcing his harsh features into amiability. 'I have been looking for a friend. Have you seen anyone – any man – up in the woods? My friend is tall and walks fast, and his clothes are grey.'

One of Alison's accomplishments was that she understood German perfectly, and spoke it with fluency and a reasonable correctness. But it occurred to her that it would not be wise to reveal this talent; so she pretended to follow Mastrovin with difficulty and to puzzle over one word, and she began to answer in the purest Ollendorff.

'You are English?' he asked. 'Speak English, please. I understand it.'

Alison obeyed. She explained that she had indeed met a man in the high woods, though she had not specially remarked his clothes. She had passed him, and thought that he must have returned soon after, for she had not seen him on her way down. She described minutely the place of meeting – on the right-hand road at the main fork, near the brow of the hill, and not far from

the rock called the Wolf Crag which looked down on Unnutz –
precisely the opposite direction from the woodcutter's hut.

Mastrovin thanked her with a flourish of his hat. 'I must now
to breakfast,' he said. 'There is a *Gasthaus* by the roadside where
I will await my friend, if he is not already there.'

II

Usually the two miles to Unnutz were the one black spot in the
morning's walk, for they were flat and dusty and meant a return
to the house of bondage. But today Alison was scarcely conscious
of them, for she was thinking hard, with a flutter at her heart
which was half-painful and half-pleasant. Prince John was here in
retreat for some purpose, and Count Casimir was in touch with
him; that must mean that things were coming to a head in
Evallonia. Mastrovin, his bitterest enemy, was on the trail of
Casimir, and must know that Prince John was in the
neighbourhood. That meant trouble. Her false witness that
morning might send Mastrovin on a wild-goose chase to the
wrong part of the forest, but it was very certain that he must
presently discover the Prince's hermitage. The Prince and
Casimir might suspect that their enemies were looking for them,
but they did not know that Mastrovin was in Unnutz. She alone
knew that, and she must warn the Prince, and that must be done
secretly when she could be certain that she was not followed. She
had begun to plan a midnight journey, for happily she had a
room giving on a balcony, from which it would be easy to reach
the ground. To her surprise she found that she looked forward
with no relish to the prospect; if she had had company it would
have been immense fun, but, being alone, she felt only the
weight of a heavy duty. She longed passionately for Jaikie.

Entering the hotel by a side door, she changed into something
more like the regulation toilet of Unnutz, and sought her father
on the verandah. For once Lord Rhynns was in a good humour.

'A little late, my dear,' he complained mildly. 'Yes, I have had a better night. I am beginning to hope that I have got even with my accursed affliction.' Then, regarding his daughter with complacent eyes, he became complimentary. 'You are really a very pretty girl, Alison, though your clothes are not such as gentlewomen wore in my young days.' With a surprising touch of sentiment he added, 'You are becoming very like my mother.'

Taking advantage of her father's urbanity, Alison broached the question of going home.

'Presently, my dear. Another week, I think, should set me right. Your mother is anxious to leave – a sudden craving for Scotland. We shall go for a little to Harriet at Castle Gay – she has been more than kind about it, and Craw has behaved admirably. I am told he has the place very comfortable, and I have always found him conduct himself like a gentleman. Money, my dear. Ample means are not only the passport to the name of gentility, but they create the thing itself. In these days it is not easy for a pauper to preserve his breeding.

'By the way,' he continued, 'some friends of ours arrived here this morning. They are breakfasting more elaborately than we are in the *salle-à-manger*. The Roylances. Janet Roylance, you remember, was old Cousin Alastair Raden's second girl.'

'What!' Alison almost shrieked. It was the best news she could have got, for now she could share her burden of responsibility. In the regrettable absence of Jaikie the Roylances were easily the next best.

'Yes,' her father went on. 'They have been at Geneva, and have come on here for a holiday. Sir Archibald, they tell me, is making a considerable name for himself in politics. For a young man in these days he certainly has creditable manners.'

His lordship finished his coffee, and announced that he proposed to go to his sitting-room till luncheon to write letters. Alison dutifully accompanied him thither, paid her respects to her mother, who was also in a more cheerful mood, and then hastened downstairs. In the big dining-room she found the pair she sought at a table in one of the windows. Alison flung herself upon Janet Roylance's neck.

'You've finished breakfast? Then come outdoors and smoke. I know a quiet corner beside the lake. I must talk to you at once. You blessed angels have been sent by Heaven just at the right moment.'

When they were seated where a little half-moon of shrubbery made an enclave above the blue waters of the Waldersee, Sir Archie offered Alison a cigarette.

'No, thank you. I don't smoke. If I did it would be a pipe, I'm so sick of the cigarette-puffing hussy. First of all, what brought you two here?'

Sir Archie grinned. 'The Conference has adjourned till Bolivia settles some nice point with Uruguay.'

'We came,' said Janet, 'because we are free people with no plans and we knew that you were here. We thought we should find you moribund with boredom, Allie, but you are radiant. What has happened? Have the parents turned over a new leaf?'

'Papa is quite good and nearly well. Mamma has actually begun to crave for Scotland. There's no trouble at present on the home front. But the foreign situation is ticklish. This place is going to be the scene of dark doings, and I can't cope with them alone. That's why I hugged you like a bear. Have you ever heard of Evallonia?'

'I have,' said Janet, 'for I sometimes read the Craw Press.'

'We've expected a revolution there,' said Sir Archie, 'any time these last two years. But something seems to have gone wrong with the timing.'

'Well, that has been seen to. The blow-up must be nearly ready, and it's going to start in this very place. Listen to me very carefully. The story begins two years ago in Castle Gay.'

Briefly but vigorously Alison told the tale of the raid on the Canonry and the discomfiture by Jaikie and Dickson McCunn of Mastrovin and his gang. ('Jaikie?' said Sir Archie. 'That's the little chap we saw with you at Maurice's? I was in a scrap alongside him years ago. Janet knows the story. Good stamp of lad.') She sketched the personalities of the three Royalists and the six Republicans, and she touched lightly upon Prince John. She described the face seen the afternoon before in the old village, and her sight that morning of the Prince and Casimir at the woodcutter's hut. The drama culminated in Mastrovin squatted like a partridge in the scrub above Casimir's car.

'Mastrovin!' Sir Archie brooded. 'He was at Geneva as an Evallonian delegate. Wonderful face of its kind, but it would make any English jury bring him in guilty of any crime without leaving the box. He was very civil to me. I thought him a miscreant but a sportsman, though I wouldn't like to meet him alone on a dark night. He looked the kind of chap who wasn't afraid of anything except the other Evallonian female. You remember her, Janet?'

His wife laughed. 'Shall I ever forget her? You never saw such a girl, Allie. A skin like clear amber, and eyes like topazes, and the most wonderful dark hair. She dressed always in bright scarlet and somehow carried it off. Archie, who as you know is a bit of a falconer, remembered that in the seventeenth century there was a hawk called the Blood-Red Rook of Turkey, so we always called her that. She was a Countess Araminta Something-or-other.'

Alison's eyes opened. 'I know her – at least, I have met her. She was in London the season before last. Her mother was English, I think, and hence her name. She rather scared me. She wasn't a delegate, was she?'

'No,' said Archie. 'She held a watching brief for something. I can tell you she scared old Mastrovin. He didn't like to be in the same room with her, and he changed his hotel when she turned up at it.'

'Never mind the Blood-Red Rook,' said Alison. 'Mastrovin is our problem. I don't care a hoot for Evallonian politics, but having once been on the Monarchist side I'm going to stick to it. Evallonia is apparently at boiling point. The Monarchist cause depends upon Prince John. Mastrovin is for the Republic or something still shadier, and therefore he is against Prince John. That innocent doesn't know his enemy is about, and Casimir has gone off in the direction of Italy. Therefore we have got to do something about it.'

'What puzzles me,' said Archie, 'is what your Prince is doing in Unnutz, which isn't exactly next door to Evallonia, and why he should want to get himself up as a peasant?'

'It puzzles me, too, but that isn't the point. It all shows that things are getting warm in Evallonia. What we have got to do is to dig Prince John out of that hut before Mastrovin murders or kidnaps him, and stow him away in some safer place. I considered it rather a heavy job for me alone, but it should be child's play for the three of us. Don't tell me you decline to play.'

During the last few minutes of the conversation Archie's face had been steadily brightening.

'Of course we'll play,' he said. 'You can count us in, Alison, but I'm getting very discreet in my old age, and I must think it over pretty carefully. It's a chancy business purloining princes, however good your intentions may be. The thing's easy enough, but it's the follow-up that matters... Wait a second. I've always believed that the best hiding place was just under the light. What about bringing him to this hotel to join our party?'

'As Prince John or as a woodcutter?' Janet asked.

'As neither,' said Archie. 'My servant got flu in Geneva, and I had to leave him behind. How would the Prince fancy taking on the job? I can lend him some of my clothes. Is he the merry class of lad that likes a jape?'

The luncheon gong boomed. 'We can talk about that later,' said Alison. 'Meanwhile, it's agreed that we three slip out of this place after dark. We'll take your car part of the way, and there's a moon, and I can guide you the rest. We daren't delay, for I'm positive that this very night Mastrovin will get busy.'

Sir Archie arose with mirth in his eye, patted his hair and squared his shoulders. A boy approached and handed him a telegram.

'It's from Bobby Despenser,' he announced. 'The Conference has resumed and he wants me back at once. Well, he can whistle for me.'

He tore the flimsy into small pieces.

'Take notice, you two,' he said, 'that most unfortunately I have not received Bobby's wire.'

III

On the following morning three people sat down to a late breakfast in a private sitting-room of the Hôtel Kaiserin Augusta. All three were a little heavy about the eyes, as if their night's rest had been broken, but in the air of each was a certain subdued excitement and satisfaction.

'My new fellow is settling down nicely,' said Sir Archie, helping himself to his third cup of coffee. 'Answers smartly to the name of McTavish. Lucky I brought the real McTavish's passport with me. Curious thing, but the passport photograph isn't unlike him, and he has almost the same measurements. I've put some sticking plaster above his left eye to correspond to the scar that McTavish got in Mespot, and I've had a go at his hair with scissors – he objected pretty strongly to that, by the way. I've put him into my striped blue flannel suit, which you could tell for English a mile away, and given him a pair of my old brown shoes. Thank God, he's just about my size. I'm going to buy him a black Homburg – the shops here are full of them – and then he'll look the very model of a gentleman's gentleman, who has had to supplement his London wardrobe locally.'

'But, Archie, he has the kind of face that you can't camouflage,' said Janet. 'Anyone who knows him is bound to recognise him.'

Her husband waved his hand. '*N'ayez pas peur, je m'en charge*, as old Perriot used to say at Geneva. He won't be recognised, because no one will expect him here. He's in the wrong environment – under the light, so to speak, which is the best sort of hiding-place. He won't go much out of doors, and I've got a cubby hole of a bedroom up in the attics. Not too comfortable, but Pretenders to thrones must expect to rough it a bit. He'll mess with the servants, who are of every nationality on earth, and I've told him to keep his mouth shut. Like all royalties, he's a dab at languages, and speaks English without an accent, but I'm teaching him to give his words a Scotch twist. He tumbled to it straight off, and says "Sirr" just like my old batman. If anyone makes trouble I've advised him to dot him one on the jaw in the best British style. He looks as if he could swing a good punch.'

The small hours of the morning had been a stirring time for the party. They had left the hotel by Alison's verandah a little before midnight, and in Archie's car had reached the foot of the forest path, meeting no one on the road. Then their way had become difficult, for it was very dark among the pines, and Alison had once or twice been at fault in her guiding. The moon rose when they were near the crest of the hill, and after that it had been easy to find the road to the hut through the dew-drenched pastures. There things marched fast. There was pandemonium with two dogs, quieted with difficulty by Alison, who had a genius for animals. The old woman, who appeared with a stable lantern, denied fiercely that there was any occupant of the hut except herself, her husband being dead these ten years and her only son gone over the mountains to a wedding. She was persuaded in the end by Alison's mention of Count Casimir, and the three were admitted.

Then Prince John had appeared fully dressed, with what was obviously a revolver in his pocket. He recognised Alison and had heard of Sir Archie, and things went more smoothly. The news that Mastrovin was on his trail obviously alarmed him, but he took a long time to be convinced about the need for shifting his residence. Clearly he was a docile instrument in the hands of the Monarchists, and hesitated to disobey their orders for fear of spoiling their plan. Things, it appeared, were all in train for a revolution in Evallonia, at any moment he might be required to act, and Unnutz had been selected as the council chamber of the conspirators. On this point it took the united forces of the party to persuade him, but in the end he saw reason. Alison clinched the matter. 'If Mastrovin and his friends get you, it's all up. If you come with us it may put a little grit in the wheels, but it won't smash the machine. Remember, sir, that these men are desperate, and won't stick at trifles. They were desperate two years ago at Castle Gay, but now it is pretty well your life or theirs, and it had better be theirs.'

When he allowed himself to be convinced his spirits rose. He was a young man of humour, and approved of Sir Archie's proposal that he should go to their hotel. He liked the idea of taking the place of the absent McTavish, and thought that he could fill the part. There only remained to give instructions to the old woman. If anyone came inquiring, she was not to deny the existence of her late guest, though she was to profess ignorance of who or what he was. Her story was to be that he had left the preceding afternoon with his belongings on his back. She did not know where he had gone, but believed that it was over the mountains to the Vossthal, since he had taken the path for the Vossjoch.

The journey back had been simple, though Alison had thought it wise to make a considerable detour. It had been slightly complicated by the good manners of the Prince, since he persisted in offering assistance to Janet and Alison, who needed it as little as a chamois. They had reached the hotel just before daybreak, and had entered, they believed, without being observed. That morning Sir Archie had explained to the manager about the delayed arrival of his servant, and the name of Angus McTavish had been duly entered in the hotel books with the Roylances' party.

'And now,' said Archie, 'he's busy attending to my dress clothes. What says the Scriptures? "Kings shall be thy ministers and queens thy nursing mothers." We're getting up in the world, Janet. I'm going to raise a chauffeur's cap for him, and I want him to take your parents, Alison, out in the car this afternoon to accustom the neighbourhood to the sight of a new menial. As for me, I propose to pay another visit to the hut. There's bound to have been developments up that way, and we ought to keep in touch with them. I'll be an innocent tourist out for a walk to observe birds.'

'What worries me,' said Janet, 'is how we are going to keep the Monarchists quiet. We may have Count Casimir here any moment, and that will give the show away.'

'No, it won't. I mean, he won't. I left a letter for him which will give him plenty to think about.'

Janet set down her coffee-cup. 'What did you say in the letter?' she demanded severely.

'McTavish wrote it – I only dictated the terms. He quite saw the sense of it. It was by way of being a piteous cry for help. It said he had been pinched by Mastrovin and his gang, and appealed to his friends to fly to his rescue. Quite affecting it was. You see the scheme? We've got to keep McTavish cool and quiet on the ice till things develop. If Casimir and his lot are looking for him in Mastrovin's hands they won't trouble us. If Mastrovin is being hunted by Casimir he won't be able to hunt McTavish. What you might call a cancelling out of snags.'

His wife frowned. 'I wonder if you've not been a little too clever.'

'Not a bit of it,' was the cheerful answer. 'Ordinary horse sense. As old Perriot said, "*N'ayez pas peur* –" '

'Archie,' said Janet, 'if you quote that stuff again I shall fling the coffee pot at you.'

IV

Sir Archie did not return till nine o'clock that evening, for he had walked every step of the road and had several times lost his way. He refreshed himself in the sitting-room with sandwiches and beer, while Janet and Alison had their after-dinner coffee.

'How did McTavish behave?' he asked Alison.

'Admirably. He drives beautifully and both Papa and Mamma thought he was Scotch. The only mistake was that he treated us like grandees, and held the door open with his cap in his hand. How about you? You look as if you had been seeing life?'

'I've had a trying time,' said Sir Archie, passing a hand through his hair. 'There has been a bit of a row up at the hut. No actual violence, but a good deal of unpleasantness.'

'Have you been fighting?' Janet asked, observing a long scratch on her husband's sunburnt forehead.

'Oh, that scratch is nothing, only the flick of a branch. But I've been through considerable physical tribulation. Wait till I get my pipe lit and you'll have the whole story...

'I reached the hut between four and five o'clock in what John Bunyan calls a pelting heat. Ye gods, but it was stuffy in the pinewoods, and blistering hot on the open hillside! I made pretty good time, and arrived rather out of condition, for my right leg – my game leg as was – wasn't quite functioning as it should. Well, there was the old woman, and in none too good a temper. Poor soul, she had been considerably chivvied since we last saw her. It seemed that we were just in time this morning, for Mastrovin and his merry men turned up about an hour after we left. It was a mercy we didn't blunder into them in the wood, and a mercy that we had the sense to hide the car a goodish distance from where the track starts. Mastrovin must have spent yesterday in sleuthing, for he had the ground taped, and knew that McTavish had been in the hut at supper. He had three fellows with him, and they gave the old lady a stiff time. They didn't believe her yarn about McTavish having started out for the Vossthal. They ransacked every corner of the place, and put in some fine detective work examining beds and cupboards and dirty dishes, besides raking the outhouses and beating the adjacent coverts. In the end they decided that their bird had flown and tried to terrorise the old lady into a confession. But she's a tough ancient, and by her account returned them as good as they gave. She wanted to know what concern her great-nephew Franz was of theirs, poor Franz that had lost his health working in Innsbruck and had come up into the hills to recruit. All their bullying couldn't shake her about great-nephew Franz, and in the end they took themselves off, leaving her with a very healthy dislike of the whole push.

'Then, very early this morning, Count Casimir turned up and got his letter. It put him in a great taking. She said he grew as white as a napkin, and he started to cross-examine her about the hour and the manner of the pinching of McTavish. That was where I had fallen down, for I had forgotten to tell her what was in the letter. So she gave a very confused tale, for she described him as going off with us, mentioning the women in the party, and she also described Mastrovin's coming, and from what she said I gathered that he got the two visits mixed up. What specially worried him was that Mastrovin should have had women with him, and he was very keen to know what they were like. I don't know how the old dame described you two – I should have liked to hear her – but anyway, it didn't do much to satisfy the Count. She said that he kept walking about biting his lips, and repeating a word that sounded like "Mintha". After that he was in a hurry to be off, but before leaving he gave her an address – I've written it down – with which she was to communicate if she got any news.

'I was just straightening out the story for her – I thought it right to get her mind clear – and explaining that we had got McTavish safe and sound, but that it was imperative in his own interests that Count Casimir should believe there had been dirty work, when what do you think happened? Mastrovin turned up, accompanied by a fellow who looked like a Jew barber out of a job. He didn't recognise me and looked at me very old-fashioned. I was sitting in a low chair, and got up politely to greet him, when I had an infernal piece of bad luck. I sprang every blessed muscle in my darned leg. You see, it hadn't been accustomed to so much exercise for a long time, and the muscles were all flabby. Gad, I never knew such pain! It was the worst go of cramp I ever heard of. My toes stuck out like agonising claws – my calf was a solid lump of torment – the riding muscle above the knee was stiff as a poker and as hard as iron. I must have gone white with pain, and I was all in a cold sweat, and I'm dashed if I could do anything except wallow in the chair and howl.

'Well, Mastrovin wasn't having any of that. He gave me some rough-tonguing in German, and demanded of the old woman what kind of mountebank I was. But she had taken her cue – pretty quick in the uptake she is – or else she thought I was having a paralytic stroke. I was all dithered with the pain and couldn't notice much, but I saw that she had got off my shoes and stockings and had fetched hot water to bathe my feet. Then the barber fellow took a hand, for he saw I wasn't playing a game. I dare say he was some kind of medico and he knew his business. He started out to massage me, beginning with the lower thigh, and I recognised the professional touch. In a few minutes he had me easier, and you know the way the thing goes – suddenly all the corded muscles dropped back into their proper places, and I was out of pain, but limp as chewing gum.

'Then Mastrovin began to ask me questions, first in German, and then in rather better English than my own. I gave him my name, and his face cleared a little, for he remembered me from Geneva. He was quite polite, but I preferred his rough-tonguing to his civility. A nasty piece of work that lad – his eyes are as cold as a fish's, but they go through you like a gimlet. I was determined to outstay him, for I didn't want him to be giving the old lady the third degree, which was pretty obviously what he had come for. So I pretended to be down and out, and lay back in her chair gasping, and drank water in a sad invalidish way. I would have stuck it out till midnight, but friend Mastrovin must have been pressed for time, for after about half an hour he got up to go. He offered to give me a hand down the hill, but I explained that I wasn't yet ready to move, but should be all right in an hour or so. I consider I brought off rather a creditable piece of acting, for he believed me. I also told him that I had just popped in to Unnutz for a night and was hurrying back to Geneva. He knew that the Conference had been resumed, but said that he himself might be a little late... That's about all. I gave him twenty minutes' law and then started home. D'you mind ringing the bell, Janet? I think I'll have an omelet and some more beer. Where's McTavish?'

'At his supper, I expect. What I want to know, Archie, is our next step. We can't go on hiding royal princes in the butler's pantry. McTavish will revolt out of sheer boredom.'

'I don't think so.' Archie shook a sapient head. 'McTavish is a patient fellow, and has had a pretty strict training these last years. Besides, life is gayer for him here than up at that hut, and the food must be miles better. We've got to play a waiting game, for the situation is obscure. I had a talk with him this morning, and by all accounts Evallonian politics are a considerable mix-up.'

'What did he tell you?' Alison asked sharply. She felt that to Archie and Janet it was all a game, but that she herself had some responsibility.

'Well, it seems that the revolution is ready to the last decimal – the press prepared, the National Guard won over, the people waiting, and the Ministers packing their portmanteaux. The Republican Government will go down like ninepins. But while the odds are all on the monarchy being restored, they are all against its lasting very long. It appears that in the last two years there has been a great movement in Evallonia of all the younger lot. They're tired of having the old 'uns call the tune and want to play a sprig themselves. I don't blame 'em, for the old 'uns have made a pretty mess of it.'

'Is that the thing they call Juventus?' Alison asked. 'I read about it in *The Times*.'

'Some name like that. Anyhow, McTavish tells me it's the most formidable thing Evallonia has seen for many a day. They hate the Republicans, and still more Mastrovin and his Communists. But they won't have anything to do with Prince John, for they distrust Count Casimir and all that lot. Call them the "old gang", the same bouquets as we hand to our elder statesmen, and want a fresh deal with new measures and new men. They're said to be more than half a million strong, all likely lads in hard condition and jolly well trained – they've specialised in marksmanship, for which Evallonia was always famous. They have the arms and the money, and, being all bound together by a blood oath, their discipline is the stiffest thing on earth. Oh, and I forgot to tell you – they wear green shirts – foresters' green. They have a marching song about the green of their woodlands, and the green of their mountain lakes, and the green shirts of Evallonia's liberators. It's funny what a big part fancy haberdashery plays in the world today.'

'Have they a leader?' Alison asked.

'That's what I can't make out. There doesn't seem to be any particular *roi de chemises* – that's what Charles Lamancha used to call me in my dressy days. But apparently the thing leads itself. The fact we've got to face is that if Casimir puts McTavish on the throne, which apparently he can do with his left hand, Juventus will kick him out in a week, and McTavish naturally doesn't want that booting. That's why he has been so docile. He sees that the right policy for him is to lie low till things develop.'

'Then our next step must be to get in touch with Juventus,' said Alison.

Janet opened her eyes. 'You're taking this very seriously, Allie,' she said.

'I am,' was the answer. 'You see, I was in it two years ago.'

'But how is it to be done?' Archie asked. 'McTavish doesn't know. He doesn't know who the real leaders are – not Casimir, and certainly not Mastrovin. You see, the thing is by way of being a secret society, sort of jumble-up of Boy Scouts, Freemasons and the Red Hand. They have their secret passwords, and the brightest journalist never sticks his head into one of their conclaves. They can spot a Monarchist or Republican spy a mile off, and don't stand on ceremony with 'em. They have a badge like Hitler's swastika – an open eye – but, apart from their songs and their green shirts, that's their only public symbol.'

'My advice,' said Janet, 'is that we keep out of it, and restore the Prince to the sorrowing Count Casimir as soon as we can get in touch with him. You go back to Scotland with your family, Allie, and Archie and I will pop down into Italy.'

There was a knock at the door and a waiter brought in the evening post. One letter was for Alison, which she tore open eagerly as soon as she saw the handwriting. She read it three times and then raised a flushed face.

'It's from Jaikie,' she said, and there was that in her voice which made Archie and Janet look up from their own correspondence. 'Jaikie, you know – my friend – Mr Galt that I told you about. He is somewhere in Evallonia.'

'My aunt!' exclaimed Archie. 'Then there will be trouble for somebody.'

'There's trouble for him. He seems to have got into deep waters. Listen to what he says.'

She read the following:

'I am in a queer business which I am bound to see through. But I can't do it without your help. Can you manage to get away from your parents for a few days, and come to Tarta, just inside the Evallonian frontier? You take the train to a place called Zutpha, where you will be met. If you can come wire Odalchini, Tarta, the time of your arrival. I wouldn't bother you if the thing wasn't rather important, and, besides, I think you would like to be in it.'

'Short and to the point,' commented the girl. 'Jaikie never wastes words. He has a genius for understatement, so if he says it is rather important it must be tremendously important... Wait a minute. Odalchini! Prince Odalchini was one of the three at Knockraw two years ago. Jaikie has got mixed up with the Monarchists.'

Archie was hunting through his notebook. 'What did you say was the name of the place? Tarta? That's the address Casimir gave the old woman to write to if she had any news. Schloss Thingumabob – the second word has about eight consonants and no vowels – Tarta, by Zutpha. Your friend Jaikie has certainly got among the Monarchists.'

'Hold on!' Alison cried. 'What's this?' She passed round the letter for inspection. It was a sheet of very common notepaper with no address on it, but in the top left-hand corner there was stamped in green a neat little open eye with some hieroglyphic initials under it.

'Do you see what that means?' In her excitement her voice sank to a whisper. 'Jaikie is in touch with the Juventus people. This letter was sent with their consent – or the consent of one of them, and franked by him.'

'Well, Allie?' Janet asked.

'Of course I'm going. I must go. But I can't go alone, for Papa wouldn't allow it. He and Mamma have decided to return to Scotland this week to Aunt Harriet at Castle Gay. You and Archie must go to Tarta and take me with you.'

'Isn't that a large order? What about McTavish?'

'We must take him with us, for then we'll have all the cards in our hands. It's going to be terribly exciting, but I can promise you that Jaikie won't fail us. You won't fail me either?'

Janet turned smilingly to her husband. 'What about it, Archie?'

'I'm on,' was the answer. 'I've been in a mix-up with Master Jaikie before. Bobby Despenser can whistle for me. The difficulty will be McTavish, who's a compromising piece of goods, but we'll manage somehow. Lord, this is like old times, and I feel about ten years younger. "It little profits that an idle king, matched with an aged wife..." Don't beat me, Janet. We're both ageing... I always thought that the Almighty didn't get old Christoph to mend my leg for nothing.'

CHAPTER 4

Difficulties of a Revolutionary

When Jaikie saw who his captor was, his wrath ebbed. Had it been Prince Odalchini it would have been an outrage, but since it was Ashie, it was only an undergraduate 'rag' which could easily be repaid in kind. But his demeanour was severe.

'What's the meaning of these monkey tricks?' he demanded.

'The meaning is,' Ashie had ceased to smile, 'that you have deceived me. What about your business with your circus friend? I had you followed – I was bound to take every precaution – and instead of feeding in a pot-house you run in circles like a hunted hare and end up at the Schloss. I had my men inside the park, and when I heard what you were up to I gave orders that you should be brought before me. You went straight from me to the enemy. What have you to say to that?'

Ashie's words were firm, but there was dubiety in his voice and a hint of uncertainty in his eye; this the other observed, and the sight wholly removed his irritation. Ashie was talking like a book, but he was horribly embarrassed.

'Well, I'm blowed!' said Jaikie. 'Who the blazes made you my keeper? Let's get this straightened out at once. First, what I said was strictly true. I was going to lunch with my friend from the circus. If your tripe-hounds had been worth their keep they would have seen me meet him – a fellow with the name of the circus blazoned on his cap. The choice of a luncheon place was his own and I had nothing to do with it. As a matter of fact, I happened to know the man he took me to, Prince Odalchini – I met him two years ago in Scotland. Have you got that into your fat head?'

'Will you please give me the gist of your conversation with Prince Odalchini?'

'Why on earth should I? What has it got to do with you? But I'll tell you one thing. He was very hospitable and wanted me to stay a bit with him – same as you. I said no, that I wanted to go home, and I was on my way back when I fell in with your push and got my head into a bag. What do you mean by it? I'm sorry to tell you that you have taken a liberty – and I don't allow liberties.'

'Prince Odalchini is the enemy, and we are in a state of war.'

'Get off it. He's not my enemy, and I don't know anything about your local scraps. I told you I would have nothing to do with them, and I told the Prince the same.'

'So you talked of Evallonian affairs?' said Ashie.

'Certainly. What else was there to talk about? Not that he told me much, except that there was likely to be trouble and that he wanted me to stay on and see the fun. I told him I wasn't interested in his tinpot politics and I tell you the same.'

This had the effect which Jaikie intended, and made Ashie angry.

'I do not permit such language,' he said haughtily. 'I do not tolerate insults to my country. Understand that you are not in your sleek England, but in a place where gentlemen defend their honour in the old way.'

'Oh, don't be a melodramatic ass. I thought we had civilised you at Cambridge and given you a sense of humour, but you've relapsed into the noble savage. I've been in Evallonia less than one day and I know nothing about it. Your politics may be all the world to you, but they're tinpot to me. I refuse to be mixed up in them.'

'You've mixed yourself up in them by having intercourse with the enemy.'

'Enemy be blowed! I talked for an hour or two to a nice old man who gave me a dashed good luncheon, and now you come butting in with your detective-novel tricks. I demand to be deported at once. Otherwise I'll raise the hairiest row about the kidnapping of a British subject. If you want international trouble, I promise you you'll get it. I don't know where we are, but here's this car, and you've got to deliver me at Kremisch by bedtime. That's the least you can do to make amends for your cheek.'

Jaikie looked out of the window and observed that they had halted on high ground, and that below them lights twinkled as if from an encampment. For a moment he thought that he had struck the Cirque Doré. And then a bugle sounded, an instrument not generally used in circuses. 'Is that your crowd down there?' he asked.

Ashie's face, even in the dim interior light of the car, showed perplexity. He seemed to be revolving some difficult question in his mind. When he spoke again there was both appeal and apology in his voice. Jaikie had an authority among his friends which was the stronger because he was wholly unconscious of it and in no way sought it. His personality was so clean-cut and his individuality so complete and secure that, while one or two gave him affection, all gave him respect.

'I'll apologise if you like,' said Ashie. 'I dare say what I did was an outrage. But the fact is, Jaikie, I badly want your help. Your advice, anyway. I'm in a difficult position, and I don't see my road very clearly. You see, I'm an Evallonian, and this is Evallonian business, but I've got a little outside the atmosphere of my own country. That's to the good, perhaps, for this thing is on the biggest scale and wants looking at all round it. That's why I need your help. Give me one night, and I swear, if you still want me to, I'll deliver you at Kremisch tomorrow morning and trouble you no more.'

Jaikie was the most placable of mortals, he had a strong liking for Ashie, and he was a little moved by the anxious sincerity of his voice. He had half expected this proposal.

'All right,' he said, 'I'll give you one night. Have your fellows pinched my kit?'

Ashie pointed to a knapsack on the floor of the car, which he promptly shouldered. 'Let's get out of this,' he said. He spoke a word to the driver, who skipped round and opened the door, standing stiffly at the salute. Then he led the way down the little slope into the meadow of the twinkling lights. Presently he had to give a password, and three times had to halt for that purpose before they reached his tent. The gathering was far larger than that which Jaikie had seen at the Tarta bridge, and he noticed a considerable number of picketed horses.

'What are these chaps after?' he asked.

'We are riding the marches,' was the answer. 'What at Cambridge they call beating the bounds. It is not desirable that for the present we should operate too near the capital.'

There were two tents side by side and separated by a considerable space from the rest, as if to ensure the commander's privacy. A sentry stood on guard whom Ashie dismissed with an order. He led Jaikie into the bigger of the tents. It was furnished with a camp mattress, two folding chairs, and a folding table littered with maps. 'You will sleep next door. You may have a companion for the night, but of that I speak later. Meantime, let us dine. I can only offer you soldiers' fare.'

The fare proved excellent. A mushroom omelet was brought in by one of the green-shirts, and cups of strong coffee. There was a dish of assorted cold meats, and a pleasantly mild cheese. They drank white wine, and Ashie insisted on Jaikie tasting the native liqueur. 'It is made from the lees of wine,' he told him. 'Like the French marc, but not so vehement.'

When the meal was cleared away Jaikie lit his pipe and Ashie a thin black cigar. 'Now for my story,' the latter said. 'There is one fact beyond question. The rotten Republican Government is doomed, and hangs now by a single hair which a breath of wind can destroy. But when the hair has gone, what then?'

He told much the same tale that Jaikie had heard that day from Prince Odalchini, but with a far greater wealth of detail. Especially he expounded the origin and nature of Juventus, with which he had been connected from the start. 'Most of this is common knowledge,' he said, 'but not all – yet. We are not a secret society, but we have our *arcana imperii*.' He described its beginnings. Ricci had designed it as a counter move against the Monarchists, but it had soon turned into something very different, a power detached indeed from the Monarchists but altogether hostile to the Republic, and Ricci, the used instead of the user, had been flung aside. 'It was no less than a resurgence of the spirit of the Evallonian nation,' he said solemnly.

He explained how it had run through the youth of the country like a flame in stubble. 'We are a poor people,' he said, 'though not so poor as some, for we are closer to the soil, and less dependent upon others. But we have been stripped of some of our richest parts where industry flourished, and many of us are in great poverty. Especially it is hard for the young, who see no livelihood for them in their fathers' professions, and can find none elsewhere. Evallonia, thanks to the jealous Powers, has been reduced to too great an economic simplicity, and has not that variety of interests which a civilised society requires. Also there is another matter. We have always made a hobby of our education, as in your own Scotland. Parents will starve themselves to send their sons to Melina to the university, and often a commune itself will pay for a clever boy. What is the consequence? We have an educated youth, but no work for it. We have created an academic proletariat and it is distressed and bitter.'

Ashie told his story well, but his language was not quite his native woodnotes. Jaikie wondered whose reflections he was repeating. He wondered still more when he launched into an analysis of the exact feelings of Evallonian youth. There was a subtlety in it and an acumen which belonged to a far maturer and more sophisticated mind.

'So that is that,' he concluded. 'If our youth is to be satisfied and our country is to prosper, it is altogether necessary that the Government should be taken to pieces and put together again on a better plan. What that plan is our youth must decide, and whatever it is it must provide them with a horizon of opportunity. We summon our people to a new national discipline under which everyone shall have both rights and duties.'

Where had Ashie got these phrases, Jaikie asked himself – '*arcana imperii*', 'academic proletariat', 'horizon of opportunity'? There must be some philosopher in the background. 'That sounds reasonable enough,' was all he said.

'It is reasonable – but difficult. Some things we will not have. Communism, for one – of that folly Europe contains too many awful warnings. We have had enough talk of republics, which are the dullest species of oligarchy. Evallonia, having history in her bones, is a natural monarchy. Her happiest destiny would be to be like England.'

'That is all right then,' said Jaikie. 'You have Prince John.'

Ashie's face clouded.

'Alas! that is not possible. For myself I have nothing against the Prince. He represents our ancient line of kings, and he is young, and he is well spoken of, though I have never met him. But he is fatally compromised. His supporters, who are about to restore him, are indeed better men than our present mis-governors, but they are relics – fossils. They would resurrect an old world with all its stupidities. They are as alien to us as Mastrovin and Rosenbaum, though less hateful. If Prince John is set upon the throne, it is very certain that our first duty will be regretfully to remove him – regretfully, for it is not the Prince that we oppose, but his following.'

'I see,' said Jaikie. 'It *is* rather a muddle. Are the Monarchists only a collection of stick-in-the-muds?'

'You can judge for yourself. You have seen Prince Odalchini, who is one of the best. He worships dead things – he speaks the language of a vanished world.'

Once again Jaikie wondered how Ashie, whose talk had hitherto been chiefly of horses, had managed to acquire this novel jargon.

'You want a king, but you won't – or can't – have the Prince. Then you've got to find somebody else. What's your fancy? Have you a possible in your own rank?'

Ashie knit his brows. 'I do not think so. We have admirable regimental officers and good brigadiers, but no general-in-chief. Juventus was a spontaneous movement of many people, and not the creation of one man.'

'But you must have leaders.'

'Leaders – but no leader. The men who presided at its birth have gone. There was Ricci, who was a trickster and a coward. He has washed himself out. There was my father, who is now dead. I do not think that he would have led, for he was not sure of himself. He had great abilities, but he was too clever for the common run of people, and he was not trusted. He was ambitious, and since his merits were not recognised, he was always unhappy, and therefore he was ineffective. I have inherited the prestige of his name, but the Almighty has given me a more comfortable nature.'

'Why not yourself?' Jaikie asked. 'You seem to fill the bill. Young and bold and not yet compromised. Ashie the First – or would it be Paul the Nineteenth? I'll come and grovel at your coronation.'

Jaikie's tone of badinage gave offence.

'There is nothing comic in the notion,' was the haughty answer. 'Four hundred years ago my ancestors held the gates of Europe against the Turk. Two centuries before that they rode in the Crusades. The house of Jovian descends straight from the Emperors of Rome. I am of an older and prouder race than Prince John.'

'I'm sure you are,' said Jaikie apologetically. 'Well, why not have a shot at it? I would like to have a pal a reigning monarch.'

'Because I cannot,' said Ashie firmly. 'I am more confident than my father, God rest his soul, but in such a thing I do not trust myself. Your wretched England has spoiled me. I do not want pomp and glory. I should yawn my head off in a palace, and I should laugh during the must solemn ceremonials, and I should certainly beat my Ministers. I desire to remain a private gentleman and some day to win your Grand National.'

Jaikie whistled.

'We have certainly spoiled you for this game. What's to be done about it?'

'I do not know,' was the doleful answer. 'For I cannot draw back. There have been times when I wanted to slip away and hide myself in England. But I am now too deep in the business, and I have led too many people to trust me, and I have to consider the honour of my house.'

'Honour?' Jaikie queried.

'Yes, honour,' said Ashie severely. 'Have you anything to say against it?'

'No. But it's an awkward word and apt to obscure reason.'

'It is a very real thing, which you English do not understand.'

'We understand it well enough, but we are shy of talking about it. Remember the inscription in the Abbey of Thelème – "*Fais ce que voudrais*, for the desires of decent men will always be governed by honour."'

Ashie smiled, for Rabelais, as Jaikie remembered, had been one of the few authors whom he affected.

'That doesn't get one very far,' he said. 'I can't leave my friends in the lurch any more than you could. I have been forced in spite of myself into a position out of which I cannot see my way, and any moment I may have to act against my will and against my judgment. That's why I want your advice.'

'There are people behind you prodding you on? Probably one in particular? Who is it?'

'I cannot say.'

'Well, I can. It's a woman.'

Ashie's face darkened, and this time he was really angry. 'What the devil do you mean? What have you heard? I insist that you explain.'

'Sorry, Ashie. That was a silly remark, and I had no right to make it.'

'You must mean something. Someone has been talking to you. Who? What? Quick, I have a right to know.'

Ashie had mounted a very high horse and had become unmistakably the outraged foreign grandee.

'It was only a vulgar guess,' said Jaikie soothingly. 'You see, I know you pretty well, Ashie. It isn't easy to shift you against your will. I couldn't do it, and I don't believe any of your friends could do it. You've become a sensible chap since we took you in hand, and look at things in a reasonable way. You're not the kind of fellow to run your head against a stone wall. Here you are with all the materials of a revolution in your hands and you haven't a notion what to do with them. It's no good talking about honour and about loyalty to your crowd when if you go on you are only going to land them in the soup. And yet you seem determined to go on. Somebody has been talking big to you and you're impressed. From what I know of you I say that it cannot be a man, so it must be a woman.'

Ashie's face did not relax.

'So you think I'm that kind of fool! The slave of a sentimental woman?... The damnable thing is that you're right. The power behind Juventus is a girl. Quite young – just about my own age. A kinswoman of mine, too, sort of second cousin twice removed. I'll tell you her name. The Countess Araminta Troyos.'

Jaikie's blank face witnessed that he had never heard of the lady.

'I've known her all my life,' Ashie went on, 'and we have been more or less friends, though I never professed to understand her. Beautiful? Oh yes, amazingly, if you admire the sable and amber

65

type. And brains! She could run round Muresco and his lot, and even Mastrovin has a healthy respect for her. And ambition enough for half a dozen Mussolinis. And her power of – what do you call the damned thing? – mass persuasion? – is simply unholy. She is the soul of Juventus. There's not one of them that doesn't carry a picture postcard of her next his heart.'

'What does she want? To be Queen?'

'Not she, though she would make a dashed good one. She's old-fashioned in some ways, and doesn't believe much in her own sex. Good sane anti-feminist. She wants a man on the throne of Evallonia, but she's going to make jolly well sure that it's she who puts him there.'

'I see.' Jaikie whistled gently through his teeth, which was a habit of his. 'Are you in love with her?'

'Ye gods, no! She's not my kind. I'd as soon marry a were-wolf as Cousin Mintha.'

'Is she in love with you?'

'No. I'm positive no. She could never be in love with anybody in the ordinary way. She runs for higher stakes. But she mesmerises me, and that's the solemn truth. When she orates to me I feel all the pith going out of my bones. I simply can't stand up to her. I'm terrified of her. Jaikie, I'm in danger of making a blazing, blasted fool of myself. That's why I want you.'

Ashie's cheerful face had suddenly become serious and pathetic, like a puzzled child's, and at the sight of it Jaikie's heart melted. He was not much interested in Evallonia, but he was fond of Ashie, now in the toils of an amber and sable Cleopatra. He could not see an old friend dragged into trouble by a crazy girl without doing something to prevent it. A certain *esprit de sexe* was added to the obligations of friendship.

'But what can I do?' he asked. 'I don't know the first thing about women – I've hardly met any in my life – I'm no match for your cousin.'

'You can help me to keep my head cool,' was the answer. 'You stand for the world of common sense which will always win in the long run. When I'm inclined to run amok you'll remind me of England. You'll lower the temperature.'

'You want me to hold your hand?'

'Just so. To hold my hand.'

'Well,' said Jaikie after a pause. 'I don't mind trying it out for a fortnight. You'll have to give me free board and lodging, or I won't have the money to take me home.'

Ashie's face cleared so miraculously that for one uncomfortable moment Jaikie thought that he was about to be embraced. Instead he shook hands with a grip like iron.

'You're a true friend,' he said. 'Come what may, I'll never forget this... There's another thing. Unless we're to have civil war there must be some arrangement. Somebody must keep in touch with the Monarchists, or in a week there will be bloody battles. Juventus has cut off all communication with the enemy and burned its boats, but it cannot be allowed to go forward blindly, and crash head-on into the other side. I want a *trait d'union*, and you're the man for it. I can't do it, for I'm too conspicuous – I should be found out at once, and suspected for treachery. But you know Prince Odalchini. You've got to be my go-between. How do you fancy the job?'

Jaikie fancied it a good deal. It promised amusement and a field for his special talents.

'It won't be too easy,' Ashie went on. 'You see, you're by way of being my prisoner. All my fellows by this time know about your visit to the Prince and my having you kidnapped. We've tightened up the screws in Juventus, and I daren't let you go now.'

'Then if I hadn't decided to stay, you'd have kept me by force?' Jaikie demanded.

'No. I would have delivered you at Kremisch according to my promise, but it would have been an uncommon delicate job, and I should have had to do the devil of a lot of explaining. I've given out that you are an English friend, who is not hostile but knows too much to be safe. So you'll have to be guarded, and your visits to the House of the Four Winds will have to be nicely camouflaged. Lucky I'm in charge of Juventus on this side of the country.'

'You've begun by handicapping me pretty heavily,' said Jaikie. 'But I'll keep my word and have a try.'

An orderly appeared at the tent door with a message. Ashie looked at his watch.

'Your stable companion for the night has arrived,' he said. 'I think you'd better clear out while I'm talking to him. He's an English journalist, and rather a swell, I believe, who has been ferreting round for some weeks in Evallonia. It won't do to antagonise the foreign press just yet – especially the English, so I promised to see him tonight and give him some dope. But I'll see that he's beyond the frontier tomorrow morning. We don't want any Paul Prys in this country at present.'

'What's his name?' Jaikie asked with a sudden premonition.

Ashie consulted a paper. 'Crombie – Dougal Crombie. Do you know him?'

'I've heard of him. He's second in command on the Craw Press, isn't he?'

'He is. And he'll probably be a sentimental royalist, like the old fool who owns it.'

Long ago in the Glasgow closes there had been a signal used among the Gorbals Die-hards, if one member did not desire to be recognised when suddenly confronted by another. So when Mr Crombie was ushered into the tent and observed beside the Juventus commander a slight shabby figure, which pinched its chin with the left hand and shut its left eye, he controlled his natural surprise and treated Ashie as if he were alone.

'May I go to bed, sir?' Jaikie asked. 'I'm blind with sleep, and I won't be wakened by my fellow guest.'

Ashie assented, and Jaikie gave the Juventus salute and withdrew, keeping his eyes strictly averted from the said fellow guest.

He did not at once undress, but sat on the sleeping valise and thought. His mind was not on the House of the Four Winds and the difficulties of keeping in touch with Prince Odalchini; it was filled with the picture of an amber and sable young woman. That he believed to be the real snag, and he felt himself unequal to coping with it. In the end, on notepaper which Ashie had given him, he wrote two letters. The first was to Miss Alison Westwater and the second to Prince Odalchini; then he got into pyjamas, curled himself inside the valise, and was almost at once asleep.

He was wakened by being poked in the ribs, and found beside him the rugged face of Dougal illumined by a candle.

'How on earth did you get here, Jaikie?' came the hoarse whisper.

'By accident,' was the sleepy answer. 'Ran into Ashie – that's Count Paul – knew him at Cambridge. I'm a sort of prisoner, but I'll be all right. Don't ask me about Evallonia, for you know far more than me.'

'I dare say I do,' said Dougal. 'Man, Jaikie, this is a fearsome mess. Mr Craw will be out of his mind with vexation. Here's everything ripe for a nice law-abiding revolution, and this dam-fool Juventus chips in and wrecks everything. I like your Count Paul, and he has some rudiments of sense, but he cannot see that what he is after is sheer lunacy. The Powers are in an easy temper, and there would be no trouble about an orderly restoration of the old royal house. But if these daft lads start running some new dictator fellow that nobody ever heard of, Europe will shut down like a clam. Diplomatic relations suspended – economic boycott – the whole bag of tricks. It's maddening that the people who most want to kick out the present Government should be working to give it a fresh lease of life, simply because they insist on playing a lone hand.'

'I know all that,' said Jaikie. 'Go away, Dougal, and let me sleep.'

'I tell you what' – Dougal's voice was rising, and he lowered it at Jaikie's request – 'we need a first-class business mind on this job. There's just one man alive that I'd listen to, and that's Mr McCunn. He's at Rosensee, and that's not a thousand miles off, and he's quite recovered now and will likely be as restless as a hen. I'm off there tomorrow morning to lay the case before him.'

'Good,' Jaikie answered. 'Now get to bed, will you?'

'I must put him in touch with Count Casimir and Prince Odalchini – the big Schloss at Tarta is the place – that's the Monarchist centre. And what about yourself? How can I find you?'

'If I'm not hanged,' said Jaikie drowsily, 'it will be at the same address. I'll turn up there sometime or other. I wish you'd put these two letters in your pocket, and post them tomorrow when you're over the frontier. And now for pity's sake let me sleep.'

CHAPTER 5

Surprising Energy of a Convalescent

Mr Dickson McCunn sat in a wicker chair with his feet on the railing of a small verandah, and his eyes on a wide vista of plain and forest which was broken by the spires of a little town. Now and then he turned to beam upon a thick-set, red-haired young man who occupied a similar chair on his left hand. He wore a suit of grey flannel, a startling pink shirt and collar, and brown suede shoes – things so foreign to his usual wear that they must have been acquired for this occasion. He was looking remarkably well, with a clear eye and a clear skin to which recent exposure to the sun had given a becoming rosiness. His hair was a little thinner than two years ago, but no greyer. Indeed, the only change was in his figure, which had become more trim and youthful. Dougal judged that he had reduced his weight by at least a stone.

He patted his companion's arm.

'Man, Dougal, I'm glad to see you. I was thinking just yesterday that the thing I would like best in the world would be to see you and Jaikie coming up the road. I've been wearying terribly for the sight of a kenned face. I knew you were somewhere abroad, and I had a sort of notion that you might give me a look in. Are they making you comfortable here? It's not just the place I would recommend for a healthy body, for they've a poor notion of food.'

71

'Me?' he exclaimed in reply to a question. 'I've never been better in my life. It's a perfect miracle. I walked fifteen miles the day before yesterday and never turned a hair. I'll give the salmon a fright this back end. I tell you, Dougal, Dr Christoph hasn't his equal on this earth. He's my notion of the Apostles that could make the lame walk and the blind see. When I came here I was a miserable decrepit body that couldn't sleep, and couldn't take his meat, and wanted to lie down when he had walked a mile. He saw me twice a day, and glowered and glunched at me, like an old-fashioned minister at the catechising, and asked me questions – he's one that would speir a whelk out of its shell. But he wouldn't deliver a judgment – not him – just told me to possess my soul in patience till he was ready. He made me take queer wee medicines, and he prescribed what I was to eat. Oh, and I had what they call massage – he was a wonder at that, for he seemed to flype my body as you would flype a stocking. And I had to take a daft kind of bath, with first hot water and then cold water dropping on me from the ceiling and every drop like a rifle bullet. I thought I had wandered into a demented hydropathic... Then after three weeks he spoke. "Mr McCunn," he says, "I'm happy to tell you that there's nothing wrong with you. There's been a heap wrong, but it's gone now, the mischief is out of your system, and all you have to do is to build your system up. You will soon be able to eat what you like," he says, "and the more the better, and you can walk till you fall down, and you can ride on a horse" – not that I was likely to try that – "and I don't mind if you tumble into the burn. You're a well man," he says, "but I'd like to keep you here for another three weeks under observation." Oh, and he wrote a long screed about my case for the Edinburgh professor – I've got a copy of it – I don't follow it all, for it is pretty technical and Dr Christoph isn't very grand at English. But the plain fact is, that I've been a sick man and am now well, and that in five days' time I'll be on the road for Blaweary, singing the 126th Psalm.

'Among the heathen say the Lord
Great things for us hath wrought.'

Mr McCunn hummed a stave from the Scots metrical version to
a dolorous tune.

'You've been enjoying yourself fine,' said Dougal.

The other pursed his lips. 'I would scarcely say that. I've
enjoyed the fact of getting well, but I haven't altogether enjoyed
the process. There were whiles when I was terrible bored, me
that used to boast that I had never been bored in my life. The
first weeks it was like being back at the school. I had my bits of
walks prescribed for me, and the hours when I was to lie on my
back and rest, and when I sat down to my meals there was a
nurse behind my chair to see that I ate the right things and didn't
forget my medicine. I had an awful lot of time on my hands. I
doddered about among the fir woods – they're a careful folk, the
Germans, and have all the hillsides laid out like gentlemen's
policies – nice tidy walks, and seats to sit down on, and directions
about the road that I couldn't read. I'll not deny that it's a
bonny countryside – in its way, but the weather was blazing hot
and I got terrible tired of these endless fir trees. It's a
monotonous place, for when you get to the top of one rig there's
another of the same shape beyond, covered with the same
woods. Man, I got fair sick for a sight of an honest bald-faced
hill.

'Indoors,' he went on, 'it was just the same. It's all very well
to be told to rest and keep your mind empty, but that was never
my way. I brought out a heap of books with me, and was looking
forward to getting a lot of quiet reading done. But the mischief
was that I couldn't settle to a book. I had intended to read the
complete works of Walter Savage Landor – have you ever tried
him, Dougal? I aye thought the quotations from him I came
across most appetising. But I might as well have been reading a
newspaper upside down, for I couldn't keep my mind on him. I
suppose that my thoughts having been so much concerned lately

with my perishing body had got out of tune for higher things. So I fell back on Sir Walter – I'm not much of a hand at novels, as you know, but I can always read Scott – but I wasn't half through *Guy Mannering* when it made me so homesick for the Canonry that I had to give it up. After that I became a mere vegetable, a bored vegetable.'

'You don't look very bored,' said Dougal.

'Oh, it's been different the last weeks, when the doctor told me I was cured, for I've been pretty nearly my own master. I've had some grand long walks – what you would call training walks, for I was out just for the exercise and never minded the scenery. I've sweated pounds and pounds of adipose tissue off my bones. I hired a car, too, and got Peter Wappit to drive it, and I've been exploring the countryside for fifty miles round. I've found some fine scenery and some very respectable public houses. You'll be surprised that I mention them, but the fact is that my mind has been dwelling shamelessly on food and drink. I've never been so hungry in all my days. I'm allowed to eat anything I like, but the trouble is that you can't get it in this house. The food is deplorable for a healthy man. Endless veal, which I cannot bide – and what they call venison, but is liker goat – and wee blue trouts that are as wersh as the dowp of a candle – and they've a nasty habit of eating plums and gooseberries with butcher's meat. I'll admit the coffee is fine, but they've no kind of notion of tea. Tea has always been my favourite meal, but here you never see a scone or a cookie – just things like a baby's rusks, and sweet cakes that you very soon scunner at. So I've had to supplement my diet at adjacent publics... I tell you what, Dougal, Peter is a perfect disgrace. It's preposterous that a man should have been two years in jyle in Germany and have picked up so little of the language. He just stammers and glowers and makes noises like a clocking hen, and it's me that has to do the questioning, with about six words of the tongue and every kind of daft-like grimace and contortion. If the Germans weren't an easy-tempered folk we'd have had a lot of trouble.

'But, thank God,' said Mr McCunn, 'that's all very near by with. I've got back my health and now I want something to occupy my mind and body.' He pushed back his chair, stood up, doubled his fists and made playful taps at Dougal's chest to prove his vigour.

'What about yourself, Dougal?' he said. 'Let's hear what you've been up to. Is Mr Craw still trying to read up the affairs of Europe?'

'He is. That's the reason I'm out here. And that's the reason I've come to see you. I want your advice.'

'In that case,' said Mr McCunn solemnly, 'we'd be the better of a drink. Beer is allowed here, and it's a fine mild brew. We'll have a tankard apiece.'

'Now,' said he, when the tankards had been brought, and he was comfortably settled again in his chair, 'I'm waiting on your story. Where have you come from?'

'From Evallonia.'

For a moment or two Dickson did not speak. The word set his mind digging into memories which had been heavily overlaid. In particular he recalled an autumn night on a Solway beach when in the moonlight a cutter swung down the channel with the tide. He saw a young man under whose greatcoat was a gleam of tartan, and he remembered vividly a scene which for him had been one of tense emotion. On the little finger of his left hand he wore that young man's ring.

'Aye, Evallonia,' he murmured. 'That's where you would be. And how are things going in Evallonia?'

'Bad. They couldn't be worse. Listen, Mr McCunn, and I'll give you the rudiments of a perfectly ridiculous situation.'

Dickson listened, and his occasional grunts told of his lively interest. When Dougal had finished, he remained for a little silent and frowning heavily. Then he began to ask questions.

'You say the Monarchists have got everything arranged and can put Prince John on the throne whenever they're so minded? Can they put up a good Government?'

'I think so. They've plenty of brains among them and plenty of experience. Count Casimir Muresco is a sort of lesser Cavour. I've seen a good deal of him and can judge. You'll remember him?'

'Aye, I mind him well. I thought he had some kind of a business head. Prince Odalchini was a fine fellow, but a wee thing in the clouds. What about the Professor – Jagon, I think they called him?'

'He has gone over to Juventus. Discovered that it fulfilled his notion of democracy. He was a maggoty old body.'

'Well, he'll maybe not be much loss. You say that there's a good Government waiting for Evallonia, but that this Juv – Juventus thing – that's Latin isn't it – won't hear of it because they didn't invent it themselves. What kind of shape would they make at running the country?'

'Bad, I think. They've brains, but no experience, and not much common sense. They're drunk with fine ideas and as full of pride as an old blackcock, but they're babes and sucklings at the job of civil administration.'

'But they've power behind them?'

'All the power there is in Evallonia. They've an armed force uncommon well trained and disciplined – you never saw a more upstanding lot of lads. The National Guard, which is all the army that is permitted under the Peace Treaty, is good enough in its way, but it's small, and the people don't give a hang for it. Juventus has captured the fancy of the nation, and with these Eastern European folk, that means that the battle is won. They can no more make a good Government than they could square the circle, but they can play the devil with any Government that they don't approve of. You may say that the real motive power in Evallonia today is destructive. But they'll have to set up some sort of figurehead – one of themselves, though there's nobody very obvious – and that will mean an infernal mess, the old futile dictatorship ran-dan, and no end of trouble with the Powers. I've the best reason to be positive on that point, for Mr Craw has seen – ' and he mentioned certain august names.

Dickson asked one other question. 'What about the Republicans?'

Dougal laughed. 'Oh, their number's up all right. Whoever is topdog, they're bound to be the bottom one for many a day. They've their bags packed waiting to skip over the frontier. But they'll do their best, of course, to make the mischief worse. Mastrovin, especially. If he's caught in Evallonia he'll get short shrift, but he'll be waiting outside to put spokes in the wheels.'

'Yon's the bad one,' said Dickson reflectively. 'When he is thrawn, he has a face that's my notion of the Devil... It seems that Juventus is the proposition we have to consider. What ails Juventus at Prince John?'

'Nothing. They've no ill will to him – only he's not their man. What they dislike is his supporters.'

'Why?'

'Simply because they're the old gang and associated in their minds with all the misfortunes and degradation of Evallonia since the War. Juventus is thinking of a new world, and won't have any truck with the old. They're new brooms, and are blind to the merits of the old besoms. They're like laddies at school, Mr McCunn – when catties come in they won't look at a bool or a girr.'

Dickson whistled morosely through his teeth.

'I see,' he said. 'Well, it looks ugly. What kind of advice do you want from me?'

'I want a business like view of the situation from a wise man, and you can't get that in Evallonia.'

'But how in the name of goodness can I give you any kind of view when I don't know the place or the folk?'

'I've tried to put the layout before you, and I want the common sense of a detached observer. You may trust my facts. I've done nothing but make inquiries for the last month, for the thing is coming between Mr Craw and his sleep. I've seen Count

Casimir and all his lot and talked with them till my brain was giddy. I've taken soundings in Evallonian public opinion, to which I had pretty good access.'

'Have you seen much of Juventus?'

Dougal drew down the corners of his mouth.

'Not a great deal. You see, it's a secret society, and you can no more get inside it than into a lodge of Masons. I've talked, of course, to a lot of the rank and file, and I can judge their keenness and their popular support. There was one of them I particularly wanted to see – a woman called Countess Troyos – but I was warned that if I went near her she would have me shot against a wall – she's a ferocious Amazon and doesn't like journalists. But I managed to get an interview with one of the chiefs, a certain Count Paul Jovian, a son of the Jovian that was once a Republican Minister. It was that interview that gave me the notion of coming to you, for this Count Paul has some rudiments of sense, and has lived a lot in England, and I could see that he was uneasy about the way things were going. He didn't say much, but he hinted that there ought to be some sort of compromise with the Monarchists, so there's one man at any rate that will accept a reasonable deal... And Jaikie whispered as much to me before I left.'

'Jaikie!' The word came almost like a scream from the startled Mr McCunn. 'I thought he was on a walking tour in France.'

'Well, he has walked into Evallonia. He was with Count Paul, whom it seems he knew at Cambridge. He told me he was a prisoner.'

'How was he behaving himself?'

'Just as Jaikie would. Pretending to be good and meek and sleepy. The same old flat-catcher. If Juventus knew the type of fellow Jaikie was they wouldn't rest till they saw him safe in bed in the Canonry.'

Dickson grinned. 'I'm sure they wouldn't.' But the grin soon faded. He strode up and down the little verandah with his head bowed and his hands clasped behind his back. He did this for perhaps five minutes, and then, with a 'Just you bide here' to his companion, he disappeared into the house.

He was absent for the better part of an hour, and when he returned it was with a gloomy and puzzled countenance.

'I got the Head Schwester to telephone for me to Katzensteg to the aerodrome. There's some jukery-pukery on, and it seems I can't get a machine for the job. The frontier is closed to private planes and only the regular air service is allowed.'

'Whatever do you want an aeroplane for?' Dougal asked.

'To get to Evallonia,' said Dickson simply. 'I've never been in one, but they tell me it's the quickest way to travel. There'll be nothing for it but to go by road. I'll have to attend strictly to the map, for Peter has no more sense of direction than a sheep.'

'But what will you do when you get there?'

'I thought of having a crack with Prince Odalchini in the first place.'

'The thing's impossible,' Dougal cried. 'Man, the country is already almost in a state of siege. Juventus won't let you near the Prince. They're sitting three-deep round his park wall. They carted me over the frontier yesterday with instructions that I wasn't to come back if I valued my life – and, mind you, I had their safe conduct.'

'All the same, I must find some way of getting to him.' In Dickson's voice there was a note of dismal obstinacy which Dougal knew well.

'But it's perfectly ridiculous,' said Dougal. 'I wish to Heaven I had never come here. You can't do a bit of good to anybody and you can do the devil of a lot of harm to yourself.'

'I can see the place and some of the folk, and give you that business advice you said you wanted.'

'You'll see nothing except the inside of a guardroom,' Dougal wailed. 'Listen to reason, Mr McCunn. I must be in Vienna tomorrow, for I have to sign a contract about paper for Mr Craw. Stay quietly here till I come back, and then maybe we'll be able to think of a plan.'

'I can't,' said Dickson. 'I must go at once... See here, Dougal. Do you observe that ring?' He held up his left hand. 'I got it two years back come October on the Solway sands. "I've gotten your ring, Sire," I says to him, "and if I get the word from you I'll cross the world." Well, the word has come. Not direct from Prince John, maybe, but from what they call the logic of events. I would think shame to be found wanting. It's maybe the great chance of my life... Where more by token is his Royal Highness?'

'How should I know?' said Dougal wearily. 'Not in Evallonia, but lurking somewhere near, waiting on a summons that will likely never come. Poor soul, I don't envy him his job... And you're going to stick your head into a bees' byke, when nobody asks you to. You say it's your sense of duty. If that's so, it's a misguided sense not very different from daftness. My belief is that the real reason is that you're looking for excitement. You're too young. You're like a horse with too much corn. You're doing this because it amuses you.'

'It doesn't,' was the solemn answer. 'Make no mistake about that, Dougal. I'm simply longing to be back at Blaweary. I want to be on the river again – I hear the water's in fine trim – and I want to get on with my new planting – I'm trying Douglas for the first time... I don't care a docken for Evallonia and its politics. But I'm pledged to Prince John, and in all my sixty-three years I've never broken my word. I'm sweir to go – I'll tell you something more, I'm feared to go. I've never had much truck with foreigners, and their ways are not my ways, and I value my comfort as much as anybody. That was why I tried to get an aeroplane, for I thought it would commit me and get the first plunge over, for I was feared of weakening. As it is I'll have to content myself with the car and that sumph Peter Wappit. But some way or other I'm bound to go.'

Dougal's grim face relaxed into an affectionate smile.

'You're a most extraordinary man. I'll not argue with you, for I know it's about as much good as making speeches to a tombstone. I'll go back to Evallonia as soon as my business is finished, and I only hope I don't see your head stuck up on a spike on Melina gatehouse.'

'Do you think that's possible?' Dickson asked with a curious mixture of alarm and rapture.

'Not a bit of it. I was only joking. The worst that can happen is that you and Peter will be sent back over the border with a flea in your ear. If Juventus catches you they'll deport you as a harmless lunatic... But for God's sake don't get into the same parish as Mastrovin.'

CHAPTER 6

Arrivals at an Inn

Sir Archibald Roylance drove a motorcar well but audaciously, so that he disquieted the nerves of those who accompanied him; his new servant McTavish drove better, and with a regard for the psychology of others which made a journey with him as smooth as a trip in the Scotch express. The party left Unnutz early in the morning before the guests of the Kaiserin Augusta were out of bed, and since they had many miles to cover, Archie insisted on taking McTavish's place for a spell every three hours. All day under a blue sky they threaded valleys, and traversed forests, and surmounted low passes among the ranges, and since the air was warm and the landscape seductive, they did not hurry unduly. Lunch, for example, on a carpet of moss beside a plunging stream, occupied a full two hours. The consequence was that when they came out of the hills and crossed the Rave and saw before them the lights of the little railway station of Zutpha, it was already evening. Clearly not a time to pay a call upon Prince Odalchini, who did not expect them. Archie inquired of McTavish where was the nearest town, and was told Tarta, where the inn of the Turk's Head had a name for comfort. All the party was hungry and a little weary, so it was agreed to make for Tarta.

The car took a country road which followed the eastern side of Prince Odalchini's great park. Passing through Zutpha village, Archie, whose turn it was then to drive, noticed a number of youths who appeared to be posted on some kind of system. They stared at the car, and at first seemed inclined to interfere with it. But something – the road it was taking or the badges on the front of its bonnet – satisfied them, a word was passed from one to the other, and they let it go. They wore shorts, and shirts of a colour which could not be distinguished in the dark.

'Juventus,' Archie turned his head to whisper. 'We've come to the right shop. Thank heaven the lads don't want to stand between us and dinner.'

Soon the road, which had lain among fields of maize and beet, turned into the shadow of woods, and was joined by many tributary tracks. Archie, who had a good sense of direction, knew the point of the compass where Tarta lay, and had an occasional glimpse of the park paling on his right to keep him straight. He was driving carelessly, for the road seemed deserted, and his mind was occupied in wondering what kind of fare the Turk's Head would give them, when in turning a corner he saw a yard or two ahead a stationary car, drawn up dangerously in a narrow place. He clapped on his brakes, for there was no room to pass it, since its nose was poked beyond the middle of the road, and came to a standstill in a crooked echelon, his off front wheel all but touching its running board.

Archie, like many casual people, was easily made indignant by casualness in others. On this occasion surprise made him indignant in his own language. 'You fool!' he shouted. 'Will you have the goodness to shift your dashed perambulator?'

One man sat stiffly at the wheel. The other was apparently engaged in examining a map with the assistance of the headlight. It was the latter who replied.

'Peter,' he said, 'they're English. Thank God for that.'

The map-student straightened himself, and stood revealed in the glare of the big acetylene lamps as a smallish man in a tweed ulster. He took off his spectacles, blinked in the dazzle, and came deferentially towards Archie. His smile was so ingratiating that that gentleman's irritation vanished.

'That's a silly thing to do,' was all he said. 'If my brakes hadn't been good we'd have had a smash.'

'I'm awful sorry. Peter lost his head, I doubt. You see, we've missed our road.'

Something in the voice, with its rich Scots intonation, in the round benignant face, and in the friendly peering eyes stirred a recollection in Archie which he could not place. But he was not allowed time to drag the deeps of his memory. Alison from the back seat descended like a tornado, and was grasping the stranger's hand.

'Dickson,' she cried, 'who'd have thought of finding you here? You're a sight for sore eyes.'

The little man beamed.

''Deed, so are you, Miss Alison. Mercy, but it's a queer world.'

'This is Sir Archie Roylance. You know him? Aren't you a neighbour of his?'

Dickson extended a grimy hand.

'Fine I know him, though I haven't seen him for years. D'you not mind the Gorbals Die-hards, Sir Archibald, and Huntingtower where you and me fought a battle?'

'Golly, it's McCunn!' Archie exclaimed. 'And not a day older – '

'And that,' said Alison, waving a hand towards the back of her car, 'is my cousin Janet – Lady Roylance.'

Dickson bowed, and, since he was too far off to shake hands, also saluted.

'Proud to meet you, mem. This is a fair gathering of the clans. I never thought when I started this morning to run into a covey of friends.' The encounter seemed to have lifted care from his mind, for he beamed delightedly on each member of the party, not excluding McTavish.

'But what are you doing here?' Alison repeated. 'I thought you were ill and at some German cure place.'

'I've been miraculously restored to health,' said Dickson solemnly. 'And I'm here because I want to have a word with a man. You know him, Miss Alison – Prince Odalchini.'

'But that's what we're here for too,' the girl said.

'You don't tell me that. Have you tried to get inside his gates? That's what I've been seeking to do, and they wouldn't let me.'

'Who wouldn't let you?'

'A lot of young lads in short breeks and green sarks. My directions were to go to a place called Zutpha, which was the proper way in. I found the lodge gates all right, but they were guarded like a penitentiary. I told the lads who I was seeking and got a lot of talk in a foreign language, I didn't understand a word, but the meaning was plain enough that if I didn't clear out I would get my neck wrung. One of them spoke German, and according to Peter what he said was the German for "Go to hell out of this". So I just grinned at them and nodded and told Peter to turn the car, for I saw it was no good running my head against a stone dyke. So now I'm looking for a town called Tarta, where I can bide the night and think things over.'

'But what do you want with Prince Odalchini?'

'It's a long story, and this is not the place to tell it. It was Dougal that set me off. Dougal Crombie – you remember him at Castle Gay?'

'Dougal! You have seen him?'

'No farther back than the day before yesterday. He's in Vienna now. He came seeking me, for Dougal's sore concerned about this Evallonia business. Jaikie is in it, too. He had seen Jaikie.'

'Where is Jaikie?' Alison asked, her voice shrill with excitement.

'Somewhere hereabouts. Dougal says he's a prisoner and in the hands of the same lads that shoo'ed me away from the Prince's gates.'

Here Archie intervened. 'This conference must adjourn,' he said. 'We're all famishing and Mr McCunn is as hungry as the rest of us. Dinner is the first objective. I'll back my car, and you'

– he addressed Peter Wappit – 'go on ahead. It's a straight road, and the town isn't five miles off. We can't talk here by the roadside, especially with Alison shrieking like a peahen. If Juventus has got the wind up, it's probably lurking three deep in these bushes.'

The hostelry of the Turk's Head drew its name from the days when John Sobieski drove the Black Sultan from the walls of Vienna. Part of it was as old as the oldest part of the Schloss, and indeed at one time it may have formed an outlying appanage of the castle. In the eighteenth century, in the heyday of the Odalchinis, it was a cheerful place, where great men came with their retinues, and where in the vast kitchen the Prince's servitors and foresters drank with the townfolk of Tarta. It still remained the principal inn of the little borough, but Tarta had decayed, and it stood on no main road, so while its taproom was commonly full, its guest rooms were commonly empty. But the landlord had been valet in his youth to the Prince's father, and he had a memory of past glories and an honest pride in his profession; besides, he was a wealthy man, the owner of the best vineyard in the neighbourhood. So the inn had never been allowed to get into disrepair; its rambling galleries, though they echoed to the tread of few guests, were kept clean and fresh; the empty stalls in the big stables were ready at a moment's notice for the horses that never came; there was good wine in the cellars against the advent of a connoisseur. It stood in an alley before you reached the marketplace, and its courtyard and back parts lay directly under the shadow of the castle walls.

The newcomers were received like princes. The landlord was well disposed to English milords, the class to which, from a glance at his card, he judged Archie to belong. Janet and Alison were his notion of handsome gentlewomen, for, being swarthy himself, he preferred them blonde; the two chauffeurs looked respectable; Dickson he could not place, but he had the carelessness of dress which in a Briton suggested opulence. So there was a scurrying of chambermaids in the galleries and a laborious preparation of hip baths; the cars were duly bestowed in one of the old coach houses, and the landlord himself consulted with Archie about dinner. McTavish and Peter were to be accommodated with their meals in a room by themselves – in old days, said the landlord, it had been the sitting-room of the Imperial couriers. The ladies and gentlemen would dine at the hour fixed in the grand parlour, which had some famous ancient carvings which learned men journeyed many miles to see. They would have the room to themselves – there were no other guests in the house... He departed to see to the wine with a candlestick as large as a soup tureen.

The dinner was all that the landlord had promised. There was trout from the hills – honest, speckled trout – and a pie of partridges slain prematurely – and what Archie pronounced to be the best beef he had eaten outside England – and an omelet of kidneys and mushrooms – and little tartlets of young raspberries. It was a meal which Dickson was to regard as an epoch in his life; for, coming after the bare commons of Rosensee, it was a sort of festival in honour of his restored health. They drank a mild burgundy, and a sweet wine of the Tokay clan, and a local liqueur bottled forty years ago, and the coffee with which they concluded might have been brewed by the Ottoman whose severed head decorated the inn's sign.

'Dickson,' Alison asked solemnly, 'are you really and truly well again?'

'I'm a new man,' was the answer. 'Ay, and a far younger man. I aye said, Miss Alison, that I was old but not dead old. I've an awful weight of years behind me, but for all that at this moment I'm feeling younger than when I retired from business. They tell me that you've been to Dr Christoph too, Sir Archibald?'

'He's a warlock,' said Archie. 'I had got as lame as a duck, and he made me skip like a he-goat on the mountains. I daren't presume too far, of course, or the confounded leg may sour on me. I got the most foul cramps the other day after a hill walk.'

'Same with me,' said Dickson. 'The doctor says I may be a well body till the end of my days if I just go easy. I'm not very good at ca'ing canny, so no doubt I'll have my relapses and my rheumatic turns. But that's a small cross to bear. It's not half as bad as the gout that the old gentry used to get.'

'Everybody,' said Archie, 'has gout – or its equivalent. It's part of man's destiny. *Chacun à son goût*, as they say in Gaul.'

The miserable witticism was very properly ignored. It was Alison who brought them back to business. 'I want to hear what Dougal said,' she told Dickson. 'I came here because Jaikie wrote telling me to. I haven't a notion where he is – I thought he was on his way home by this time. Archie and Janet came to keep me company. We're all bound for the same house – if we can get in. Now tell me – very slowly – everything that Dougal said.'

Dickson, as well as he could, expounded Dougal's reading of Evallonian affairs. There was nothing new to his auditors in the exposition, for it was very much what they already knew from McTavish.

'What I don't understand,' said Alison, 'is what Dougal thought you could do, Dickson.'

'I suppose,' was the modest answer, 'that he wanted a businesslike view of the situation.'

'But how could you give him that when you know so little about it?'

'That's just what I told him. I said that before I could help to read up the mischief I had to discover exactly what the mischief was. That's why I came on here.'

'You're a marvel,' said Alison with wide eyes. 'I didn't know you were so keen about Evallonia.'

'I'm not. I don't care a docken about Evallonia. But, you see, I'm under a kind of bond, Miss Alison. You'll mind the night in the Canonry when I saw Prince John off in a boat. He gave me this ring' – he held up his left hand – 'and I said to him that if ever I got the word I would cross the world to help him.'

'He sent for you?'

'Not exactly. But the poor young man is evidently in sore difficulties, and I – well, I remembered my promise. I dare say he'll be the better of a business mind to advise him. Dougal, I could see, thought me daft, but I'm sane enough. I don't particularly fancy the job, for I'm wearying to get home, but there it is. I thought I'd first have a crack with Prince Odalchini and get the layout right. And then – '

'Then?'

'Then I must find Prince John, and the dear knows how I'll manage that.'

A glance from Alison prevented Archie from saying something.

'It's more important,' she said, 'that you should find Jaikie.'

'I dare say that will be the way of it,' Dickson smiled. 'He's a prisoner, and at Zutpha today I thought I would soon be a prisoner too, and would run up against Jaikie in some jyle.'

'Jaikie,' said Alison, 'told me to come here, for he needed me. That means that sooner or later he'll be here too. They can't prevent us getting into the House of the Four Winds if we're Prince Odalchini's friends. It isn't war yet.'

'It is not a bad imitation.' A new voice spoke, and the four at the table, who had been intent on their talk, turned startled faces to the door. A tall man had quietly insinuated himself into the room, and was now engaged in turning the key in the lock. He had a ragged blond beard, and a face the colour of an autumn beech leaf: he wore an ill-cut grey suit and a vulgar shirt; also he had a Brigade tie.

'Good evening,' he said pleasantly. 'How are you, Roylance? Proser – that's the landlord – is a friend of mine and told me you were here.' He smiled and bowed to Janet, and then he stopped short, registering extreme surprise on a face not accustomed to such manifestations. 'Cousin Alison! My dear, what magic spirited you here?'

'Thank God!' Alison exclaimed fervently. 'I've been thinking of you all day, Ran, and longing to get hold of you. This is Mr Dickson McCunn, who is a friend of Jaikie – you remember Jaikie at the Lamanchas? I don't know why you're here – I don't quite know why any of us are here – but here we are, and we must do something. By the way, you were saying as you slunk in – ?'

'I was observing that the present state of affairs was a rather good imitation of war. How shall I put it? The Monarchists control the centre of Evallonia and the capital and can strike there when they please. Juventus is in power round the whole circumference of the country. They control its outlets and inlets – a very important point.'

'That's why they are besieging the castle here?'

'Not besieging. Keeping it under observation. There has been as yet no overt act of hostility.'

'But they are taking prisoners. They've pinched Jaikie.'

Mr Glynde's *nil admirari* countenance for a second time in five minutes registered surprise.

'Jaikie?' he cried. 'What do you mean?'

'He is in the hands of Juventus. He has been seen in captivity. Do you know anything about him?' Alison's voice had the sharpness of anxiety.

'I had the pleasure of meeting your Jaikie a few days ago up in the hills. I encouraged him to pay a visit to Evallonia. I helped to entertain him at luncheon with Prince Odalchini, when we tried to make him prolong his visit. You see, I had taken a fancy to Mr Jaikie and thought that he might be useful. I was to meet him that evening, but he never turned up, so I assumed that he was tired of my company, and had gone back across the frontier as he intended. It seems that I have misjudged him. He is a prisoner of Juventus, you say? That must be the doing of his friend Count Paul, and it looks as if all parties were competing for his company. Well, it may not be a bad thing, for it gives us an ally in the enemy's camp. You look troubled, Alison dear, but you needn't worry. Count Paul Jovian is not a bad sort of fellow, and I am inclined to think that Jaikie is very well able to look after himself.'

'I'm not worrying about Jaikie, but about ourselves. I came here because Jaikie sent for me, and that means that he expects to meet me. He named Prince Odalchini's house. But how are we to get into it, if Juventus spends all its time squatting round it?'

'I think that can be managed,' said Mr Glynde. 'You have greatly relieved my mind, my dear. If Jaikie means to come to the House of the Four Winds, he will probably manage it, and he may be a most valuable link with the enemy. You must understand that Juventus is by no means wholly the enemy, but may with a little luck become a friend... By the way, just how much do you know about the situation?'

He proceeded by means of question and answer to probe their knowledge, directing his remarks to Alison at first, but later to Dickson, when he perceived that gentleman's keenness.

'I must tell you one piece of bad news,' and his voice became grave. 'I have just heard it. Prince John was in hiding in a certain place, waiting for the summons, for everything depends on his safety, and all precautions had to be taken. But his enemies discovered his retreat, and he has been kidnapped. We know who did it – Mastrovin, the most dangerous and implacable of them all.'

He was puzzled to find that the announcement did not solemnise his hearers. Indeed, with the exception of Dickson, it seemed to amuse them. But Dickson was aghast.

'Mercy on us!' he cried. 'That's an awful business. I mind Mastrovin, and a blackguard murdering face he had. I must away at once – '

'It is the worst thing that could have happened,' Mr Glynde continued. 'They may kill him, and with him the hope of Evallonia. In any case it fatally disarranges the Monarchist plans… What on earth is amusing you, Roylance?' he concluded testily.

Archie spoke, in obedience to a nod from Alison.

'Sorry,' he said. 'But the fact is we got in ahead of old Mastrovin. We were at Unnutz, and saw what he was up to, so we nipped in and pinched the Prince ourselves.'

'Good God!' Mr Glynde for a moment could only stare. 'Who knows about that?'

'Nobody, except us.'

'Where have you put him?'

'At this moment he is upstairs having his supper along with Mr McCunn's chauffeur. His present job is to be my servant – name of McTavish – passport and everything according to Cocker.'

For the third time that evening Mr Glynde was staggered. He rose and strode about the room, and his blue eyes had a dancing light in them.

'I begin to hope,' he cried. 'No, I begin to be confident. This freak of fate shows that the hussy is on our side.' He took a glass from the sideboard and filled himself a bumper of the local liqueur. 'I drink to you mountebanks. You have beaten all my records. I have always loved you, Janet. I adore you, Alison, my dear, and I have been writing you some exquisite poetry. *Eructavit cor meum* as the Vulgate says – now I shall write you something still more exquisite. Roylance, you are a man after my own heart. Where are you going?' he asked, for Dickson had risen from the table.

'I thought I would go up and have a word with His Royal Highness.'

'You'll do nothing of the kind. Sit down. And drop the Royal Highness business.' Mr Glynde pulled a chair up to the table and leaned his elbows on it. 'We must go very carefully in this business. You have done magnificently, but it's still dangerous ground. You say nobody knows of it except ourselves. Well, not another soul must know of it. Mastrovin is out to kill or spirit away Prince John – he must believe that the Prince is lost. Casimir and the Monarchists must believe that Mastrovin is the villain and go out hot on his trail – that will have the advantage of demobilising the Monarchists, which is precisely what is wanted at present. The Prince must be tucked away carefully till we want him – and when and how we will want him depends on the way things go. Oh, I can tell you we have scored one mighty big point which may give us the game and the rubber. But he can't stay here as your servant.'

'It's a pretty good camouflage,' said Archie. 'He's the image of a respectable English valet, and I'm dashed if he hasn't picked up a Scotch accent, like the real McTavish. You'd have to examine him with a microscope before you spotted the Prince. He's a first-class actor, and it amuses him, so he puts his heart into it.'

'Nevertheless it is too dangerous. You people will be moving in the wrong circles, and sooner or later he'll give himself away, or somebody will turn up that has known him from childhood. Luckily he hasn't been much in Evallonia since he was a boy, but you never know. We must bury him deeper... Wait a moment. I have it. He shall go into my circus. You may not know that I'm a circus proprietor, Alison dear – the Cirque Doré – Glynde, late Aristide Lebrun – the epochal, the encyclopaedic, the grandiose. We are encamped in the environs of Tarta, and every night sprigs of Juventus, who are admitted at half price, applaud our performances. The Prince shall join my staff – I will devise for him some sort of turn – he will be buried there as deep as if he were under the Rave. It will be a joyful irony that the enemies who are looking for him will applaud his antics. Then some day, please God, we will take him out of tights and greasepaint and give him a throne.'

Mr Glynde had become a poet, but he had not ceased to be a conspirator. 'Tomorrow morning,' he told Archie, 'you will inform the landlord that you are sending your chauffeur home by road with your car. The cars will take your baggage to

Zutpha, while you will walk there at your leisure through a pleasant country to catch the evening train. Proser is a good man, but it is unkind to burden even a good man with too much knowledge. Roylance's chauffeur will not again be heard of. I will arrange about your baggage and the cars.'

'And what about us?' Archie asked.

'Before the evening – well before the evening, I hope – you will be in the House of the Four Winds.'

The party took an affectionate farewell of the landlord next morning, their baggage was piled into the cars, luncheon baskets were furnished, and Proser was informed that they meant to drive a mile or two till they cleared the town, and then to spend the day walking the woods on the left bank of the Rave, and catch the evening train at Zutpha. The cars would go straight to the railway station. There was no sign of Mr Randal Glynde.

McTavish, however, had been well coached. They crossed the Rave Bridge, passed the common where Jaikie had first met Count Paul, and plunged into a thick belt of woodland which covered all the country between the foothills and the river. Here there was no highway but many forest tracks, one in especial much rutted by heavy wagons and showing the prints of monstrous feet. The reason of this was apparent after a mile or so, when a clearing revealed the headquarters of the Cirque Doré. It was not its showground – that was in the environs of Tarta – but its base, where such animals were kept as were not immediately required. It was guarded by a stout palisade, and many notices warning the public that wild beasts lived there, and that they must not enter.

Mr Glynde was awaiting them, and one or two idlers hung around the gate. Archie caught, too, what he thought was a glimpse of a green shirt. Randal received them with the elaborate courtesies of a circus proprietor welcoming distinguished patrons. The chauffeurs of the two cars he directed how to proceed to Zutpha. 'They will return by another road in due course,' he whispered to Alison, 'but it is altogether necessary that they should be seen to leave this place.'

Of what followed no member of the party had a very clear recollection. They were taken to a tent less odoriferous than the rest, and provided with white caps on which the name of the circus was embroidered in scarlet. 'We give a matinee today,' said Randal, 'an extra performance asked for by Tarta. It will be in a dancehall, and the programme is in Luigi's hands – gipsy dances and songs and fiddling, for we are no mere vulgar menagerie. You will accompany the artistes back to Tarta. Trust me, you will not be suspected. The Cirque Doré has become a common object of the seashore.'

So Archie and Janet, Alison and Dickson, joined a party which crowded into an old Ford bus, and jolted back the way they had come. The dancehall proved to be a building not far from the Turk's Head, and it was already packed when the company arrived and entered by a side door. Randal deposited the four in a little room behind the stage. 'You will lunch out of your baskets,' he told them, 'while I supervise the start of the show. When it is in full swing I will come back.'

So while fiddles jigged a yard or two off and the feet and hands of Tarta citizens applauded, the four made an excellent meal and conversed in whispers. The circus cap was becoming to Alison and Janet, and it made Archie look like a professional cricketer, but on Dickson's head it sat like an incongruous cowl out of a Christmas cracker. 'A daft-like thing,' he observed, 'but I'm long past caring for appearances. I doubt,' he added prophetically, 'that there'll be a lot of dressing up before we're through with this business. It's a pity that I've the kind of face you cannot properly disguise. Providence never meant me to be a play-actor.'

Randal did not return for a good hour. He seemed satisfied. 'The coast is clear,' he said, 'and I've just had word from my camp that everything is all right there. Now we descend into the deeps, and I'm afraid it will be rather a dusty business. You can leave the circus caps behind, and put on your proper headgear. I hope you two women have nothing on that will spoil.'

He led them down a rickety wooden stair into a basement in which were stored many queer properties; then out of doors into a small dark courtyard above which beetled the walls of the castle. In a corner of this was a door, which he unlocked, and which led to further stables, this time of ancient stone. There followed a narrow passage, another door, and then a cave of a room which contained barrels and shelves and smelt of beer.

'We are now in the cellars of the Turk's Head,' Randal expounded. 'Proser knows this road, and he knows that I know it, but he does not know of our present visit.'

From the beer cellar they passed into a smaller one, one end of which was blocked by a massive wooden frame containing bottles in tiers. Randal showed that one part of this frame was jointed, and that a section, bottles and all, formed a door. He pulled this back, and his electric torch revealed a low door in a stone wall. It was bolted with heavy ancient bolts, but they seemed to have been recently in use, for they slipped easily back. Now he evidently expected it to open, but it refused. There was a keyhole, but no key.

'Some fool must have locked it,' he grumbled. 'It must have been Proser, and I told him to leave the infernal thing open. I'm extremely sorry, but you'll have to wait here till I get a key. It's filthy dirty, but you won't suffocate.'

They did not suffocate, but they had a spell of weary waiting, for the place was pitch-dark and no one of them had a light. Dickson tried to explore in the blackness, and ran his head hard against an out-jutting beam, after which he sat down on the floor and slept. Archie smoked five cigarettes, and did his best to keep up a flow of conversation. 'This is the Middle Ages right enough,' he said. 'We're making burglarious entry into an ancient Schloss, and I feel creepy down the spine. We didn't bargain for this Monte Cristo business, Janet, when we left Geneva. And the last thing I heard that old ass Perrier say there was that the mediaeval was out of date.' But by and by he too fell silent, and it was a dispirited and headachy company that at last saw the gleam of Mr Glynde's torch.

'I humbly apologise,' said Randal, 'but I had a devil of a hunt for Proser. He had gone to see a cousin about his confounded vines. He swears he never locked the door, so it must have been done from the other side. The people in the Schloss are evidently taking no chances. But I've got the key.'

The thing opened readily, and the explorers repeated their recent performance, threading a maze of empty cellars till they came to a door which led to a staircase. For a long time they seemed to be climbing a spiral inside a kind of turret, and came at last to a stage where thin slits of windows let in the daylight. Archie peered out and announced that in his opinion it must be about six o'clock. At last they reached a broad landing, beyond which further steps appeared to ascend. But there was also a door, which Randal tackled confidently as if he expected it to open at once.

It refused to budge. He examined it and announced that it was locked. 'It is always kept open,' he said. 'I've used it twenty times lately. What in thunder is the matter with it today?'

It was very plain what the matter was. It had been barricaded by some heavy object on the other side. It moved slightly under his pressure, but the barricade held fast.

'The nerves of this household have gone to blazes,' he said. 'Roylance, lend a hand, and you, McCunn. We must heave our weight on it.'

They heaved their weight, but it did not yield; indeed, they heaved till the three men had no breath left in them. There was a creaking and grinding beyond, but the heavy body, whatever it was, held its ground. They laboured for the better part of an hour, and by and by made a tiny aperture between door and doorpost. The door was too strong to splinter, but Archie got a foot in the crack and, supported by vigorous pressure from behind, slowly enlarged it. Then something seemed to topple down with a crash beyond the door, and they found that it yielded. They squeezed past a big Dutch armoire, from the top of which had fallen a marble torso of Hercules.

Randal was now on familiar ground. The noise they had made had woken no response in the vast silent house. He led them through stone passages, and then into carpeted corridors, and through rooms hung with tapestries and pictures. There was no sign of servants or of any human life, but Janet and Alison, feeling the approach of civilisation, tried to tidy their hair, and Mr McCunn passed a silk handkerchief over a damp forehead. At last, when it seemed that they had walked for miles, Randal knocked at a door and was bidden enter.

It was a small room lined with books, aglow with the sunset which came through a tall window. In a chair sat an old man in a suit of white linen, and on a couch beside him a youthful and dishevelled figure which was refreshing itself with a glass of beer.

CHAPTER 7

'Si Vieillesse Pouvait'

Mr John Galt had reason to seek refreshment, for he had had an eventful afternoon.

He had spent two days not unpleasantly in the camp of that wing of Juventus which Ashie commanded. ('Wing' was their major unit of division: they borrowed their names from the Romans, and Ashie was 'Praefectus Alae.') He was a prisoner, but in honourable captivity – an English friend of the Commander, detained not because he was hostile, but because of the delicacy of the situation. Ashie introduced him to the subordinate officers, and he found them a remarkable collection. There were old soldiers among them who attended to the military side, but there were also a number of young engineers and businessmen and journalists, who all had their special duties. Juventus, it appeared, was not only a trained and disciplined force, the youth of a nation in arms for defence and, it might be, offence; it was also an organisation for national planning and economic advancement. The recruits were brigaded outside their military units in groups according to their training and professions, and in each group were regular conferences and an elaborate system of education. Jaikie attended a meeting of an oil group, oil being one of Evallonia's major industries, and was impressed by the keenness of the members and the good sense of the discussions, so far as they were explained to him. This was no mere ebullition of militarism, but something uncommonly like a national revival. He realised that it was not one man's making. A leader would no doubt be necessary when Juventus took a hand in politics, but the movement itself had welled up from below. It was the sum of the spontaneous efforts of a multitude of people of all types and degrees, who had decided that they were tired of toyshops and blind alleys and must break for open country.

Jaikie was a good mixer and very soon had made friends among the rank and file as well as among the officers. His meek cheerfulness and the obvious affection which the Commander showed for him were passports to their goodwill. The language he found to be scarcely a difficulty at all. Most of the Evallonian youth had at least a smattering of English and many spoke it well, for it had long been in the schools the one obligatory foreign tongue. The second day he played in a Rugby game, a purifying experience on a torrid afternoon. Sports and gymnastics had a large part in Juventus, and every afternoon was consecrated to them. Ashie must have spread his fame, for he was invited to join the Blue fifteen, and was permitted to fill his old place at right wing three-quarters. It was a fierce, swift and not very orthodox game, the forwards doing most of the work, and the tackling being clumsy and uncertain. But he found that one or two of his side had a fair notion of the business, and some of them had certainly a fine turn of speed. One especially, the centre three-quarter next him, had clearly played a good deal, and now and then there was quite a creditable bout of passing. Jaikie had not a great deal of work to do, but in the second half he got the ball and scored a try, after a spectacular but not very difficult run down the field. However, that kind of run was apparently new to Evallonia, and it was received by the spectators with delirious applause.

Afterwards, when he was having a drink, Ashie introduced him to the centre, whose name was Ivar. The boy regarded him with open-eyed admiration.

'You have played for the English college of the Praefectus?' he asked respectfully.

'For a good deal more than that,' said Ashie. 'Mr Galt is one of the most famous players in the world. He is what they call an international, and is the pride of his nation, which is Scotland.'

Ivar gasped.

'Scotland! That is a famous land. I have read romances about it. Its men dress like women but fight like lions. It loves freedom and has always helped other people to become free.'

Jaikie had a walk with Ivar within the limits of the cantonment and discovered a strong liking for the boy's solemn enthusiasm. Ivar, it appeared, was a young electrical engineer and had been destined to a post in Brazil when Juventus called him. Now his ambition was limited to the immediate future, the great patriotic effort which the next few weeks would demand. He did not talk of it, for Juventus was schooled to reticence, but the light of it was in his eyes. But he spoke much of Evallonia, and Jaikie learned one thing from him – there was complete loyalty to the ideal of the cause, but no one leader had laid his spell upon it. Ivar mentioned with admiration and affection many names – Ashie's among them – but there was no one that dominated the rest. 'When we triumph,' he said, 'we will call to our aid all good men.'

'Including the Monarchists?' Jaikie asked.

'Including the Monarchists, if they be found worthy.'

They stood for a little on a ridge above the camp, where ran the high road along which Ashie's car had brought him. It was a clear evening and there was a wide prospect. Jaikie, who had his countrymen's uneasiness till he had the points of the compass in his head, was now able to orientate his position. The camp was in a crook of the Rave before it bent eastward in the long curve which took it to Melina. To the south he saw the confines of a big park, and to the east the smoke of a faraway train.

Ivar was glad to enlighten him.

'That is the nearest railway,' he said. 'The station of Zutpha is four miles off, beyond where you see the cornfield in sheaf. Yes, that is a nobleman's park, the castle called the House of the Four Winds. At the other side is the little city of Tarta, once a busy place, but now mouldering.'

Jaikie asked who owned the castle.

'It is Prince Odalchini,' said the boy with a grave face. 'A famous house, the Odalchinis, and we of Juventus are not rootless Communists to despise ancient things. But this Prince Odalchini is an old man and he becomes foolish. He is a crazy Monarchist, and would bring back the old ways unchanged. Therefore he is closely watched by us. We do not permit any entry into his domain, or any exit except by our leave.'

Jaikie cast his eye over the wide expanse of forest and pasture.

'But how can you watch so big a place when you have so many other things to do? It must be eight or nine miles round.'

'It is part of our training,' said Ivar simply. 'The main entrances are of course picketed. For the rest, we have our patrols, and they are very clever. We Evallonians have sharp eyes and a good sense for country, and we have been most of us in our time what you call Boy Scouts, and many of us are hill-bred or forest-bred. We have our woodcraft and our field-craft. Believe me, Prince Odalchini is as securely guarded as if battalions of foot lined his park fence. Not a squirrel can enter without our knowing it.'

'I see,' said Jaikie, feeling a little depressed. His eye crossed the Rave and ran along a line of hills ten miles or so to the west. They were only foothills, two thousand feet high at the most, but beyond he had a glimpse of remote mountains. He saw to his left the horseshoe in which Tarta and its Schloss lay – he could not see the pass that led to Kremisch, since it was hidden by a projecting spur. To the north the hills seemed to dwindle away into a blue plain. Just in front of him there was a deeply-recessed glen, the containing walls of which were wooded to the summit, but at the top the ridge was bare, and there was a cleft shaped like the backsight of a rifle. In that cleft the sun was most spectacularly setting.

Ivar followed his gaze. 'That is what we call the Wolf's Throat. It is the nearest road to the frontier. There in that cleft is the western gate of Evallonia.'

As Jaikie looked at the nick, sharp cut against the crimson sky, he had a sudden odd sensation. Beyond that cleft lay his old life. Down here in this great shadowy cup of Evallonia was a fantastic world full of incalculable chances. These chances pleasurably excited him, but there were dregs of discomfort in his mind; he felt that he had been enticed here and that something in the nature of a trap might close on him. Now Jaikie had a kind of claustrophobia, and anything like a trap made him feel acutely unhappy, so it comforted him to see the outlet. That blazing rifle backsight among the hills was the road to freedom. Some day soon he might have to use it, and it was good to know that it was there.

That night he observed after supper that he must be getting on with his job, and Ashie agreed. 'I was just going to say the same thing myself,' he said. 'The air is full of rumours, and we can't get a line on what the Monarchists mean to do. There must be some hitch in their plans. We hear from Melina that there's not a Minister left in the place, only clerks carrying on, and that the National Guard are standing to, waiting orders. We shall probably come on a Minister or two very soon trying to cross the frontier, but our orders are to speed their journey. We don't want a pogrom. What worries me is Cousin Mintha. She is in the south, among the oilfields, and it looks as if she were on the warpath and moving towards Melina. We are nothing like ready for that, and she may put everything in the soup. The Monarchists must be allowed to show their hand first, but in this darned fog nobody knows anything. So the sooner you get inside the House of the Four Winds, my lad, the better for everybody.'

'Can't you release me on parole?' Jaikie asked.

'Impossible. If you were caught in this neighbourhood and I had let you out on parole, I should be suspected of double-dealing, and I can't afford that with Mintha on her high horse. No, you must escape and go off on the loose, so that if you are caught I can deal with you firmly. I may have to put you in irons,' he added with a grin.

'It won't be easy to get into that castle,' said Jaikie. 'I've had a word with the young Ivar and they seem to have taped every yard.'

'Well, that's just where your genius comes in, my dear. I put my Evallonians high, but I'm prepared to back you as a strategist against them every time. Look at the way you ran round the Green backs this afternoon –'

'Then there's the getting in here again.'

'That will be all right if you don't take too long. I can have your tent shut up all day and give out that you've a touch of malaria and mustn't be disturbed... We can make sure that you leave camp unnoticed, for I'll tell you the dispositions. Then it's up to you to get inside the Schloss and out again and be back here early in the night. I can tell you the best place to enter our lines.'

'All right,' said Jaikie a little dolefully. 'My only job is to dodge your lads and have a heart-to-heart talk with the Prince. What about him, by the way? Mayn't he have a posse of keepers taking pot-shots at any intruder?'

'No, that's not his way. You have only us to fear. Be thankful that you can reduce your enemies to one lot. Ours seem to produce a fresh crop daily. I've just heard that one of Mastrovin's gang has been seen pretty near here. If Mastrovin turns up there's likely to be dirty work.'

Jaikie went out literally with the milk. Every morning the neighbouring farms sent up milk for the camp in great tin drums borne in little pony carts, and with them a batch of farm boys. Discipline was relaxed on these occasions, and Ashie had indicated one route which the milk convoy invariably followed. Jaikie, in much-stained flannel bags and a rough tweed jacket and ancient shoes, might easily pass as an Evallonian rustic. So he trotted out of camp behind a milk cart, his hands assisting an empty drum to keep its balance. A hundred yards on and he slipped inconspicuously into the roadside scrub.

The weather was cooler than it had been of late, and there was a light fresh wind blowing from the hills. Jaikie felt rejuvenated, and began to look forward to his day's task with a mild comfort. He did not believe that any patrols of Juventus could prevent him from getting inside the park. After that the job would be harder. He remembered the gentle fanaticism in Prince Odalchini's eyes, and considered that it might be difficult to get him to agree to any counsels of moderation, or even to listen to them. He might regard Jaikie as one who had deliberately gone over to the other side. But Randal Glynde, if he were there, would help – Jaikie hoped he would be there. And there was just a chance that Alison might have turned up. It was this last thought that strung up his whole being to a delicious expectation.

As he expected, it was not very difficult to get inside the park. His prospect from the ridge the night before had given him his bearings. He realised that his former entrance with Luigi had been on the east side, not far from the road between Zutpha and Tarta; now he was on the north side, where there was no road following the boundary, and thick coverts of chestnut undergrowth extended right up to the paling. He did not find it hard to locate the Juventus cordon. The patrols made their rounds noiselessly and well, but he discovered from their low whistles the timing of their beats, and when it would be safe to make a dash. But it took an unconscionable time, and it was midday before his chance came, for he was determined to take no needless risks. There was a point where the high paling was broken by the mossy and ruinous posts of an old gateway. That was the place he had selected, and at exactly seventeen minutes past twelve he slipped over like a weasel and dropped into the fern of the park.

He travelled a few hundred yards, and then halted to lunch off some biscuits and chocolate provided by Ashie. Then with greater freedom he resumed his journey. Beneath him the ground fell away to a small stream, a tributary of the Rave, which had been canalised in a broad, stone channel. There was no bridge, but for the convenience of the estate labourers a plank had been laid across it. Beyond was a glade of turf, at the end of which he could see the beginning of a formal garden. This was very plain sailing, and he became careless, forgetting that Juventus might have their patrols inside the park as well as without... Suddenly, when he was within a few yards of the culvert, swinging along and humming to himself, he found his feet fly from beneath him. He had been tripped up neatly by a long pole, and the owner sat himself heavily on his chest.

Convinced after the first movement that he was hopelessly outmatched in physical strength, Jaikie did not struggle. Vain resistance he had always regarded as folly. His assailant behaved oddly. He ejaculated something as the result of a closer inspection, and then removed himself from his prisoner's chest. But he did not relax a tight grip on his arm. Jaikie observed with some surprise that he was in the hands of Ivar.

Ivar's surprise was greater. His arms imprisoned Jaikie's to his sides, and to a spectator the couple must have had a lover-like air.

'Mr Galt!' he gasped. 'What the devil are you doing here?'

'You may well ask,' said Jaikie pleasantly. 'The fact is, I've broken bounds. I wanted to have a look at that Schloss. D'you mind not gripping my shoulder so hard? You've got me safe enough.'

'You have escaped?' said Ivar solemnly. 'You have not been permitted to come here on parole?'

'No. Count Paul did not give me permission – he knows nothing about it – this is my own show. But look here, Ivar, you're a sensible chap and must listen to reason. I'm on your side, and I'm trying to help your cause in my own way. I have special reasons for being here which I can't explain to you now. I mean to be back in camp this evening – I'll pledge you my word of honour for that. So if you're wise you'll let me go and never say a word about having seen me.'

Ivar's face showed the confusion of his feelings.

'You know all about me,' Jaikie went on. 'You know I'm a friend of the Praefectus. Well, I'm trying to help him, without his knowledge – that's why I'm here. You won't interfere with me if you've the interests of Juventus at heart.'

The boy's face had changed from bewilderment to sternness.

'I cannot let you go. You are my prisoner and you must return with me. It is not for me to use my discretion. I must obey my orders, and the orders are clear.'

There was that in his eye which warned Jaikie that argument was futile. The discipline of Juventus allowed no quibbling. But Jaikie continued to plead, judging meantime the distance from the culvert and the plank. Then he seemed to give it up as a bad job. 'All right,' he said. 'So be it. I dare say it's the only thing you can do, but it's infernal hard luck on me. The Praefectus will think I have been trying to double-cross him, and I honestly wanted to help him. You believe that, don't you?'

Ivar, remembering his admiration of yesterday, relented so far as to say that he did. Jaikie's surrender, too, caused him to relax the tightness of his grip, and in an instant Jaikie acted. With an eel-like twist he was out of his clutches and Ivar found himself sprawling on the slope. Before he had found his feet Jaikie had skipped over the culvert and had kicked the plank into the water. The two faced each other across a gully which was too broad to jump, and to cross which meant the descent and ascent of slimy stone walls.

'Let's talk sense,' said Jaikie. 'You know you haven't an earthly chance of catching me. You've done your duty, in arresting me – only I've escaped, which is your rotten luck. Now listen. I'm going on to reconnoitre that house, never mind why.

But, as I told you, I'm on your side, and on Count Paul's side, and I'm coming back. I'll have to wait till it's darkish – eight or nine o'clock perhaps, I daresay. Will your lads be on duty then?'

Something in Jaikie's tone impressed Ivar. 'I shall be on duty,' he said. 'I return here for my second tour at eight o'clock.'

'Well, I'll come back this way, and I'll surrender myself to you. I don't want to outrage your discipline. You can march me to the camp, and hand me over to the Praefectus, and it will be my business to make my peace with him. Have you got that right?'

But Ivar's sense of duty was not to be beguiled. He started to climb down into the culvert. 'Ass!' said Jaikie as he turned and trotted off in the direction of the castle. He dived into one of the side glades, and when he had reached the first terrace wall and looked back he saw that his pursuer had halted not very far from the culvert. Perhaps, he thought, there was some order of Juventus which confined their patrols to a certain distance inside the park bounds.

Jaikie, as he threaded the terrace paths, and climbed stairways between neglected creepers and decaying statuary, discovered that he had come to the northern end of the Schloss, which was one of the last-century additions, castellated, battlemented, topped with bogus machicolations. The great house had looked deserted on his first visit, but now it had the air of a forsaken mausoleum. He turned the flank of it and moved along the weedy upper terrace, looking for the door by which he and the Prince had entered after luncheon. He found it, but it was locked and apparently barricaded. He found other doors, but they were in the same condition. The House of the Four Winds seemed to have prepared itself for a siege.

This was discouraging. It occurred to him that the Prince might have departed, but in that case Juventus would have known of it and would not be maintaining its vigilant beleaguerment. He retired to the terrace wall, from which he could get a good view of the tiers of windows. All of them were blind and shuttered. If there were people in the castle they were dwelling in the dark. This he knew was the side where the chief living-rooms were, and if there were inmates anywhere it would be here.

At last his quick eyes caught sight of something on the third floor. It was a window open a little at the top. It was dark, but that might be because of blinds and not of shutters – the sun was so placed that it was hard to judge of that. By that window, and by that window only, he might effect an entrance.

It was an easy conclusion to reach, but the ways and means were not easy. Beneath each line of windows ran a narrow ledge along which it might be just possible to make a traverse. But the question was how to reach that ledge, for there were no friendly creepers on the great blank stone facade. Jaikie, moving stealthily in the cover of pots and statues, for he had an ugly feeling that he might be under hostile observation, reconnoitred carefully the whole front. Something told him that he was not alone in this business; he had the sense that somewhere else on that terrace there were human beings engaged perhaps in the same enterprise. Could Juventus have flung out their scouts thus far? He scarcely believed it, judging from Ivar's behaviour, but he had no time for nervousness, for the day was getting on and he had still his main work to do.

The front yielded him nothing. But at the flanking tower which he had first approached he got a glimmer of hope. There was a fire escape which had been allowed to fall into disrepair, but which was certainly still climbable. The question was would it give access to the ledge below the window? He thought that it might, and started to ascend.

Many of the rungs were rotten, and he had to move with extreme caution; indeed, at one moment he feared that the whole contraption would break loose from the wall. Now his early training proved its worth, for he was without a suspicion of vertigo, and could look down unmoved from any height. The fire escape led up to the third story, and he found that by stepping to his left he could stand on the sill of a narrow window in the gap between the tower and the main facade. He got his hands on the ledge and to his relief found it broader than he had hoped – at least a foot and a half of hard stone. The difficulty would be to draw himself up on to it.

He achieved this, not without some tremor of the heart, for a foot and a half is not much of a landing place. Very cautiously he laid himself along it, and then slowly raised himself to his feet. By turning his head he had a glimpse of a great swimming landscape running out into blue distances he did not look twice, for even his cool head grew a little giddy at the sight. With his face to the wall of the castle he began to sidestep along the ledge.

It proved far simpler than he had feared, for the stone was firm. He passed window after window, all closed and shuttered, till his heart began to sink. Had he blundered after all? Surely the window he had marked had been the fifth from the right... And then he came to one which, as he approached it, seemed suddenly to move. A hand was lifting the lower sash, and an old face looked out into the sunlight.

Jaikie took a firm grip of the inner sill, for he felt that anything might happen, and the terrace was a long way below. 'Prince Odalchini,' he said, 'I've come back.'

The old face scarcely changed. Its eyes peered and blinked a little at the uncouth figure which seemed to be hanging in air.

'I'm Galt,' said the figure. 'Do you mind me coming in?'

'Ah, yes – Mr Galt,' said the voice. 'Certainly come in. You are very welcome. I do not think anyone has attempted that ledge since for a bet I did it as a boy. But my effort was limited to the traverse between two windows. You have come all the way from the North Tower! Magnificent! You will desire, I think, some refreshment.'

Dickson McCunn sat in a deep armchair sipping a mammoth cup of tea. Prince Odalchini had offered every kind of refreshment, but it had taken time to dig the old housekeeper and the older butler out of the cavernous lower regions, and indeed Janet and

Alison had had to descend themselves and help to make tea. All seven were now sitting in the Prince's cabinet, and for the last quarter of an hour the conversation had been chiefly an examination of Jaikie by the Prince and Randal Glynde. Dickson listened with only half an ear, for Jaikie was confirming what they already knew. He was more intent on savouring the full strangeness of this experience.

Two days ago he had been an ordinary convalescent at a German *Kurhaus*, on the eve of returning to the homely delights of Blaweary. Now he found himself inside an old stone palace which was in a state of siege, a palace which he had entered like a rat through mysterious cellars. His mind kept casting back to the spring morning nine – or was it ten? – years ago, when, being freed for ever from the routine of business, he had set out on a walking tour, and had found himself in another great house among desperate folk. He remembered his tremors and hesitations, and that final resolve which he had never regretted, which indeed had been the foundation of all his recent happiness. Was he destined to face another crisis? Looking back, it seemed to him that everything had been predestined. He had left the shop and set out on his travels because he was needed at Huntingtower. Had Providence decreed that Dr Christoph should give him back his health simply that he should come here?

Dickson felt solemn. He had that Calvinistic belief in the guidance of Allah which is stronger than any Moslem's, and he had also the perpetual expectation of the bigoted romantic... But he was getting an old man, too old for cantrips. His eye fell upon Prince Odalchini, who was also old, though he seemed to have grown considerably younger in the past half-hour. He felt that he had misjudged the Prince; his face was shrewder than he had thought, and he seemed to be talking with authority. Jaikie, too. Dickson was not following the talk, but Jaikie's gravity was impressive, and the rest were listening to him eagerly. He felt a sudden uprush of pride in Jaikie. He was a different being now from the pallid urchin of Huntingtower, who had wept bitterly when he was getting dangerous.

His eyes roamed round the walls, taking in a square of old tapestry, and a line of dark kit-cat portraits. The window showed a patch of golden evening sky. The light caught Alison's hair, and he began to wonder about her and Jaikie. Would they ever be man and wife? It would be a queer match between long descent and no descent at all – but it was a queer world, and nothing could be queerer than this place. Janet and Archie belonged to a familiar sphere, but Mr Glynde was like nothing so much as the Pied Piper of Hamelin. What was he, Dickson McCunn, doing among such outlandish folk? Dougal had said that they wanted his advice; but he felt as impotent as Thomas the Rhymer no doubt felt when he was consulted on the internal affairs of Fairyland... Still, common sense was the same all the world over. But what if common sense was not wanted here, but some desperate quality of rashness, some insane adventurousness? He wished he were twenty years younger, for he remembered Prince John. He was sworn to do his best for the exiled monarch, and that very morning with a break in his voice he had renewed the pledge to the chauffeur McTavish.

By this time he was coming out of his dreams, and hearing something of the conversation. As he finished his tea Jaikie was putting the heart of his problem in staccato sentences, and Prince Odalchini and Mr Glynde with gloomy faces were nodding their assent. Something in the words stirred a reminiscence...

'I mind,' said Dickson out of the depths of his chair.

It was the first time he had spoken, and the others turned to him, so that he felt a little embarrassed.

'I mind,' he said, 'when Jimmy Turnbull was running for Lord Provost of Glasgow. He was well liked and far the best man for the job, but the feck of the Town Council didn't fancy his backers, and if it had come to the vote Jimmy would have been beat. So Tam Dickson – he was my own cousin and was Baillie then and afterwards Lord Provost himself – Tam was the wily one and jerked his brains to think of a way out. What he did was this. He got Jimmy's friends to drop Jimmy and put up one David Duthie, who was a blethering body that was never out of the papers. He had a sore job persuading them, he told me, but he managed it in the end. The consequence was that the very men that were opposed to Jimmy's backers, now that he was quit of them, took up Jimmy, and since they were a majority of the Council he was triumphantly elected.'

Dickson's apologue was received with blank faces by the others, with the exception of Randal Glynde. Into that gentleman's eyes came a sudden comprehending interest, and Dickson saw it and was encouraged. His own mind was awaking to a certain clearness.

'If Prince John didn't exist,' he asked, 'is there anybody else the Monarchists could put up?'

'There is no one,' said Prince Odalchini sadly. 'There is, of course, his uncle, the late king's brother, the Archduke Hadrian, but he is impossible.'

'Tell us about the Archduke,' said Dickson.

'He is an old man, and very frail. He has not been in Evallonia for many years, and even his name is scarcely remembered. He is believed to be one of the greatest living numismatologists, and he has given his life to his hobby. I alone of the Evallonian nobility have kept in touch with him, and it was only yesterday that I had a letter from his secretary. His Royal Highness is a bachelor, and for long has lived in a chateau in France near Chantilly, scarcely going beyond his park walls. He is as strict a recluse as any mediaeval hermit. Now he is bedridden, and I fear cannot have many months to live.'

Prince Odalchini rose, opened a cabinet, and took out a photograph.

'That is His Royal Highness, taken two years ago at my request, for I desired to have a memento of him. In my youth he was kind to me.'

He handed it to Dickson, who studied it carefully. It showed a man not unlike Mr Pickwick or the great Cavour, with a round face, large innocent eyes, and grey hair thinning on the temples – a man of perhaps seventy years, but, so far as could be judged from the photograph, still chubby and fresh-complexioned. It was passed round the company. Janet and Archie scarcely glanced at it, but Mr Glynde looked at it and then looked at Dickson, and his brow furrowed. Jaikie did the same, and when it came to Alison she cried out – 'Why, Dickson, it might be you, if your hair was greyer.'

'I was just thinking that,' was the answer. Dickson retrieved the photograph and studied it again.

'What size of a man is he?' he asked. His clearness of mind was becoming acid.

'Shortish, about your own height,' said the Prince.

'Umphm! Now what hinders you to do the same with the Archduke as my cousin Tam Dickson did with David Duthie? Jaikie says that Juventus would be for Prince John but for you and your friends. Well, if you run the Archduke, they'll take up Prince John, and since you tell me they'll have the upper hand of you, they'll put Prince John on the throne. D'you see what I mean? It's surely common sense.'

This speech had a considerable effect on the others. Archie laughed idiotically, and Mr Glynde found it impossible to remain seated. But Prince Odalchini only shook his head.

'Ingenious,' he said, 'but impossible. His Royal Highness is old and frail and bedridden. He would not consent, and even if he consented, he would he dead before he reached Evallonia.'

Dickson's mind was moving by leaps to a supreme boldness.

'What for should he come near Evallonia? He need never leave his chateau, and indeed the closer he lies there the better. It's not his person, but his name that you want... See here, Prince. You say that nobody in Evallonia knows him, and few have ever seen him, but that there's a general notion of what he looks like. Can you persuade your friends to change their minds about Prince

John and declare for the Archduke as the older and wiser man and more suited for this crisis? If you do that, and put him or something like him on the throne, Juventus will come along in a week and fling him out and set up Prince John, and then you'll be happy together.'

The company was staring at him open-mouthed and wide-eyed, all except Prince Odalchini, who seemed inclined to be cross.

'But I tell you we cannot get His Royal Highness,' he said.

'I said "or something like him",' was Dickson's answer. His mind was now as limpid as an April morning.

'What on earth do you mean?'

'I mean somebody you can pass off as the Archduke.'

'And where shall we find him?' The Prince's tone was ironical.

'What about myself?' said Dickson.

For an instant there was utter silence.

Prince Odalchini's face showed a range of strong emotions, anger, perplexity, incredulity and then something that was almost hope. When he spoke, his words were inadequate to his feelings. 'Are you mad?' he asked.

' 'Deed I'm not. I came here as a businessman to give you my advice, and there it is. It's a perfectly simple proposition, and there's just the one answer. By the mercy of God I'm reasonably like the old man, though I'm a good deal younger, and anyway there is nobody to tell the differ. I'm willing to take the chance, though I suppose it will be high treason if I'm grippit, for I'm not going back on my word to Prince John. I'll see yon lad with his hinder parts on the throne before I leave Evallonia, or my name's not Dickson McCunn.'

'You realise that you would be running tremendous risks?'

'Ugh, ay, but I've taken risks before this. The only thing I stipulate is that I'm not left too long on the throne, for I wouldn't be up to the job. I might manage a week before I went skelping across the frontier – but not more.'

Prince Odalchini's expression had changed. There was now respect in it, and excitement, and a twitching humour.

'I think you are the boldest man I have ever met,' he said.

'Never heed that,' said Dickson. 'My knees will likely be knocking together before I've done. What I want to know is, can you persuade the rest of your lot, Muresco particularly, to agree to this plan?'

The Prince considered. 'It may be difficult, but I think it can be done. After all, it is the only way.'

'And can you upset the Republic and set up the Archduke?'

'Beyond doubt. For a little while – that is to say.'

'Last and most important, can Juventus be persuaded to accept Prince John?'

It was Jaikie who answered.

'I believe they could. Count Paul would jump at him, and so would the rank and file. I don't know about the leaders. There's a woman who matters a good deal.'

'Prince John must marry her then. That's all. We're desperate folk and we're not going to stick at trifles.' Dickson was in that mood of excited authority which always with him followed the taking of a great resolution. 'But, Jaikie, it's terrible important that, if I get that far, Juventus must force me to abdicate in a week – I couldn't manage longer. It would be an awful business if at my time of life I was kept cocked up on a throne I didn't want. There's just the one job for you, and that's to manage Juventus, and, mind, I've trusted you often and never known you fail. Away with you back to your camp, for there's no time to lose.'

'We dine in half an hour,' said Prince Odalchini.

'Well, let's get pencil and paper and work out the details.'

But they did not immediately get to business, for Alison rose and ceremoniously embraced Mr McCunn. Her kiss was like that of Saskia's years before in the house of Huntingtower; it loosed a force of unknown velocity upon the world.

116

The twilight had fallen when Jaikie emerged from one of the terrace doors, which was promptly locked behind him. He proposed to return the way he had come and surrender himself to Ivar. After that he and Ashie must hold high converse. He had a task before him of immense difficulty and his head was already humming with plans. But Dickson's certainty had given him hope, and he thanked his stars that he had not gone home, for now he was in the kind of adventure he had dreamed of, and his comrades were the people he loved best in the world. This was his notion of happiness.

He must hurry, if he was not to miss Ivar, so he short-circuited his route, by dropping from the successive terrace walls instead of going round by the stairways... At the last of them he found that he had dropped into a human embrace which was strict and powerful, but not friendly.

His instinct of the afternoon had been right. Others besides himself had been lurking among the paths and statues of the terraces.

CHAPTER 8

Splendide Mendax

Jaikie's captors, whoever they were, meant business. Before the sack was slipped over his head a cloth, sticky and sweet-smelling, was twisted round his mouth. He was vaguely aware of struggling against an immense suffocating eiderdown, and that was his last conscious moment for perhaps ten minutes. These minutes should have been hours if the intentions of his ill-wishers had been fulfilled. But in Jaikie they had struck a being oddly constituted. Just as it was nearly impossible to make him drunk, so he was notably insensitive to other forms of dope. Had he ever had to face a major operation, the anaesthetist would have had a difficult time with him. Moreover, his nose had come into contact with something hard and was bleeding copiously, which may have counteracted the stuff on the bandage. The consequence was that he presently regained his senses, and found himself in a position of intense bodily discomfort. He was being borne swiftly along by persons who treated him with no more respect than as if he were a bundle of faggots.

He was a good deal frightened, but his anger was greater than his fright, and it was directed against himself. For the third time become of the caution on which he had prided himself? He had seen Ivar that very day, and now some enemy unknown. What had become of the caution on which he had prided himself? He had been an easy victim, because he had had no thought for anything but the immediate future, and had not recognised that he had been walking among hidden fires. He reproached himself bitterly. Ashie had trusted him, Prince Odalchini had trusted him, and he had proved himself only a blundering child. What especially rankled was that he must break his pledge to Ivar. That dutiful youth would be looking for him near the boundary of the park, and would set him down as a common liar.

Indignation, especially against one's self, is a wonderful antidote to fear. It also tends to sharpen the wits. Jaikie, with a horrid crick in his neck and a back aching from rough treatment, began to think hard and fast. Who was responsible for this outrage? Certainly not Prince Odalchini or anyone connected with the House of the Four Winds. Not Juventus. Ivar was the only Greenshirt who knew of his visit to the castle, and Ivar was too much of a gentleman to resort to these brigand tricks. So far his conclusions were clear, but they were only negative. Who would want to capture him? Somebody who knew about his new job? – But the only people in the secret were his friends in the castle. Somebody who had a grudge against Prince Odalchini – But that could only be Juventus, and he had ruled Juventus out. Somebody who had a grievance against himself? – But he was a humble stranger unknown in Evallonia. Somebody who hated Juventus and the Prince alike and who suspected him as a liaison between them? – Now, who filled that bill? Only the present Republican Government in Evallonia. But all his information was to the effect that that Government was shaking in its shoes, and that its members were making their best speed to the frontier. They could have neither leisure nor inclination to spy thus effectively on a castle at whose gates the myrmidons of Juventus were sitting.

And then suddenly he remembered what Ashie had told him and Prince Odalchini had repeated. Behind the effete Republic was a stronger and darker power... A horrid memory of Mastrovin came to his mind, the face which had glowered on him in the room in the Portaway Hydropathic, the face which he had seen distorted with fury in the library of Castle Gay – the heavy shaven chin, the lowering brows, the small penetrating eyes the face which Red Davie had described as that of a maker of revolutions... The thought that he might be in Mastrovin's hands sent a shiver down his aching spine. The man had tried to kidnap Prince John and had been foiled by Alison. He must be desperate with all his plans in confusion, a mad dog ready to tear whatever enemy he could get his fangs into.

Jaikie's fears must have stopped well short of panic, for he had enough power of reflection left to wonder where he was being taken. He was no longer in the park or the garden, for the feet of his bearers sounded as if they were on some kind of pavement. He had an impression, too, that he was not in the open air, but inside a masoned building. It could not be the castle, for he had heard that evening from Alison of her entry through the cellars and the difficulties of the route; if that approach was so meticulously guarded, it was probable that the same precautions had been taken with all... And then it occurred to him that, since the great building abutted on the town of Tarta, there must be other ways into the streets from the park, through outhouses and curtilages, for once the burgh had been virtually part of the castle. No doubt these were now disused and blocked up, but some knowledge of them might linger in queer places.

His guess was confirmed, for presently it was plain that his bearers were in a low and narrow passage. There seemed to be at least three of them, and they went now in Indian file – crouching as he could tell from their movements, and now and then pushing him before them. He felt his legs grating on rough stone. Once his foot caught in a crevice, and his ankle was nearly twisted when it was dragged out of it. The place was a sort of drain, and it seemed to him miles long; the air was warm and foul, and he was inert not from policy, but from necessity, for he could hardly breathe inside the sack. Once or twice his bearers seemed to be at fault, for they stopped and consulted in muffled voices. These halts were the worst of all, for there loomed before Jaikie the vision of the death of a sewer rat.

Then the passage manifestly widened, the air grew fresher, and there came the sound of flowing water. He remembered that he had seen runnels of water in the Tarta streets, effluents from the Rave, and he realised that he had been right – they were now underneath the town. After that he was only dimly conscious of his whereabouts. He believed that the party were ascending – not stairs, but an inclined tunnel. There came a point in which they moved with extreme caution, as if people were near, people who must not hear or see them. There followed the grating of an opening door, then another and another, and even through the folds of the sack Jaikie recognised that they were in some kind of dwelling. There was the feel in the air of contiguity to human uses...

The end came when he was suddenly dumped on a wooden floor, and one of the party struck a light. The sack was taken from his head, and he was laid on a truckle-bed where were some rough blankets and an unbleached pillow. He had already decided upon his course, so he kept his eyes shut and breathed heavily as if he were still under the opiate. The three men left the room, taking the candle with them, and locking the door behind them, so that all he saw was their retreating backs and these told him nothing. They looked big fellows in nondescript clothes, indoor or outdoor servants.

Jaikie's first feeling was of intense relief. Whatever happened to him, at any rate he was not going to be stifled in a drain. He lay for a little breathing free air and gasping like a fish on the shingle. His second feeling was that all his bones were broken, but that he was too tired to care. There were various other feelings, but they all blended into a profound fatigue. In about three minutes Jaikie was asleep.

He must have slept a round of the clock, and he awoke in a state of comparative bodily ease, for Rugby football had inured him to rough handling. The room was a small one, evidently little used, for it had no furniture but a bed; it looked like an attic in an unprosperous inn. Its one dormer window looked over a jumble of roofs to a large blank wall. But since it faced east, it caught the morning sunlight, and the dawn of the wholesome day had its effect on Jaikie's spirits. The ugly little fluttering at his heart had gone. He had only himself to thank for his troubles, he decided, and whatever was in store for him he must keep his head, and not be the blind fool of the past week. He had awakened with one thought in his mind. Prince John was the trump card. It was Prince John that Mastrovin was looking for – if indeed Mastrovin was his captor – and it was for him, Jaikie, to be very wary at this point. Was there any way in which he could turn his present predicament to the advantage of his mission? He had a shadow of a notion that there might be.

The door was unlocked and breakfast was brought him, not by one of his bearers of the night before, but by an ancient woman with a not unpleasing face. She gave him '*Grüss Gott*' in a friendly voice. Since she spoke German like all the Tarta people, and since the breakfast of coffee and fresh rolls looked good, he was encouraged to ask for some means of washing. She nodded, and fetched a tin basin of water, soap, a towel, a cracked mirror and a broken comb, doubtless part of her own toilet equipment. Jaikie washed the blood from his face, scrubbed from his hands some of the grime of last night's cellars, dusted his clothes, and tidied up his unruly hair. Then he made a hearty meal, lit a pipe and lay down on the bed to think.

He was not left long to his reflections. The door opened and two men entered, who may or may not have been his captors. They were clearly not countrymen, for they had the pallor of indoor workers, and the stoop which comes from bending many hours in the day. They had solemn flat faces with a touch of the Mongol in them, and one of them very civilly restored to Jaikie a knife which had dropped out of his pocket. They beckoned to him to follow them, and when he obeyed readily they forbore to take his arm, but one went before and one behind him. He was escorted down a narrow wooden staircase, and along a passage to a room at the door of which they knocked ceremonially. Jaikie found himself thrust into a place bright with the morning sun, where two men sat smoking at a table.

He recognised them both. One was a tall man with a scraggy neck and a red, pointed beard, a creature of whipcord muscles and large lean bones, who seemed to be strung on wires, for his fingers kept tapping the table, and his eyelids were always twitching. Jaikie remembered his name – it was Dedekind, who had been left with the Jew Rosenbaum to keep guard in the Castle Gay library when the others searched the house. The second was beyond doubt Mastrovin, a little older, a little balder, but formidable as ever. It was not the library scene that filled Jaikie's mind as he looked at them, but that earlier episode, in the upper room of the Portaway Hydropathic, when they had cross-examined an alcoholic little journalist. That scene stuck in his memory, for it had been for him one of gross humiliation. They had bullied him, and he had had to submit to be bullied, and that he could not forget. Hate was a passion in which he rarely indulged, but he realised that he cordially hated Mastrovin.

Could they recognise him? Impossible, he thought, for there could be no link between that cringing little rat and the part he now meant to play. He also was two years older, and in youth one changes fast. So he confronted the two men with a face of cold wrath, but there was a tremor beneath his coolness, for Mastrovin's horrid little eyes were very keen.

'Your name?' Mastrovin barked. 'You are English?'

'I should like to know first of all who you are and what you mean by your insolence?' Jaikie spoke in the precise accent of a Cambridge don, very unlike the speech of the former reporter of the Craw Press.

Mastrovin bent his heavy brows. 'You will be wise to be civil – and obedient. You are in our power. You have been found at suspicious work. We are not men to be trifled with. You will speak, or you will be made to speak, and if you lie you will suffer for it. A second time, your name?'

For some obscure reason the man's tone made Jaikie feel more cheerful. This was common vulgar bullying, bluffing on a poor hand. He thought fast. Who did they think he was? He had noticed that at the first sight of him the faces of both men had fallen. Had he been arrested because they believed that he was Prince John?

'I am English,' he said. 'An English traveller. Is this the way that Evallonia welcomes visitors?'

'You are English, no doubt, and therefore you are suspect. It is known that the English are closely allied with those who are plotting against our Government.'

'Oh, I see.' Jaikie shrugged his shoulders and grinned. 'You think I'm taking a hand in your politics. Well, I'm not. I don't know the first thing about them, and I care less. But if you're acting on behalf of the Government, then I dare say you're right to question me. I'll tell you everything about myself, for I've nothing to conceal. My name is John Galt. I've been an undergraduate at Cambridge and I have just finished with the University. I've been taking a holiday walking across Europe, and I came into Evallonia exactly four days ago. I'll give you every detail about what I've been doing since.'

While smoking his after-breakfast pipe, he had made up his mind on his course. He would tell the literal truth, which he hoped to season with one final and enormous lie.

'You have proof of what you say?' Mastrovin asked.

Jaikie took from his breast pocket the whole of its contents, which were not compromising. There was a lean pocketbook with very little money in it, his passport, the stump of a cheque book, and one or two Cambridge bills. Fortunately, Alison's letters from Unnutz were in his rucksack.

'There's every paper I've got,' he said and laid them on the table.

Mastrovin studied the bundle and passed it to Dedekind.

'Now you will recount all your doings since you came to Tarta. Be careful. Your story can be checked.'

Jaikie obliged with a minute recital. He described his meeting with his Cambridge friend, Count Paul Jovian. He explained that he knew Prince Odalchini slightly and had letters to him, and that he had called on him at the castle and stayed to lunch. He described his ambush by Ashie, and his life in the Juventus camp. On this Mastrovin asked him many questions, to which he replied with a great air of unintelligent honesty. 'They were always drilling and having powwows,' he said, 'but I couldn't make out what they were after. All I did was to play football. I'm rather good at that, for I play for Scotland.'

'Now we will have your doings of yesterday,' said Mastrovin grimly.

Jaikie replied with expansive details. 'I was getting tired of the camp. You see, I was a sort of prisoner, though Heaven knows why. I suppose it had something to do with your soda-water politics. Anyway, I was fed up and wanted a change – besides, I had promised to see Prince Odalchini again. So I slipped out of the camp and had a pretty difficult time getting into the castle grounds. The Juventus people were patrolling everywhere, and I had a bit of a scrap with one of them. Then I had a still more difficult time getting inside the castle. I had to climb in like a cat burglar.' Jaikie enlarged with gusto on the sensational nature of that climb, for he believed that Mastrovin's people had been somewhere on the terrace and must have seen him. It looked as if the guess was correct, for Mastrovin seemed to accept his story.

'Within the castle you saw – whom?' he barked. He had a most unpleasant intimidating voice.

'I saw the Prince, and dined with him. There were one or two other people there, but I didn't catch their names. One was an English Member of Parliament, I think.'

'So!' Mastrovin nodded to Dedekind. 'And when you had dined you left? Where were you going?'

'I was going back to the camp. I hadn't given my parole or anything of the kind, but I felt that I was behaving badly to my friend. Though he had made me prisoner he treated me well, and I am very fond of him. I proposed to go back and tell him what I had done.'

'He knew of your visit to the castle?'

'Not he. I took French leave. But I didn't like to leave Evallonia without having an explanation with him. Besides, I doubt if I could have managed it with his scouts everywhere. When your ruffians laid hands on me, I was going back the way I had come this morning.'

Mastrovin talked for a little with Dedekind in a tongue unknown to Jaikie. Then he turned upon him again his hanging countenance.

'You may be speaking the truth. You say you have no interest in the affairs of Evallonia. If that be so, you can have no objection to doing the Government of the Republic a service. It is threatened by many enemies, with some of whom you have been consorting. You must have heard talk – much talk – in the camp of your friend Jovian and in the castle of Prince Odalchini. You will tell me all that you heard. It will be to your interest, Mr Galt, to be frank, and it will be very much to your disadvantage to be stubborn.'

Jaikie put up a very creditable piece of acting. He managed to produce some sort of flush on his pale face, and he put all the righteous indignation he could muster into his eyes. It was not all acting, for once again this man was threatening him, and he felt that little shiver along the forehead which was a sign of the coming of one of his cold furies.

'What the devil do you mean? Do you think that I spy on my friends? I know that Juventus is opposed to your Government, and being a stranger I take no sides. There was much talk in the camp, and I didn't understand what it was all about. But if I had I would see you and your Government in Tophet before I repeated it.'

Dedekind looked ugly and whispered something to Mastrovin, which was no doubt a suggestion that means might be found for making Jaikie speak. Mastrovin whispered back what may have been an assurance that such means would come later. Jaikie could not tell, for he knew no Evallonian. But he was a little nervous lest he should have gone too far. He did not want to put a premature end to these interrogations.

Mastrovin's next words reassured him. He actually forced his heavy face into a show of friendliness.

'I respect your scruples,' he said. 'We have no desire to outrage your sense of honour. Besides, there is not much that Juventus does of which we are not fully informed. They are our declared enemies and against them we use the methods of war. But your friend Prince Odalchini is surely in a different case. He has lived peacefully under republican rule, though he has no doubt a preference for a monarchy. We bear him no ill will, but we are anxious that he should not compromise himself by an alliance with Juventus. It was for that reason that you were brought here, that we might probe what relation there was between the two, for we were aware that you had come from the Juventus camp. You can have no objection to telling us what is Prince Odalchini's frame of mind and what things were spoken of in the castle.'

Jaikie smiled pleasantly. 'That's another pair of shoes... The Prince is sick of politics. He is angry with Juventus, and asked me pretty much the same questions as you. But he is an old man and a tired one, and all he wants is to be left alone. He doesn't like these patrols sitting round his park and letting nobody in that they don't approve of. When I met him in England he was a strong Monarchist, but I don't think there is much royalism left in him now.'

Mastrovin was interested. 'No? And why?'

'Because he thinks the Monarchists so feeble. He was very strong on that point with the English Member of Parliament –

what was his name? Sir Archibald Something-or-other.' Jaikie was now talking like a man wholly at his ease.

'He thinks them feeble, does he? What are his reasons?'

'Well, one of them is that they have mislaid their trump card – their Prince John. I must say that sounds fairly incompetent.'

'So he said that?' Mastrovin's interest had quickened.

'Yes. But it wasn't only losing Prince John that he blamed them for, but their failure to discover who had got him. It seems that they believe he has been kidnapped by your people, or rather by the left wing of your people. Prince Odalchini mentioned a name – something like Merovingian – it began with an M, anyway. But that appears to have been a completely false scent.'

'Prince Odalchini thinks it a false scent?' Mastrovin's voice was suddenly quiet and gentle.

'Yes, because they now know where he is.' Jaikie had ceased to be a witness in the box, and was talking easily as if to a club acquaintance. He launched his mendacious bombshell in the most casual tone, as if it were only a matter of academic interest. 'It's Juventus that have Prince John. Not the lot here, but the division a hundred miles south that is holding the oilfields. There's a woman in command. I remember her name, because it was so fantastic – the Countess Araminta Troyos.'

There was dead silence for a second or two. Mastrovin's eyes were on the table, and Dedekind's fingers ceased to beat their endless tattoo.

'So you see,' Jaikie concluded lightly, 'Prince Odalchini is naturally sick of the whole business. I would like to see him out of the country altogether, for Evallonia at present seems to me no place for an old gentleman who only asks for a quiet life.'

Mastrovin spoke at last. If Jaikie's news was a shock to him he did not show it. He was smiling like a large, sleepy cat.

'What you tell us is very interesting,' he said. 'But we have much more to learn from you, Mr Galt.'

'I can't tell you anything more.'

'I think you can. At any rate, we will endeavour to help your memory.'

Jaikie, who had been rather pleased with himself, found his heart sink. There was a horrid menace behind that purring voice. Only the little shiver across his forehead kept him cool.

'I demand to be released at once,' he said. 'As an Englishman you dare not interfere with me, since you have nothing against me.'

'You propose?'

'To go back to the Juventus camp, and then to go home to England.'

'The first cannot be permitted. The second – well, the second depends on many things. Whether you will ever see England again rests with yourself. In the meantime you will remain in our charge – and at our orders.'

He rasped out the last words in a voice from which every trace of urbanity had departed. His face, too, was as Jaikie remembered it in the Canonry, a mask of ruthlessness.

And then, like an echo of his stridency, came a grinding at the door. It was locked and someone without was aware of that fact and disliked it. There was a sound of a heavy body applied to it, and, since the thing was flimsy, the lock gave and it flew open. Jaikie's astonished eyes saw a young Greenshirt officer, and behind him a quartet of hefty Juventus privates.

He learned afterwards the explanation of this opportune appearance. A considerable addition had been made to Ashie's wing, and it was proposed to billet the newcomers in the town. Accordingly a billeting party had been despatched to arrange for quarters, and it had begun with the principal inns. At this particular inn, which stood in a retired alley, the landlord had not been forthcoming, so the party had explored on their own account the capacities of the building. They had found their way obstructed by sundry odd-looking persons, and, since Juventus did not stand on ceremony, had summarily removed them from their path. A locked door to people in their mood seemed an insult, and they had not hesitated to break it open.

With one eye Jaikie saw that Mastrovin and Dedekind had their fingers on pistol triggers. With the other he saw that the Greenshirt had no inkling who the two were. His first thought was to denounce them, but it was at once discarded. That would mean shooting, and he considered it likely that he himself would stop a bullet. Besides, he had at the back of his head a notion that Mastrovin might *malgré lui* prove useful. By a fortunate chance he knew the officer, who had been the hooker of the forwards against whom he had played football, and to whom he had afterwards been introduced. He saw, too, that he was recognised. So he gave the Juventus salute and held out his hand.

'I'm very glad to see you,' he said. 'I was just coming to look for you. I surrender myself to you. It's your business to arrest me and take me back to camp. The fact is, I broke bounds yesterday and went on the spree. No, there was no parole. I meant to return last night, but I was detained. I shall have to have it out with the Praefectus. I deserve to be put in irons, but I don't think he'll be very angry, for I have a good many important things to tell him.' Jaikie had managed to sidle towards the door, so that he was close to the Greenshirts.

The officer was puzzled. He recognised Jaikie as a friend of the Praefectus and one for whose football capacities he had acquired a profound respect. Moreover, the frankness of his confession of irregular conduct disarmed him.

'Why should I arrest you?' he stammered in his indifferent English.

'Because I am an escaped prisoner. Discipline's discipline, you know, though a breach of it now and then may be good business.'

The young officer glanced at the morose figures at the table. Happily he did not see the pistols which they fingered. 'Who are these?' he asked.

'Two people staying in this inn. Bagmen – of no consequence... By the way, I wonder what fool locked that door?'

The young man laughed. 'It is a queer place this, and I do not like it. Few of the rooms are furnished, and the landlord has vanished, leaving only boorish servants. But I have to find billets for three companies before evening, and in these times one cannot be fastidious.' He paused. 'You are not – how do you say it? – pulling my foot?'

'Lord, no. I'm deadly serious, and the sooner I see the Praefectus the better.'

'Then I will detail two men to escort you back to camp. We will leave this place, which is as bare as a rabbit warren. I apologise, sirs, for my intrusion.' He bowed to the two men at the table, and, to Jaikie's amusement, they stood up and solemnly bowed in return.

Jaikie spent a somnolent afternoon in the tent of the Praefectus, outside of which, at his own request, an armed sentry stood on guard.

'Don't curse me, Ashie,' he said when its owner returned. 'I know I've broken all the rules, so you've got to pretend to treat me rough. Better say you're deporting me to headquarters for punishment. I want some solid hours of your undivided attention this evening, for I've the deuce of a lot to tell you. After dinner will be all right. Meantime, I want a large-scale map of Evallonia – one with the Juventus positions marked on it would be best. Any word of the Countess Araminta?'

'Yes, confound her! She has started to move. Moving on Krovolin, which is the Monarchists' headquarters. Devil take her for an abandoned hussy. Any moment she may land us in bloody war.'

'All the more reason why you and I should get busy,' said Jaikie.

'You have blood on your forehead,' Ashie told him that evening, when at last the Praefectus was free from his duties. 'Have you been in a scrap?'

'That comes of having a rotten mirror. I thought I had washed it all off. No, I had no scrap, but I got my nose bled. By Mastrovin – or rather by one of his minions.'

Ashie's eyes opened. 'You seem to have been seeing life. Get on with your story, Jaikie. We're by ourselves, and if you tantalise me any longer I'll put you in irons.'

Jaikie told the last part first – a sober narrative of kidnapping, an unpleasant journey, a night's lodging, a strictly truthful talk with two dangerous men, and the opportune coming of the Greenshirt patrol. Ashie whistled.

'You were in a worse danger than you knew. I almost wish it had come to shooting, for there were enough Greenshirts in Tarta this morning to pull that inn down stone by stone. I should love to see Mastrovin in his grave. But I dare say he would have taken you with him, and that would never do... Well, I've got the end of your tale. Now get back to the beginning. How did you get into the park?'

'Easily enough, but your people made it a slow business. By the way, I wish you would have up a lad called Ivar and explain to him that I was unavoidably prevented from keeping my engagement with him. He's a pleasant chap, and I shouldn't like him to think me a crook. The park was easy, but the castle was a tougher proposition. I had to do rather a fine bit of roof-climbing, and it was then that Mastrovin's fellows saw me, when I was spidering about the battlements. However, in the end I found an open window and got inside and met a pleasant little party. English all of them, except Prince Odalchini.'

'Good Lord, what were they doing there?'

'Justifying Mastrovin's suspicion that England is mixed up with the Evallonian Monarchists. I think they are going to be rather useful people, for they are precisely of your own way of thinking. So is Prince Odalchini, and he believes he can persuade

Count Casimir and the rest of his crowd. At any rate, he is going to have a dashed good try.'

'But I don't understand,' said the puzzled Ashie. 'Persuade him about what?'

'Listen very carefully and you'll hear, and prepare for shocks.' Jaikie proceeded to recount the conversation at the castle, and when he mentioned the Archduke Hadrian, Ashie sat up. 'He's my godfather,' he said; 'but I never saw him. No one has. I thought he was dead.'

'Well, he isn't. He's alive but bedridden, and it's only his name we want. Ashie, my dear, within a week the Monarchists are going to put the Archduke Hadrian on the throne. Only it won't be the Archduke, but another, so to speak, of the same name. One of the visitors at the castle is sufficiently like him to pass for him – except with his intimates, of whom there aren't any here. Then in another week Juventus butts in in all the majesty of its youth, ejects the dotard, and sets up Prince John, and everybody lives happy ever after.'

Ashie's reactions to this startling disclosure were many. Bewilderment, doubt, incredulity, even a scandalised annoyance chased each other across his ingenuous face. But the final residuum was relief.

'Jaikie,' he asked hoarsely, 'was that notion yours?'

'No. My line is tactics, not grand strategy. The notion came from the man who is going to play the part of the Archduke. He's an old Scotsman, and his name is McCunn, and he's the best friend I ever had in my life. Ashie, I want to ask a special favour of you. Mr McCunn is playing a bold game, and I'll back him to see it through. I don't know how much you'll come into it yourself, but if you do I want you to do your best for him. There may be a rough-house or two before he escapes over the frontier, and if you have a chance, do him a good turn. Promise.'

'I promise,' said Ashie solemnly. 'But for heaven's sake tell me more.'

'*You* tell me something. Would the rank and file of Juventus stand for Prince John?'

'They would. Ninety-nine per cent of them.' But his face was doubtful, so that Jaikie asked where the snag was.

'It's Cousin Mintha. I don't know how she'll take it.'

'That's my job. I'm off tomorrow at break of day. You'll have to let me go, and find me a motor bicycle.'

'You're going to Mintha?'

'I must. Every man to his job, and that's the one I've been allotted. I can't say I fancy it. I'd sooner have had any other, but there it is, and I must make the best of it. You must give me all the tips you can think of.'

'You'd better get hold of Doctor Jagon first. He is Mintha's chief counsellor.'

'Good. I know him – met him in Scotland. A loquacious old dog, but honest.'

'How are you going to get Prince John out of the Monarchist crowd into Mintha's arms?'

'He isn't with the Monarchists. He's lost.'

'Lost! That spikes our guns.'

'Officially lost. He disappeared a few days ago from the place in the Tirol where Count Casimir had him hidden. The Count thought that Mastrovin had pinched him, and Mastrovin – well, I don't know what Mastrovin thought, but he's raking heaven and earth to find him. Nobody knows where he is except the little party that dined last night in the castle. That's why Casimir will be friendly to the idea of the Archduke, for he has mislaid his Prince.'

'Where is he?' Ashie demanded.

'I had better not tell you. It would be wiser for you not know – at present. But I promise you I can lay my finger on him whenever we want him. What you've got to do is to put it about that he's with Juventus. That will prepare people's minds and maybe force your cousin's hand. I did a useful bit of work this morning, for I told Mastrovin that Prince John was with the

Countess Araminta. That means, I hope, that he will go there after him and annoy your cousin into becoming a partisan.'

Ashie looked at his friend with admiration slightly tempered by awe.

'Mintha is a little devil,' he said slowly; 'but she's a turtle-dove compared to you.'

CHAPTER 9

Night in the Woods

The great forest of St Sylvester lies like a fur over the patch of country through which the little river Silf – the Amnis Silvestris of the Romans – winds to the Rave. At the eastern end, near the Silf's junction with the main river, stands the considerable town of Krovolin; south of it stretch downs studded with the ugly headgear of oil wells; and west is the containing wall of the mountains. It is pierced by one grand highway, and seamed with lesser roads, many of them only grassy alleys among the beeches.

At one of the crossroads, where the highway was cut at right angles by a track running from north to south, two cars were halted. The Evallonian summer is justly famed for its settled weather, but sometimes in early August there falls for twenty-four hours a deluge of rain, if the wind should capriciously shift to the west. The forest was now being favoured with such a downpour. All day it had rained in torrents, and now, at eleven o'clock at night, the tempest was slowly abating. It was dark as pitch, but if the eyes had no work for them, the ears had a sufficiency, for the water beat like a drum in the tops of the high trees, and the drip on the sodden ground was like the persistent clamour of a brook.

One of the cars had comprehensively broken down, and no exploration of its intestines revealed either the reason or the cure. It was an indifferent German car, hired some days before in the town of Rosensee; the driver was Peter Wappit, and the occupants were Prince Odalchini and Dickson McCunn. The party from the other car, which was of a good English make, had descended and joined the group beside the derelict. Three men and two women stood disconsolately in the rain, in the glow of the two sets of headlights.

Prince Odalchini had not been idle after the momentous evening session in the House of the Four Winds. He had his own means of sending messages in spite of the vigilance of the Juventus patrols, and word had gone forthwith to the Monarchist leaders and to the secretaries of the Archduke Hadrian far away in the French chateau. It had been a more delicate business getting the castle party out of the castle confines. The road used was that which led through the cellars of the Turk's Head, and the landlord Proser, who had now to be made a confidant, had proved a tower of strength. So had Randal Glynde, whose comings and goings seemed to be as free and as capricious as the wind. The cars – and Peter Wappit – had been duly fetched from the Cirque Doré or wherever else they had been bestowed, and early that morning, before Tarta was astir, two batches of prosperous-looking tourists had left the inn, after the hearty farewells which betoken generous tipping. Their goal was the town of Krovolin, but the route they took was not direct. Under Prince Odalchini's guidance – no one would have recognised the Prince, for Mr Glynde had made him up to look like an elderly American with a goatee – they made a wide circuit among the foothills, and entered the Krovolin highway by a route from the south-west.

The weather favoured them, for the Tarta streets were empty when they started, and they met scarcely a traveller on the roads. There was one exception, for about four miles from the town their journey was impeded by part of a travelling circus, which seemed to he bearing south. Its string of horses and lurching caravans took a long time to pass in the narrow road, and during the delay the proprietor of the circus appeared to offer his apologies. This proprietor, a tall, fantastically dressed being with a ragged beard, conversed with various members of the party while the block ahead was being cleared, and much of his conversation was in low tones and in a tongue which was neither German nor Evallonian.

The five figures in the rain had a hurried conference. The oldest of them seemed to be the most perturbed by the *contretemps*. He peered at a map by the light of the lamps, and consulted his watch.

'Krovolin is less than thirty kilometres distant,' he said. 'We could tow this infernal car if we had such a thing as a rope, which we haven't. We can wait here for daylight. Or one car can go on to Krovolin and send out help.'

'I'm for the last,' said Sir Archie. 'I would suggest our all stowing into my car, but it would mean leaving our kit behind, and in these times I don't think that would be safe. I tell you what. You and Mr McCunn get into my car and Peter will drive you. Janet and Alison and I will wait behind with the crock, and you can send help for us as soon as you can wake up a garage.'

Prince Odalchini nodded. 'I think that will be best,' he said. 'I can promise that you will not have long to wait, for at Casimir's headquarters there is ample transport. I confess I do not want to be delayed, for I have much to do. Also it is not wise for me to be loitering in St Sylvester's woods, since at present in this country I am somewhat contraband goods. Mr McCunn too. It is vital no mishap should befall him. You others are still free people.'

'Right,' said Archie, and began moving the kit of his party from his own car to the derelict. 'You'd both be the better of a hot bath and a dressing down, for you've been pretty well soaked all day. We'll begin to expect the relief expedition in about an hour. If I can get this bus started, where do I make for in Krovolin?'

'The castle of Count Casimir,' was the answer. 'It is a huge place, standing over Krovolin as the House of the Four Winds stands over Tarta.'

When the tail lights of his own car had disappeared, Archie set himself to make another examination of Dickson's, but without success. It was a touring car with a hood of an old-fashioned pattern, which during the day had proved but a weak defence against the weather. The seats were damp and the floor was a shallow pool. Since the rain was lessening, Archie managed to dry the seats and invited the women to make themselves comfortable. Janet Roylance and Alison had both been asleep for the past hour, and had wakened refreshed and prepared to make the best of things. Janet produced chocolate and biscuits and a thermos of coffee, and offered supper, upon which Alison fell ravenously. Archie curled his legs up on the driver's seat and lit his pipe.

'I'm confoundedly sleepy,' he said. 'A long day in the rain always makes me sleepy. I wonder why?' A gout of wet from the canvas of the hood splashed on his face. 'This is a comfortless job. Looks as if the fowls of the air were one up on us tonight. I'll get a crick in my neck if I stick here longer, and I'd get out and roost on the ground if it weren't so sloppy. "A good soft pillow for my good grey head" – how does the thing go?'

' "Were better than this churlish turf of France." ' Alison completed the quotation. 'Have some coffee. It will keep you awake.'

'It won't. That's my paradoxical constitution. Coffee makes me sleepier.' He looked at his watch. 'Moon's due in less than an hour. I call this a rotten place – not the sound of a bird or beast, only that filthy drip. I say, you know, you two look like a brace of owls in a cage.'

It was not an inept comparison for the women in their white waterproofs, which caught dimly the back-glow of the side-lamps. The place was sufficiently eerie, for the trees were felt

139

rather than seen, and the only food for the eye was the glow made by the headlights on the shining black tarmac of the highway. The car had been pushed on to the turf with its nose close to the main road, opposite where the track from the north debouched. Archie to cheer himself began a song, against which his wife stoutly protested.

'That's sacrilege,' she said. 'This is a wonderful place, for there must be fifteen miles of trees round us in every direction. Be quiet, Archie, and, if you can't doze and won't have any supper, think good thoughts.'

'The only good thought I have is the kind of food Count Casimir will give us. Is he the sort of fellow that does himself well, Alison? You're the only one of us that knows him. I want beefsteaks – several of 'em.'

'I think so,' the girl answered. 'He praised our food at Castle Gay and he gave me a very good breakfast at Knockraw. But the breakfast might have been Prince John's affair, for he was a hungry young man... I wonder where *he* is now. I don't think he was with Ran's outfit when we passed it this morning.'

'We have properly dissipated our forces,' said Archie. 'However, that's a good rule of strategy if you know how to concentrate them later. I wonder where Jaikie is?'

'Poor Jaikie!' Alison sighed. 'He has an awful job before him, for he is as shy as an antelope really, though he does brazen things. He'll be scared into fits by the Countess Araminta. Dickson was the one to deal with her.'

'He may fall in love with her,' said Archie. 'Quite possible, though she's not the sort I fancy myself. Very beautiful, you know. When I first saw her I thought her wonderful sunburn came out of a bottle, and I considered her too much of a movie star, but when I found it was the gift of Heaven I rather took to her. But Jaikie will have to stand up to her or she'll eat him. I say, Janet, how much use do you think Prince Odalchini is?'

'Good enough for a day with the bitch pack on the hills,' was the drowsy answer. 'Not much good for the Vale and the big fences.'

'Just my own notion. He's too old, and though he's a brave old boy, I don't see him exactly leading forlorn hopes. What about Count Casimir, Alison?'

The girl shook her head. 'I'm not sure. He talks too much.'

'Too romantic, eh?'

'Too sentimental. Dickson's romantic, which is quite a different thing.'

'I see. Well, I take it there's no question about the Countess. By all accounts she's a high-powered desperado. Apart from her it looks as if this show was a bit short of what Bobby Despenser calls "dynamic personages", and that what there are are mostly our own push. There's McCunn – no mistake about him. And Jaikie – not much mistake about Jaikie. And there's your lunatic cousin Glynde. To think that when I saw him at Charles Lamancha's party two months ago, I thought him rather a nasty piece of work – too much the tailor's model and the pride of the Lido. Who'd have guessed that he was a cross between a bandit and a bard?'

Conversation had dispelled Archie's languor.

'This promises to be a merry party,' he said. 'The trouble is to know how and when it will stop and what kind of heads we'll have in the morning. Do you realise the desperate way we're behaving? We're taking a hand in another fellow's revolution, and some of us have taken charge of it. And, more by token, who are we? A retired Glasgow grocer that wants to keep a crazy promise – and a Rugger tough from Cambridge – and a girl I've purloined from her parents – and a respectable married woman – and myself, an ornament of the Mother of Parliaments, who should be sitting at Geneva before a wad of stationery making revolutions for ever impossible... Hullo, what's this?'

There was a noise like that of a machine-gun which rapidly grew louder, and down the side road from the north came the lights of a motor bicycle. Its rider saw the lamps of the car, slowed down, skidded on the tarmac, and came to a standstill in a clump of fern. A soaked and muddy figure stood blinking in the car lights. So dirty was his face that two of the three did not recognise him. But Alison in a trice was out of the car with a cry of 'Jaikie'.

Mr John Galt had had a laborious day. Ashie had prepared for him a pass, giving him safe conduct to the camp of the Countess Araminta, but had warned him that, except for Juventus, it was of no use, and that Juventus had few representatives in the piece of country through which he must travel. He had also provided a map, and the two had planned an ingenious course, which would take him to the oilfields by unfrequented byways. It had proved too ingenious, for Jaikie had lost his way, and gone too far west into the foothills. The blanket of low clouds and the incessant rain made it impossible for him to get a prospect, and the countryside seemed empty of people. The only cottages he passed were those of woodcutters whose speech he could not understand, and when he mentioned place names he must have mispronounced them, for they only shook their heads. His only clue was the Silf, of which he struck the upper waters after midday. But no road followed the Silf, which ran in a deep ravine, and he was compelled to bear north again till he found a road which would take him south through the forest. But he knew now his position on the map, and he hoped to reach his destination before dark, when his machine began to give trouble. Jaikie was a poor mechanic and it took him three hours before he set the mischief right. By this time the dark skies were darkening further into twilight. There was no shelter for the night in the forest, so he decided to struggle on till at any rate he was out of the trees. The map showed a considerable village on the southern skirts which would surely provide an inn.

His lamp gave him further trouble, for it would not stay lit. He had been soaked since early in the day, for Ashie could not provide him with overalls, and his shabby mackintosh was no protection against the deluge. He was also hungry, for he had long ago finished his supply of biscuits and chocolate. The consolations of philosophy, of which he had a good stock, were nearly exhausted when he skidded on the tarmac of the trunk highway.

Archie laughed boisterously.

'I was just saying that we had dangerously dispersed our forces, but now we've begun to concentrate. Where have you been, my lad?'

Jaikie, grinning sheepishly at Alison, shook the water from his ancient hat, and pushed back a lock of hair which had straggled over his left eye.

'I've been circumnavigating Evallonia. I dare say I've come two hundred miles.'

'Was that purpose or accident?'

'Accident. I've been lost most of the day up on the edge of the hills. And I've got a relic of a bicycle. But what are you doing here?'

'Accident, too. This car of McCunn's soured on him, so we sent him and the Prince on to Krovolin in mine, and Janet and Alison and I are waiting here like Babes in the Wood till we're rescued.'

'Have you any food to spare?' Jaikie asked. He had recovered his spirits, and saw his misadventures in a more cheerful light, since they had led to this meeting.

Alison gave him some coffee out of the thermos and the remains of the biscuits.

'You're a grisly sight, Jaikie,' she said severely. 'I've seen many a tattie-bogle that looked more respectable.'

'I know,' he said meekly. 'I've been looking a bit of a ragamuffin for a long time, but today has put the lid on it.'

'You simply can't show yourself to the Countess like that. You look like a tramp that has been struck by lightning and then drowned.'

'I thought I might find an inn where I could tidy up and get my clothes dried.'

'Nothing will tidy you up. Juventus are a dressy lot, you know and they'll set the dogs on you.'

'But I have letters from Ashie.' He dived into his inner pocket and drew forth a sodden sheaf. 'Gosh! they're pulp! The rain's got at them and the ink has run. They're unreadable. What on earth am I to do?'

'You're a child of calamity. Didn't you think of oilskin or brown paper?... You'd better come on with us to Krovolin for a wash and brush up, and Prince Odalchini will find you more decent clothes.'

Jaikie shook his head. 'I must obey orders. That's the first rule of Juventus, and I belong to Juventus now. Properly speaking, I'm at present your enemy... I must be getting on, for I've a big job before me. I'm glad you pushed off the Prince and Mr McCunn, for they also have their job. You three are only camp followers.'

'You're an ungrateful beast,' said Alison indignantly, 'to call us camp-followers, when you know I came hundreds of miles before you said you needed me... Get off then to your assignation. A pretty figure you'll cut in a lady's bower!'

Jaikie's face fell. 'Lord, but duty is an awful thing! I funk that interview more than anything I remember. What, by the way, is her proper name? I must get that right, for Ashie, who's her cousin, calls her Mintha.'

'She is the Countess Araminta Troyos – have you got that? How do you propose to approach her? Mr Galt to see the Countess on private business? Or a courier from the Praefectus of the Western Wing?'

'I'm going first to the Professor man – what's his name – Doctor Jagon. He won't make much of this mass of pulp, but he may remember me from the Canonry. Anyway, I think I can persuade him that I'm honest.'

Jaikie was in the act of wheeling his machine into the track which ran south when he started at a shout of Archie's, and turning his head saw the glow of a great car lighting up the aisle among the trees.

'Well done the Prince,' said Archie. 'Gad, he's done us proud and sent two cars – there's another behind.'

'But they're coming from the wrong direction,' said Janet.

An avalanche of light sped through the darkness, and the faces of the waiting four took on an unearthly whiteness. This was a transformation so sudden and startling that each remained motionless – Jaikie with his hand on his bicycle, Alison holding the thermos, Janet with her head poked out of the car, and Archie with one foot on the step. The lights halted, and the two cars were revealed. They were big roadsters with long rakish bonnets, and in each were two men.

Jaikie happened to be nearest, and he was the first to recognise the occupants. The man at the wheel he did not know, and what he could see of his face was only a long nose between his hat and the collar of his waterproof. But the other who sat beside him was unmistakable. He saw the forward-thrusting jaw, the blunt nose, and the ominous eyes of Mastrovin.

His first thought was to get off, for he considered that he alone of the four was likely to be interfered with. But unfortunately the recognition had been mutual. Mastrovin cried a sharp word of command which brought the two men out of the second car, and he himself with surprising agility leaped on to the road. Jaikie found himself held by strong hands and looking into a most unfriendly face.

'I am in luck,' said Mastrovin. 'We did not finish our conversation the other day, Mr – Galt, I think you said the name was? I am glad to have the opportunity of continuing it, and now I think we shall not be interrupted.'

'Sorry,' said Jaikie, 'but I can't wait.'

'Sorry,' was the answer, 'but you must.'

Jaikie found his hands wrenched from the bicycle handles and his person in the grip of formidable arms. He observed that Mastrovin had turned his attention to the others.

'How are you, Mr Mastrovin?' he heard Archie say in a voice of falsetto cheerfulness. 'We met, you remember, at Geneva?'

'We have met since,' was the answer. 'We met in a hut in the mountains at Unnutz.' There was an unpleasant suggestion in his tone that that meeting had not been satisfactory.

Mastrovin peered within the car and saw Janet, who apparently did not interest him. But Alison was a different matter. He must have had a good memory for faces, for he instantly recognised her.

'Another from Unnutz,' he said. 'A young lady who took early morning walks in the hills. So!' He cried a word to the driver of his car, which Jaikie did not understand. Then he faced Sir Archie, his brows drawn to a straight line and his mouth puckered in a mirthless smile.

'You are the English who have been in the House of the Four Winds. I did not think I was mistaken... Two of you I have seen elsewhere – at the time I suspected you and now I know. You have meddled in what does not concern you, and you must take the consequences.'

He rasped out the final words in a voice which made it plain that these consequences would not be pleasant. Archie, whose temper was rising, found himself looking into the barrel of a pistol held in a very steady hand.

'Do not be foolish,' Mastrovin said. 'We are four armed men, and we do not take chances. You will accompany us you and the women. You are in no danger if you do as I bid you, but it is altogether necessary that for a little you should be kept out of mischief.'

Archie's angry protests were checked on his lips, they were so manifestly futile. Janet and he were ordered into the first car, where Mastrovin took the seat opposite them. They were permitted to take their baggage, and that was bundled into the second car, whither Alison accompanied it. The man who was holding Jaikie asked a question, oddly enough in French, to which Mastrovin replied by bidding him put the 'little rat' beside the luggage. Jaikie found himself on a folding seat with a corner of Archie's kitbag in his ribs and Alison sitting before him.

The cars sped down the Krovolin road, and after some miles they passed another car coming in the opposite direction. That, thought Jaikie, must be the relief sent by Prince Odalchini... He was in what for him was a rare thing, a mood of black despair. Partly it was due to his weary and sodden body, but the main cause was that he had suddenly realised the true posture of affairs. He had slipped idly into this business, as had the others, regarding it only as an amusing game, a sort of undergraduate 'rag'. There was a puzzle to solve, where wits and enterprise could come into play, but the atmosphere was *opéra bouffe*, or at the best comedy. The perplexed Ashie was a comic figure; so were Prince Odalchini and the Monarchists; so was the formidable Countess Mintha; so even two days ago had seemed Mastrovin. Alison and Janet and Archie were all votaries of the comic spirit.

But now he realised that there were darker things. Mastrovin's pistol had suddenly dispelled the air of agreeable farce, and opened the veils of tragedy. The jungle was next door to the formal garden – and the beasts of the jungle. As in the library of Castle Gay two years before, he had a glimpse of wolfish men and an underworld of hideous things. That night for the second time he had been called a rat by Mastrovin and his friends, but the insult did not sting him, for he was in the depths of self-abasement. The bitter thought galled his mind that he had brought Alison into a grim business. For that he was alone responsible, and he saw no way out. It was bad that he should be compelled to fail Ashie, for his mission was now hopeless, but it was worse that Alison should have to pay for his folly. Mastrovin would never let them go, and if things went ill with Mastrovin's side he would make them pay the penalty... And he was utterly helpless. He knew nothing of the country and could not speak the tongue, he had no money, and only a boy's strength. Prince Odalchini and Dickson might persist in their plot and Juventus continue its high career, but Alison and Janet and Archie and he were out of it forever, prisoners in some dim underworld of Mastrovin's contriving.

They came out of the forest to find that the rain had stopped and that the moon was rising among ragged clouds. He saw a gleam of water and what looked like the spires of a city. They were being taken to Krovolin, and presently they approached the first houses of its western *faubourg*... And then something happened which brought a thin ray of hope to Jaikie's distressed soul. There were lights in an adjacent field, and from them came the strains of a fiddle. It was playing Dvořák's *Humoresque*, and that was the favourite tune of Luigi of the Cirque Doré.

CHAPTER 10

Aurunculeia

The familiar melody brought only a momentary refreshment to Jaikie's spirit. The feeling was strong upon him that he had stumbled out of comedy into a melodrama which might soon darken into tragedy. As they entered the city of Krovolin, this mood was increased by the sight of unmistakable pistols in the hands of his guards. Some kind of watch was kept at the entrance, for both cars were stopped and what sounded like pass-words were exchanged. Krovolin he knew was the headquarters of the Monarchists, but Mastrovin, having spent all his life in intrigue, was not likely to be stopped by so small a thing as that. It was like his audacity to have domiciled himself in the enemy's camp, and he probably knew most of that enemy's secrets. Jaikie dismissed the thought of appealing to these Monarchist sentries and demanding to be taken to Count Casimir, for he was convinced that at that game he would be worsted. Besides, he could not talk the language.

The hour was late, and there were few people in the well-lit street which descended to the bridge of the river. The cars turned along the edge of the water over vile cobbles, and presently wove their way into a maze of ancient squalor. This was the Krovolin of the Middle Ages, narrow lanes with high houses on both sides, the tops of which bent forward so as to leave only a slender ribbon of sky. Up a side alley they went, and after many twistings came to the entrance of a yard. Here they were clearly expected, for a figure stood on watch outside, who after a word with Mastrovin opened a pair of ancient rickety gates. The car scraped through with difficulty, and Jaikie found himself in a cobbled space which might once have been the courtyard of a house, Now the moon showed it as a cross between a garage and a builder's yard, for it held two other cars, a motor lorry, and what looked like the debris of a recent earthquake. When he got out he promptly fell over a heap of rubble and a sheaf of spades. Somebody had recently been digging there.

He was given no time to prospect. Mastrovin came forward, bowed to Alison and shepherded her to the side of Janet and Archie. Two men took charge of the baggage, and the party were conducted indoors. For a moment Jaikie was left alone, and his hopes rose – perhaps he was too humble for Mastrovin's attentions. He was speedily undeceived, for the man who had been with Mastrovin at Tarta gave an order, and the fellow who had been outside the gate clutched Jaikie's arm. He was also a prisoner, only a more disconsidered one than the others. He was pushed through a door and prodded down a passage and up a narrow staircase, till he reached a little room smelling abominably of garlic. It was a bedroom, for there was a truckle-bed and a deal table carrying on it the stump of a candle. His conductor nodded to the bed, on which he flung Jaikie's rucksack, and then departed, after locking the door.

There was a window which seemed to look out upon a pit of darkness. It was not shuttered, but the sashes were firmly bolted. By bending low Jaikie could see upwards to a thin streak of light. The room must be on the street side, and what he saw was a strip of moonlit sky. It must also be on the first floor, for he had ascended only one flight of stairs. If this was meant as a prison it was an oddly insecure one.

But all thought of immediate escape was prevented by the state of his body. He was immeasurably weary, and so sleepy that his eyes were gummed together; a condition which with him usually followed a day of hard exercise in the rain. The stuffiness of the place increased his drowsiness. He sat on the edge of the bed and tried to think, but his mind refused to work. He must have sleep before he could do anything. He stripped off his sodden clothes, and found that he was not so wet as he had feared – of his undergarments only the collar and sleeves of his shirt had suffered. He hung them to dry on rusty nails with which the walls were abundantly provided. There were plenty of bedclothes and they seemed clean, so, wrapping his naked body in them, he was presently asleep.

He woke to a dusty twilight, but there was a hum out of doors which suggested that it was full day. A glance from the window showed him that though the sun had not yet got into the alley the morning's life had begun. The place was full of people, and by standing on the sill he could see their heads beneath him. He had been right – the room was on the first story. It bulged out above the street, so his vision was limited; he saw the people in the middle and on the other side, but not those directly beneath him.

He was very hungry, for he had had scanty rations the day before, and he wondered if breakfast was included in this new regime. There was no sign of it, so he turned his attention to the window. It was of an old-fashioned type, with folding sashes secured by slim iron bars which ran into sockets where they were held by padlocks. Jaikie was a poor mechanic, but he saw that these bolts would be hard to tamper with. If the place were kept sealed up like this no wonder the air was foul. Fortunately the sun could not make itself felt in that cavern of a street, but, all the same, by noon it would be an oven.

This was a disheartening thought, and it took the edge off his appetite. What he particularly wanted was something to drink, beer for preference, but he would have made shift with water. He lay down on the bed, for to look out of the sealed window only distressed him.

As the morning advanced he must have slept again, for the opening of the door woke him with a start. The newcomer was Mastrovin.

He looked very square and bulky in that narrow place, and he seemed to be in an ugly temper. He walked to the window and examined the fastenings. Jaikie observed for the first time that there were no shutters. What if he smashed the glass and dropped into the street? It could not be more than ten yards, and he was as light on his feet as a cat.

Mastrovin may have guessed his thought, for he turned to him with a sour smile.

'Do not delude yourself, Mr – Galt, isn't it? That window is only the inner works of this fortress. Even if you opened it you would be no better off. The outer works would still have to be passed, and they are human walls, stronger than stone and lime.'

'Am I to have any breakfast?' Jaikie asked. 'I don't suppose it's any good asking you what you mean by bringing me here. But most gaolers feed their prisoners.'

'I am the exception. Life at present is too hurried with me to preserve the amenities. But a word from you will get you breakfast; liberty also – conditional liberty. You cannot be released just at once, but I will have you taken to a more comfortable place. That word is the present address of Prince John.'

Mastrovin spoke as Jaikie remembered once hearing a celebrated statesman speak when on a visit to Cambridge – slowly, pronouncing his words as if he relished the sound of them, giving his sentences an oratorical swing. It was certainly impressive.

'I haven't the remotest idea,' he said, speaking the strictest truth.

'Let me repeat,' said Mastrovin with a great air of patience. 'The English have long been suspected of dabbling in Monarchist plots. That I have already told you. You have been at Tarta in the House of the Four Winds, which is the home of such plots. Did not my people pick you out of it? You admitted to me that you were acquainted with Prince Odalchini. Where, I ask you now, is Prince Odalchini's master?'

'I tell you, I don't know. As I told you at Tarta, I heard a rumour that he was with some lady called the Countess Troyos.'

'That rumour is a lie,' said Mastrovin fiercely. 'For a moment I believed it, but I have since proved it a lie. What is more, when you told it me you knew it was a lie. I repeat my question.'

The formidable eyebrows were drawn together, and the whole man became an incarnate menace. Jaikie, empty, headachy, sitting in his shabby clothes on the edge of the bed, felt very small and forlorn. He sometimes felt like that, and on such occasions he would have given all he possessed for another stone of weight and another two inches of height.

'I don't know,' he said. 'How should I know? I'm an ordinary English tourist who came to Evallonia by accident. I don't know anybody in it except Prince Odalchini...and Count Paul Jovian – and you.'

'You will know a good deal more about me very soon, my friend. Listen. You are lying – I am a judge of liars, and I can read your face. You are a friend of the three other English – the man and the two women – I find you in the forest in their company. Of these other English I know something. I last saw them in the neighbourhood of Prince John, and it is certain that they know where he has gone and what he is now doing. That knowledge I demand to share – and at once.'

'I don't know what the others know, but I know what I don't know. Though you kept me here till I had a long grey beard I couldn't give you any other answer.'

'You will not stay long enough to grow a beard. Only a little time, but it will not be a pleasant time. You will do what I ask, I think. The others – the others are, as you say in England, of the gentry – a politician and baronet – two ladies of birth. I hold such distinctions as less than rotten wood, but I am a man of the world, and now and then I must submit to the world's valuation... But you are of a different class. You are of the people, the new educated proletariat on which England prides herself... With you I can use elementary methods... With the others in time, if they are stubborn...but with you, now.'

He spat out the last words with extraordinary venom. No doubt he thought that in that moment he was being formidable, but as a matter of fact to Jaikie he had ceased to be even impressive. He had insulted him, threatened him, had wakened the small efficient devil that lived at the back of his mind. Jaikie was very angry, and with him wrath always blanketed fear. He saw Mastrovin now, not as a sinister elemental force, but as a common posturing bully.

He yawned.

'I wish you'd send me up some breakfast,' he said. 'A cup of coffee, if you've nothing else.'

Mastrovin moved to the door.

'You will get no food until you speak. And no drink. Soon this room will be as hot as hell, and may you roast in it!'

The exhilaration of Jaikie's anger did not last long, though it left behind it a very solid dislike. He realised that he had got himself into an awkward place, from which every exit seemed blocked. But what struck cold at his heart was the peril of Alison. He had heard at the House of the Four Winds of her days at Unnutz, and he realised that Mastrovin had good grounds for connecting her and Janet and Archie with Prince John's disappearance. He must have suspected them from the start, and the sight of the trio at Tarta had clinched his suspicions.

Jaikie tried to set out the case soberly and logically. Prince John was for Mastrovin the key of the whole business. If he could lay hands on him he could render the Monarchists impotent. He was probably clever enough to have foreseen the possibilities of Juventus taking up the Prince's cause, for without the Prince or somebody like him Juventus would spend its strength on futilities. So long as it had no true figurehead it was at the mercy of Mastrovin and his underworld gang. The settlement of

Evallonia was the one thing the latter must prevent: the waters must be kept troubled, for only then could he fish with success... Jaikie saw all that. He saw Mastrovin's purpose, and knew that he would stop at nothing to effect it, for he was outside the pale of the decencies. He meant to try to starve Jaikie himself into submission; but, far worse, he would play the same game with Alison and Janet. All four had stumbled out of a bright world into a mediaeval gloom which stank horribly of the Inquisition.

For a moment his heart failed him. Then his sense of feebleness changed into desperation. He knew that the lives of the other three depended on him, and the knowledge stung him into action. Never had he felt so small and feeble and insignificant, but never so determined. A memory came to him of that night long ago at Huntingtower when the forlorn little band of the Gorbals Diehards had gone into action. He remembered his cold fury, which had revealed itself in copious tears. Nowadays he did not weep, but if there had been a mirror in the room it would have shown a sudden curious pallor in his small face.

He set to work on the window. His rucksack had been searched for weapons, but he had in his pocket what is known as a sportsman's knife, an implement with one blade as strong as a gully, and with many gadgets. He could do nothing with the bolts and the padlocks, but he might cut into the supporting wood.

It proved an easier task than he had feared. The windows across the street were shuttered, so he could work without fear of detection. The socket of the lower bolt had a metal plate surrounding it, but the upper was fair game for his knife. The wood was old and hard, but after labouring for an hour or two he managed to dig out the square into which the bolt fastened. That released the top of one window, and he turned to the harder job of the bottom.

Here he had an unexpected bit of luck. There seemed something queer about the lower padlock, and to his joy he found that he could open it. It had been locked without the tongue being driven home. This was providential, for the lower part was solidly sheathed in metal and his knife would have been useless. With some difficulty he drew the stiff bolts, and one half of the window was at his disposal.

Very gingerly he pushed it open. A hot breath of air came in on him from the baking alley, but it was fresh air and it eased his headache. Then cautiously he put his head out and looked down upon the life of the street.

Mastrovin had not been bluffing. There were strong outworks to this fortress, and the outworks were human. Few people were about, perhaps because it was the time for the midday meal. It was a squalid enough place, with garbage in the gutters, but it had one pleasant thing, a runnel of water beside the pavement on the other side, no doubt a leat from the Rave or the Silf. The sight of the stream made his thirst doubly vexatious, but he had no time to think of it, for something else filled his eye. There were men on guard – two below his window, and one on the kerb opposite. This last might have seen him, but happily he was looking the other way.

Jaikie drew in his head and shut the window.

That way lay no hope of escape. If he dropped into the street it would be into such arms as had received him on Prince Odalchini's terrace.

This was disheartening, but at first he was not greatly disheartened. The fact that he had made an opening into the outer world had given him an illogical hope. Also he could now abate the stuffiness of his prison house. The place was still an oven, but the heat was not stifling. In time evening would come – and night. Might not something be done in the darkness? He had better try to sleep.

But as he lay on the bed he found that his thoughts, quickened by anxiety for Alison, ran in a miserable whirligig and that hope was very low. Mastrovin was taking no chances. Before night he would probably examine the window; in any case his ruffians below were likely to be on stricter duty. His own bodily discomfort added to his depression, for his tongue was like a stick and he was sick with hunger. A man, he knew, could fast for many days if only he had water, but if he had neither food nor drink his strength would soon ebb.

What, he wondered, was Alison doing? Enduring the same misery? Not yet – though that would come unless he could bestir himself. But she and Janet and Archie must he pretty low in mind... He remembered that he was failing Prince Odalchini and Ashie, and doing nothing about the duty which had been assigned him. But that was the least of his troubles. This infernal country might go hang for all he cared. What mattered was Alison.

One thought maddened him that the four of them had gone clean out of the ken of their friends. It would be supposed that at the moment he was with the Countess Araminta, and no one would begin to ask questions. About the other three there might be some fuss, for the relief car would find the derelict in the forest. Also his motor bicycle, though again that would mean nothing to anybody. Archie and his party were expected to join Dickson and Prince Odalchini at Count Casimir's headquarters. When they did not arrive and the derelict was found there would no doubt be a hue and cry. But to what effect? Mastrovin would have covered his tracks, and the last place to look for the missing would be the slums of Krovolin. The best hiding place was under the light.

The street had been almost noiseless in the early afternoon, when good citizens were taking their siesta. About three it woke up a little. There was a drunken man who sang, and from the window Jaikie saw the tops of greengrocers' carts moving countrywards, after the forenoon market. After that there was silence again, and then the tramp of what sounded like a police patrol. Between four and five there was considerable movement and the babble of voices. Perhaps the street was a short cut between two popular thoroughfares; at any rate it became suddenly quite a lively place. There were footsteps outside his door, and Jaikie closed the window in a hurry and lay back on the bed. Was Mastrovin about to pay him another visit? But whoever it was thought better of it, and he heard the steps retreating down the stairs. They had scarcely died away, when out of doors came a sound which set Jaikie's nerves tingling. Someone was playing on a flute, and the tune was Dvořák's *Humoresque.*

He flew to the window and cautiously looked out. There was no watcher on the opposite pavement. Quite a number of people were in the street, shop-girls and clerks for the most part on their way home. A beggar was playing in the gutter, playing a few bars and then supplicating the passers-by. His face was towards Jaikie, who observed that he wore a gipsy cap of cats' skins and for the rest was a ruin of rags. Underneath the cap there was a glimpse of dark southern eyes and a hairy unshaven face.

The man as he played kept an eye on Jaikie's window when he was not ogling the shopgirls. The light in the street was poor, and he seemed to be looking for something and to be uncertain if he had found it. Jaikie stuck his head farther out, and this seemed to give the man what he sought. He took his eyes off the window, finished his tune, and held out his cap for alms. Jaikie saw the gleam of earrings. Then he blew into his flute, pocketed it, and started to shamble inconspicuously down the gutter till in a minute he was lost to view.

Jaikie shut the window and resolutely stretched himself on the bed. But now his mood had wholly changed. Luigi had seen him. The Cirque Doré knew his whereabouts. Soon it would be dark, and then Randal Glynde would come to his rescue.

So complete was his trust in Mr Glynde that he forebore to speculate on the nature of the rescue. Had he done so he might have been less confident. Here in this squalid place Mastrovin was all powerful, and he had his myrmidons around him. The Cirque Doré could produce no fighting men; besides, any attempt at violence would probably mean death for those on whose behalf it was used. Mastrovin had the manners of the jungle... Jaikie thought of none of these things. His only fear was of a second visit from his gaoler, when, if he proved recalcitrant, he might be removed to other quarters in this dark rabbit warren. At all costs he must remain where Luigi had seen him.

Jaikie had now forgotten both his thirst and hunger. As the room darkened into twilight he lay listening for footsteps on the stairs. The falling of plaster, the scurrying of rats, the creaking of old timbers threw him into a sweat of fear. But no steps came. The noises of the street died away, and the place began to settle into its eery nightly quiet.

Suddenly from out of doors came a tumultuous and swelling sound. At first Jaikie thought that a rising had broken out in some part of the city, for the noise was that of many people shouting. But there were no shots, and the tumult had no menace in it. It grew louder, so it was coming nearer. He looked into the darkness, and far on his right he saw wavering lights, which from their inconstancy must be torches held in unsteady hands. The thing, whatever it was, was coming down this street.

There was a patter of feet below him, and he saw a mob of urchins, the forerunners of the procession, who trotted ahead with frequent backward glances. The light broadened till the alley was bright as day, but with a fearsome murky glow. It was torches, sure enough, carried and waved by four half-naked figures with leopard-skin mantles and chaplets of flowers on their heads. Behind them came four cream-coloured ponies, also garlanded, drawing a sort of Roman chariot, and in that chariot was a preposterous figure who now and then stood on its head, now and then balanced itself on the chariot's rim, and all the time kept up a shrill patter and the most imbecile grimaces. He recognised Meleager, the clown of the Cirque Doré.

Jaikie knew that the moment had come. The rescue party had arrived and he must join it. But how? It was not halting; in a moment Meleager's chariot had passed on, and he was looking down on zebras ridden by cowboys. It was not a big circus, and the procession could not last long, so he must get ready for action.

He noticed that it was hugging his side of the street, so that the accompanying crowd was all on the far pavement. That meant that Mastrovin's watchers could not keep their places just below him. Did Randal Glynde mean him to drop down and move under the cover of the cavalcade? That must be it, he thought. He opened the window wide, and sat crouched on the sill.

Then he noticed another thing. The whole procession was not lit up, but clusters of torches and flares alternated with no lights at all, and the dark patches were by contrast very dark. He must descend into one of these tracts of blackness.

Marie Antoinette, or somebody like her, had just passed in a gaudy illuminated coach, and he made ready to drop into her wake. But a special tumult warned him that something odd was following. Though an unlit patch succeeded, the crowd on the opposite kerb seemed to be thicker. Straining his eyes to the right he saw a huge shadow moving up the alley, so close to his side of the street that it seemed to be shouldering the houses. It was high, not six feet below his perch, and it was broad, for it stretched across to the very edge of the runnel of water. And it moved fast, as fast as the trotting ponies, though the sound of its movement was lost in the general din.

It was under him, and, clutching his rucksack, he jumped for it. A hand caught his collar, and dumped him between two pads. He found himself looking up at the stars from the back of the elephant Aurunculeia.

He lay still for a time, breathing in the clean air, while Mr Glynde was busy with his duties as mahout. Presently they were out of the narrow street, and Aurunculeia swung more freely now that dust was under her and not cobbles.

'You did well,' said Mr Glynde. 'I did not overrate your intelligence.'

Jaikie roused himself.

'Thank God you came,' he said. 'I don't know how to thank you. But the job isn't finished, for there are three other people left in that beastly house.'

'So I guessed,' said Mr Glynde. 'Well, everything in good time. First we must get you safely off. We cut things pretty fine, you know. Just as you joined our convoy someone came into your room with a light. I got a glimpse of his face and it was familiar. At present he is probably looking for you in the street... But he may push his researches farther.'

CHAPTER 11

The Blood-Red Rook

Jaikie was not conscious of most of that evening's ride. Thirty-six hours of short commons and the gentle swaying of Aurunculeia made him feel slightly seasick and then very drowsy. He found a strap in the trappings through which he crooked his arm, and the next he knew he was being lifted down a stepladder by Randal Glynde in a place which smelt of horses and trodden herbage.

Mr Glynde was a stern host. He gave him a bowl of soup with bread broken into it, but nothing more. 'You must sleep before you eat properly,' he said, 'or you'll be as sick as a dog.' Jaikie, who was still a little light-headed, would have gladly followed his advice, when something in Randal's face compelled his attention. It was very grave, and he remembered it only as merry. The sight brought back to him his immediate past, and the recollection of the stifling room in the ill-omened house effectively dispelled his drowsiness. He had left Alison behind him.

'I can't stay here,' he croaked. 'I must get the others out… That man's a devil. He'll stick at nothing… What about Count Casimir? He's a big swell here, isn't he? and he has other Monarchists with him… Where are we now? I should get to him at once, for every hour is important.' Then, as Randal remained silent, with the same anxious eyes, he said, 'Oh, for God's sake, do something. Make a plan. You know this accursed country and I don't.'

'You have just escaped from the most dangerous place in Europe,' said Randal solemnly. 'I think you are safe now, but it was a narrower thing than you imagine. The wild beast is in his lair, and a pretty well-defended lair it is. You may smoke him out, but it may be a bad thing for those he has got in the lair beside him.'

Jaikie's wits were still muddled, but one feeling was clear and strong, a horror of that slum barrack in the mean street.

'Are there no police in Krovolin?' he demanded.

'The ordinary police would not be much use in what has been a secret rendezvous for years. The place is a honeycomb. You might plant an army round it, and Mastrovin would slip out – and leave ugly things behind him.'

Jaikie shuddered.

'Then I'm going back. You don't understand... I can't go off and leave the others behind. You see, I brought your cousin here... Alison – ' He ended his sentence with something like a moan.

Randal for the first time smiled. 'I expected something like that from you. It may be the only way – but not yet. Alison and the Roylances are not in immediate danger. At present to Mastrovin they are important means of knowledge. When that fails they may become hostages. Only in the last resort will they be victims.'

'Give me a cigarette, please,' said Jaikie. He suddenly felt the clouds of nausea and weariness roll away from him. He had got his second wind. 'Now tell me what is happening.'

Randal nodded to a sheaf of newspapers on the floor of the caravan.

'The popular press, at least the Monarchist brand of it, announces that the Archduke Hadrian has crossed the Evallonian frontier. One or two papers say that he is now in Krovolin. They all publish his portrait – the right portrait. Prince Odalchini's staff work is rather good.'

Jaikie found himself confronted with a large-size photograph of Dickson McCunn. It must have been recently taken, for Mr McCunn was wearing the clothes which he had worn at Tarta.

'I have other news,' Randal continued, 'which is not yet in the press. The Archduke, being an old man, is at present resting from the fatigue of his journey. Tomorrow afternoon, accompanied by his chief supporters, he will move to Melina through a rejoicing country. It has all been carefully stage-managed. His escort, two troops of the National Guard, arrive here in the morning. The distance is only fifteen miles, and part of the road will be lined with His Royal Highness' soldiers. Melina is already occupied on his behalf, and the Palace is being prepared for his reception.'

'Gosh!' said Jaikie. 'How are people taking that?'

'Sedately. The Evallonians are not a politically-minded nation. They are satisfied that the hated Republic is no more, and will accept any Government that promises stability. As for His Royal Highness, they have forgotten all about him, but they have a tenderness for the old line, and they believe him to be respectable.'

'He is certainly that. How about Juventus?'

'Juventus is excited, desperately excited, but not about the Archduke. They regard him as a piece of antiquated lumber, the last card of a discredited faction. But the rumour has gone abroad that Prince John has joined them, and that has given them what they have been longing for, a picturesque figurehead. I have my own ways of getting news, and the same report has come in from all the Wings. The young men are huzzaing for the Prince, who like themselves is young. Their presses are scattering his photograph broadcast. Their senior officers, many of whom are of the old families, are enthusiastic. Now at last the wheel has come full circle for them – they have a revolution of youth which is also a restoration, and youth will lead it. They are organised to the last decimal, remember, and they have the bulk of the national feeling behind them, except here in Krovolin and in the capital. They are sitting round the periphery of Evallonia waiting for the word to close in. Incidentally they have shut the frontier, and are puzzled to understand how the Archduke managed to cross it without their knowledge. When the word is given there will be a march on Melina, just like Mussolini's march on Rome. There is only one trouble – the Countess Araminta.'

'Yes. What about her?' was Jaikie's gloomy question.

'That young woman,' said Randal, 'must be at present in a difficult temper and not free from confusion of mind. She has not been consulted about Prince John; therefore she will be angry. All Juventus believes that the Prince is now with her Wing, but she knows that to be untrue. She has not seen His Royal Highness since she was a little girl... Besides, there's another complication. I said that Juventus was waiting. But not the Countess. Some days ago she took the bit between her teeth, and started to march on Krovolin. My information is that tonight she is encamped less than ten miles from this city. Tomorrow should see her at its gates.'

'Then she'll pinch Mr McCunn before he starts.'

'Precisely. At any rate there will be fighting, and for the sake of the future it is very necessary that there should be no fighting. At the first rifleshot the game will get out of hand.'

'Can't you get him off sooner?'

'Apparently no. Some time is needed for the arrangements in Melina, and already the programme has had to be telescoped.'

'What a hideous mess! What's to be done? She must be stopped.'

'She must. That is the job to which I invite your attention.'

'Me!' The ejaculation was wrung from Jaikie by a sudden realisation of the state of his garments. His flannel bags were shrunken and to the last degree grimy, his tweed jacket was a mere antique, his shoes gaped, his hands and presumably his face were black with dust. Once again he felt, sharp as a toothache, his extreme insignificance.

Randal followed his glance. 'You are certainly rather a scarecrow, but I think I can make you more presentable. You must go. You see, you are the last hope.'

'Couldn't you – ?' Jaikie began.

'No,' was the decided answer. 'I have my own work to do, which is as vital as yours. There is one task before you. You must get her to halt in her tracks.'

'She won't listen to me.'

'No doubt she won't – at first. She'll probably have you sent to whatever sort of dungeon a field force provides. But you have one mastercard.'

'Prince John?'

'Prince John. She must produce him or she will be put to public shame, and she hasn't a notion where to look for him. She is a strong-headed young woman, but she can't defy the public opinion of the whole of Juventus. You alone know where the Prince is.'

'I don't.'

'You will be told... So you can make your terms. From what I remember of her you will have a rough passage, but you are not afraid of the tantrums of a minx.'

'I am. Horribly.'

Randal smiled. 'I don't believe you are really afraid of anything.'

'I'm in a desperate funk of one thing, and that is, what is going to happen to Alison.'

'So am I. You are fond, I think, of Cousin Alison. Perhaps you are lovers?'

Jaikie blushed furiously.

'I have been in love with her for two years.'

'And she?'

'I don't know. I hope...some day.'

'You are a chilly Northern pair of children. Well, she is my most beloved and adored kinswoman, and for her sake I would commit most crimes. We are agreed about that. It is for the sake of Alison and the sweet Lady Roylance that you and I are going into action. I wait in Krovolin and keep an eye on Mastrovin. He is a master of ugly subterranean things, but I also have certain moles at my command. There will be a watch kept on the Street of the White Peacock – that is the name of the dirty alley – a watch of which our gentleman will know nothing. When the Cirque Doré mobilises itself it has many eyes and ears. For you the task is to immobilise the Countess. Your price is the revelation of Prince John. Your reason, which she will assuredly ask, is not that the Archduke should get safely off to Melina – for remember your sympathies are with Juventus. It is not even that the coming revolution must not be spoiled by bloodshed, and thereby get an ill name in Europe. She would not listen to you on that matter. It is solely that your friends are in the power of Mastrovin, whom she venomously hates. If she enters Krovolin Mastrovin will be forced into action, and she knows what that will mean.'

Jaikie saw suddenly a ray of hope.

'What sort of woman is she?' he asked. 'Couldn't I put it to her that she has not merely to sit tight, but has to help to get my friends out of Mastrovin's clutches? I can't do anything myself, for I don't know the place or the language. But she is sure to have some hefty fellows with her to make up a rescue party. She can't refuse that if she's anything of a sportsman. It's a fair deal. She'll have the Prince if she gives me my friends. By the way, I suppose you can produce the man when I call for him?'

'I can. What's more, I can give you something if she asks for proof. It's the mourning ring prepared for his late Majesty, which only the royal family possess. She'll recognise it.'

Randal's gravity had slightly melted. 'I think you could do with a drink now,' he said. 'Brandy and soda. I prescribe it, for it's precisely what you need. Do you know, I think you have hit upon the right idea. Get her keen on doing down Mastrovin, and she won't bother about the price. She's an artist for art's sake. Make it a fight between her and the Devil for the fate of three innocents and she'll go raging into battle. I believe she has a heart, too. Most brave people have.'

As he handed Jaikie his glass, he laughed.

'There's a good old English word that exactly describes your appearance. You look "varminty" – like a terrier that has been down a badger's earth, and got its nose bitten, and is burning to go down again.'

The car, a dilapidated Ford, fetched a wide circuit in its southward journey, keeping well to the west of Krovolin, and cutting at right angles the road from the forest of St Sylvester. The morning was hazy and close, but after the last two days it seemed to Jaikie to be as fresh as April. They crossed the Silf, and saw it winding to its junction with the Rave, with the city smoking in the crook of the two streams. Beyond the Rave a rich plain stretched east towards the capital, and through that plain Dickson that afternoon must make his triumphant procession. Even now his escort would be jingling Krovolin-wards along its white roads.

Jaikie had recovered his bodily vigour, but never in his life had he felt so nervous. The thought of Alison shut up in Mastrovin's den gnawed like a physical pain. The desperate seriousness of his mission made his heart like lead. It was the kind of thing he had not been trained to cope with; he would do his best, but he had only the slenderest hope. The figure of the Countess Araminta grew more formidable the more he thought about her. Alison at Tarta had called her the Blood-red Rook – that had been Lady Roylance's name for her – and had drawn her in colours which suggested a cross between a vampire and a werewolf. Wild, exotic, melodramatic and reckless – that had been the impression left on his mind. And women were good judges of each other. He could deal with a male foreigner like Ashie whom Cambridge had partially tamed, but what could he do with the unbroken female of the species? He knew less about women than he knew about the physics of hyperspace.

His forebodings made him go over again his slender assets. He knew the line he must take, provided she listened to him. But how to get an audience? The letters which Ashie had given him, being written on official flimsies, had been reduced to a degraded pulp by the rain, and he had flung them away. He had nothing except Randal's ring, and that seemed to him an outside chance. His one hope was to get hold of Dr Jagon. Jagon would remember him from the Canonry – or on the other hand he might not. Still, it was his best chance. If he were once in Jagon's presence he might be able to recall himself to him, and Jagon was the Countess' civilian adviser. But his outfit might never get near Jagon; it might be stopped and sent packing by the first sentry.

It was not a very respectable outfit. The car was a disgrace. He himself had been rigged up by Randal in better clothes than his own duds, but he realised that they were not quite right, for the Cirque Doré, was scarcely abreast of the fashions. He had a pair of riding breeches of an odd tubular shape, rather like what people at Cambridge wore for beagling, and they were slightly too large for him. His coat was one of those absurd Norfolk jacket things that continentals wear, made of smooth green cloth with a leather belt, and it had been designed for someone of greater girth than himself. He had, however, a respectable pair of puttees, and his boots, though too roomy, were all right, being a pair of Randal's own. He must look, he thought, like a shopboy on a holiday, decent but not impressive.

Then for the first time he took notice of the chauffeur. He was one of the circus people, whom Randal had vouched for as a careful driver who knew the country. The chief point about the man's appearance was that he wore a very ancient trench Burberry, which gave him an oddly English air. He was apparently middle-aged, for he had greying side-whiskers. His cheeks had the pallor which comes from the use of much grease-paint. There was nothing horsy about him, so Jaikie set him down as an assistant clown. He looked solemn enough for that. He wondered what language he spoke, so he tried him in French, telling him that their first business was to ask for Professor Jagon.

'I know,' was the answer. 'The boss told me that this morning.'

'Where did you learn English?' Jaikie asked, for the man spoke without the trace of an accent.

'I am English,' he said. 'And I picked up a bit of French in the war.'

'Do you know Evallonia?'

'I've been here off and on for twenty years.'

The man had the intonations of a Londoner. It appeared that his name was Newsom, and that he had first come to Evallonia as an under-chauffeur in a family which had been bankrupted by the war. He had gone home and fought on the British side in a Royal Fusilier battalion, but after the Armistice he had again tried his fortune in Evallonia. His luck had been bad, and Mr Glynde had found him on his uppers, and given him a job in the circus. Transport was his principal business, but he rather fancied himself as a singer, and just lately had been giving Meleager a hand. 'We're a happy family in the old Cirque,' he said, 'and don't stick by trade-union ways. I can turn my hand to most anything, and I like a bit of clowning now and then. The trouble is that the paint makes my skin tender. You were maybe noticing that I'm not very clean shaved this morning.' And he turned a solemn mottled face for Jaikie's inspection.

In less than an hour they came out of the woods into a country of meadows which rose gently to a line of hills. They also came into an area apparently under military occupation. A couple of Greenshirts barred the road. Jaikie tried them in English, but they shook their heads, so he left it to Newsom, who began to explain in Evallonian slowly, as if he were hunting for words, and with an accent which to Jaikie's ears sounded insular. There was a short discussion, and then the Greenshirts nodded and stood aside. 'They say,' said Newsom, 'that Dr Jagon's quarters are at the farm a kilometre on, but they believe that he is now with the Wing-Commander. But they don't mind our calling on him. I said you were an old friend of his, and brought important news from Krovolin.'

The next turn of the road revealed a very respectable army on the march. The night's bivouac had been in a broad cup formed by the confluence of two streams. There was a multitude of little tents, extensive horselines, and a car park, and already there were signs that movement was beginning. Men were stamping out the breakfast fires, and saddling horses, and putting mule teams to transport wagons, and filling the tanks of cars. 'I must hurry,' thought Jaikie, 'or that confounded woman will be in Krovolin this afternoon.' His eye caught a building a little to the rear of the encampment which had the look of a small hunting lodge. The green and white flag of Juventus was being lowered from its flagstaff.

There was no Jagon at the farm, but there was a medical officer who understood English. To him Jaikie made the appeal which he thought most likely to convince. He said he was a friend of the Professor – had known him in England and brought a message to him of extreme importance.

The officer rubbed his chin. 'You are behind the fair,' he said. 'You come from Krovolin? Well, we shall be in Krovolin ourselves in three hours.'

'That is my point,' said Jaikie. 'There's something about Krovolin which you should hear. It concerns Mastrovin.'

The name produced an effect.

'Mastrovin! You come from him?' was the brusque question.

'Only in the sense that I escaped last night from his clutches. I've something to tell the Professor about Mastrovin which may alter all your plans.'

The officer looked puzzled.

'You are English?' he demanded. 'And he?' He nodded towards Newsom.

'Both English, and both friends of Juventus. I came here as a tourist and stumbled by accident on some important news which I thought it my duty to get it to Professor Jagon. He is the only one of you I know. I tell you, it's desperately important.'

The officer pondered.

'You look an honest little man. I have my orders, but we of the special services are encouraged to think for ourselves. The Professor is at this moment in conference with the Praefectus, and cannot be interrupted. But I will myself take you to headquarters, and when he is finished I will present you. Let us hurry, for we are about to march.'

He stood on the footboard of the car, and directed Newsom along a very bumpy track, which skirted the horselines, and led to the courtyard of the hunting lodge. Here was a scene of extreme busyness. Greenshirts with every variety of rank badges were going in and out of the building, a wagon was being loaded with kit, and before what seemed to be the main entrance an orderly was leading up and down a good-looking chestnut mare. Out of this door merged the burly figure of a man, with a black beard and spectacles, who was dressed rather absurdly in khaki shorts and a green shirt, the open neck of which displayed a hairy chest.

'The Professor,' said the medical officer. He saluted. 'Here is an Englishman, sir, who says he knows you and has an urgent message.'

'I have no time for Englishmen,' said Jagon crossly. His morning conference seemed to have perturbed him.

'But you will have time for me,' said Jaikie. 'You remember me, sir?'

The spectacled eyes regarded Jaikie sourly. 'I do not.'

'I think you do. Two years ago I came to breakfast with you at Knockraw in Scotland. I helped you then, and I can help you now.'

'Tchut! That is a long-closed chapter.' But the man's face was no longer hostile. He honoured Jaikie with a searching stare. 'You are that little Scotsman. I recall you. But if you come from my companions of that time it is useless. I have broken with them.'

'I don't come from them. I come from the man you beat two years ago – I escaped from him twelve hours ago. I want to help you to beat him again.'

Jagon looked at the medical officer and the medical officer looked at Jagon. The lips of both seemed to shape, but not to utter, the same word. 'I think the Englishman is honest, sir,' said the officer.

'What do you want?' Jagon turned to Jaikie.

'Five minutes' private talk with you.'

'Come in here. Keep an eye on that chauffeur' – this to the officer. 'We know nothing about him.'

'I'm an Englishman, too,' said Newsom, touching his cap.

'What the devil has mobilised the British Empire this morning?' Jagon led Jaikie into a little stone hall hung with sporting trophies and then into a cubby hole where an orderly was packing up papers. He dismissed the latter, and shut the door.

'Now let's have your errand. And be short, for we move in fifteen minutes.'

Jaikie felt no nervousness with this hustled professor. In half a dozen sentences he explained how he had got mixed up in Evallonia's business, but he did not mention Prince Odalchini, though he made much of Ashie. 'I want to see the Countess Araminta. And you, who know something about me, must arrange it.'

'You can't. The Praefectus sees no strangers.'

'I must. If I don't she'll make a godless mess of the whole business.'

'You would tell her that?' said Jagon grimly. 'The Praefectus is not so busy that she cannot find time to punish insolence.'

'It isn't insolence – it's a fact. I didn't talk nonsense to you at Knockraw, and it was because you believed me that things went right. You must believe me now. For Heaven's sake take me to the Countess – and let's waste no more time.'

'You are a bold youth,' said the Professor. 'Bold with the valour of ignorance. But the Praefectus will see no one. Perhaps this evening when we have entered Krovolin – '

'That will be too late. It must be now.'

'It cannot be. I have my orders. The Praefectus is not to be disobeyed.' The eyes behind the spectacles were troubled, and the black beard did not hide the twitching of the lips. He reminded Jaikie of a don of his acquaintance in whom a bonfire in the quad induced a nervous crisis. His heart sank, for he knew the stubbornness of the weak.

'Then I am going direct to the Countess.'

A clear voice rang outside in the hall, an imperative voice, and a woman's. Jaikie's mind was suddenly made up. Before Jagon could prevent him, he was through the door. At the foot of the stairs were two Greenshirts at attention, and on the last step stood a tall girl.

Indignation with the Professor and a growing desperation had banished Jaikie's uneasiness. He saluted in the Greenshirt fashion and looked her boldly in the face. His first thought was that she was extraordinarily pretty. What had Alison meant by drawing the picture of a harpy? She was dressed like Ashie in green riding breeches and a green tunic, and the only sign of the Blood-red Rook was her scarlet collar and the scarlet brassard on her right arm. Her colouring was a delicate amber, her eyes were like pools in a peaty stream, and her green forester's hat did not conceal her wonderful dead-black hair. Her poise was the most arrogant that he had ever seen, for she held her little head so high that the world seemed at an infinite distance beneath her. As her eyes fell on him they changed from liquid topaz to a hard agate.

She spoke a sharp imperious word and her voice had the chill of water on a frosty morning.

Audacity was his only hope.

'Madam,' said Jaikie. 'I have forced myself upon you. I am an Englishman, and I believe that you have English blood. I implore your help, and I think that in turn I can be of use to you.'

She looked over his head, at the trembling Jagon and the stupefied Greenshirts. She seemed to be asking who had dared to disobey her.

'I take all the blame on myself,' said Jaikie, trying to keep his voice level. 'I have broken your orders. Punish me if you like, but listen to me first. You are leading a revolution, and in a revolution breaches of etiquette are forgiven.'

At last she condescended to lower her eyes to him. Something in his face or his figure seemed to rouse a flicker of interest.

'Who is this cock sparrow?' she asked, and looked at Jagon.

'Madam,' came the trembling answer, 'he is a Scotsman who once in Scotland did me a service. He is without manners, but I believe he means honestly.'

'I see. A *revenant* from your faulty past. But this is no time for repaying favours. You will take charge of him, Professor, and be responsible for him till my further orders.' And she passed between the sentries towards the door.

Jaikie managed to plant himself in her way. He played his last card.

'You must listen to me. Please!' He held out his hand.

It was his face that did it. There was something about Jaikie's small, wedge-shaped countenance, its air of innocence with just a hint of devilry flickering in the background, its extreme and rather forlorn youth, which most people found hard to resist. The Countess Araminta looked at him and her eyes softened ever so little. She looked at the outstretched hand in which lay a ring.

It was a kind of ring she had seen before, and the momentary softness left her face.

'Where did you get that?' she demanded in a voice in which imperiousness could not altogether conceal excitement.

'It was given me to show to you as a proof of my good faith.'

She said something in Evallonian to the guards and the Professor, and marched into the cubby hole which Jaikie had lately left. 'Follow,' said the Professor hoarsely. 'The Praefectus will see you – but only for one minute.'

Jaikie found himself in a space perhaps six yards square, confronting the formidable personage the thought of whom had hitherto made his spine cold. Rather to his surprise he felt more at his ease. He found that he could look at her steadily, and what he saw in her face made him suddenly change all his prearranged tactics. She was a young woman, but she was not in the least a young woman like Alison or Janet Roylance. He was no judge of femininity, but there was not much femininity here as he understood it... But there was, something else which he did understand. Her eyes, the way she held her head, the tones of her voice had just that slightly insecure arrogance, that sullen but puzzled self-confidence, which belonged to a certain kind of public-school boy. He had studied the type, for it was not his own, and he had had a good deal to do with the handling of it. One had to be cautious with it, for it was easy to rouse obstinate, half-comprehended scruples, but it was sound stuff if you managed it wisely. His plan had been to propose a bargain with one whom he believed to be the slave of picturesque ambitions. In a flash he realised that he had been mistaken. If he suggested a deal it would be taken as insolence, and he would find himself pitched neck-and-crop into the yard. He must try other methods.

'Countess,' he said humbly. 'I have come to you with a desperate appeal. You alone can help me.'

He was scrupulously candid. He told how he had come to Evallonia, of his meeting with Ashie, of his visit to Prince

Odalchini. He told how he had brought Alison and the Roylances to the House of the Four Winds. 'It was none of my business,' he admitted. 'I was an interfering fool, but I thought it was going to be fun, and now it's like a tragedy.'

'The Roylances,' she repeated. 'They were at Geneva. I saw them there. The man is the ordinary English squire, and the woman is pleasant. Miss Westwater too I know – I have met her in England. Pretty and blonde – rather fluffy.'

'Not fluffy,' said Jaikie hotly.

She almost smiled.

'Perhaps not fluffy. Go on.'

He told of Mastrovin, sketching hurriedly his doings in the Canonry two years before. He described the meeting in the Forest of St Sylvester, when he himself had been on the way to the Countess with letters from Ashie. 'I can't give you them,' he said, 'for the rain pulped them.' He described the house in the Street of the White Peacock and he did not mince his words. But he skated lightly over his escape, for he felt that it would be bad tactics to bring Randal Glynde into the story at that stage.

There could be no question of her interest. At the mention of Mastrovin her delicate brows descended and she cross-examined him sharply. The Street of the White Peacock, where was it? Who was with Mastrovin? She frowned at the name of Dedekind. Then her face set.

'That rabble is caught,' she said. 'Trapped. Tonight it will be in my hands.'

'But the rabble is desperate. You have an army, Countess, and you can surround it, but it will die fighting with teeth and claws. And if it perishes my friends will perish with it.'

'That I cannot help. If fools rush in where they are not wanted they must take the consequences.'

'You don't wish to begin with a tragedy. You have the chance of a bloodless revolution which for its decency will be unlike all other revolutions. You mustn't spoil it. If it starts off with the murder of three English its reputation will be tarnished.'

'The murders will have been done by our enemies, and we shall avenge them.'

'Of course. But still you will have taken the gloss off Juventus in the eyes of England – and of Europe.'

'We care nothing for foreign opinion.'

Jaikie looked her boldly in the eyes.

'But you do. You must. You are responsible people, who don't want merely to upset a Government, but to establish a new and better one. Public opinion outside Evallonia will mean a lot to you.'

Her face had again its arrogance.

'That is dictation,' she said, 'and who are you to dictate?'

'I am nobody, but I must plead for my friends. And I am hot on your side. I want you to begin your crusade with an act of chivalry.'

'You would show me how to behave?'

'Not I. I want you to show me and the world how to behave, and prove that Juventus stands for great things. You are strong enough to be merciful.'

He had touched the right note, for her sternness patently unbent.

'What do you want me to do?' Her tone was almost as if she spoke to an equal.

'I want you to halt where you are. I want you to let me have half a dozen of your best men to help me to get my friends out of Mastrovin's hands. If we fail, then that's that. If we succeed, then you occupy Krovolin and do what you like with Mastrovin. After that you march on Melina with a good conscience and God prosper you!'

She looked at him fixedly and her mouth drew into a slow smile. 'You are a very bold young man. Are you perhaps in love with Miss Westwater?'

'I am,' said Jaikie, 'but that has nothing to do with the point. I brought her to this country, and I can't let her down. You know you could never do that yourself.'

Her smile broadened.

'I am to stop short in a great work of liberation to rescue the lady-love of a preposterous Englishman.'

'Yes,' said Jaikie, 'because you know that you would be miserable if you didn't.'

'You think you can bring it off?'

'Only with your help.'

'I am to put my men under your direction?'

'We'll make a plan together. I'll follow any leader.'

'If I consent, you shall lead. If I am to trust you in one thing I must trust you in all.'

Jaikie bowed. 'I am at your orders,' he said.

She continued to regard him curiously.

'Miss Westwater is noble,' she said. 'Are you?'

Jaikie puzzled at the word. Then he understood.

'No, I'm nobody, as I told you. But we don't bother about these things so much in England.'

'I see. The Princess and the goose-boy. I do not quarrel with you for that. You are like our Juventus, the pioneer of a new world.'

Jaikie knew that he had won, for the agate gleam had gone out of her eyes. He had something more to say and he picked his words, for he realised that he was dealing with a potential volcano.

'You march on Melina,' he said, 'you and the other wings of Juventus. But when you march you must have your leader.'

Her eyes hardened. 'What do you know of that?' she snapped.

'I have seen the newspapers and I have heard people talking.' Jaikie walked with desperate circumspection. 'The Republic has fallen. The Monarchists with their old man cannot last long. Juventus must restore the ancient ways, but with youth to lead.'

'You mean?' Her eyes were stony.

'I mean Prince John,' he blurted out, with his heart sinking. She was once more the Valkyrie, poised like a falcon for a swoop. He saw the appropriateness of Alison's name for her.

'You mean Prince John?' she repeated, and her tone was polar ice.

'You know you can't put a king on the throne unless you have got him with you. Juventus is wild for Prince John, but nobody knows where he is. I know. I promise to hand him over to you safe and sound.'

There were many things in her face – interest, excitement, relief, but there was also a rising anger.

'You would make a bargain with me?' she cried. 'A huckster's bargain – with *me*!'

Strangely enough, the surprise and fury in her voice made Jaikie cool. He knew this kind of tantrum, but not in the Countess' sex.

'You mustn't talk nonsense, please,' he said. 'I wouldn't dare to make a bargain with you. I appealed to you, and out of your chivalry you are going to do what I ask. I only offer to show my gratitude by doing what I can for you. Besides, as I told you, I'm on your side. I mean what I say. You can go back on me and refuse what I ask, and I'll still put you in the way of getting hold of Prince John, if you'll give me a couple of days. I can't say fairer than that. A mouse may help a lion.'

For a second or two she said nothing. Then her eyes fell.

'You are the first man,' she said, 'who has dared to tell me that I was a fool.'

'I didn't,' Jaikie protested, with a comfortable sense that things were going better.

'You did, and I respect you for it. I see that there was no insult. What I do for you – if I do it – I do because I am a Christian and a good citizen... For the other thing, what proof have you that you can keep your word?'

Jaikie held out the ring. The Countess took it, studied the carving on the carnelian, and returned it. She was smiling.

'It is a token and no more. If you fail – '

'Oh, have me flayed and boiled in oil,' he said cheerfully. 'Anything you like as long as you get busy about Mastrovin.'

She blew a silver whistle, and spoke a word to the orderly who entered. Then Jagon appeared, and to him she gave what sounded like a string of orders, which she enumerated on her slim gloved fingers. When he had gone she turned to Jaikie.

'I have countermanded the march for today. Now we go to choose your forlorn hope. You will lunch with me, for I have some things to say to you and many to ask you. What is your name, for I know nothing of you except that you are in love with Miss Westwater and are a friend of my cousin Paul?'

'Galt,' she repeated. 'It is not dignified, but it smells of the honest earth. You will wait here, Galt, till I send for you.'

Jaikie, left alone, mopped his brow, and, there being no chairs in the place, sat down on the floor, for he felt exhausted. He was not accustomed to this kind of thing.

'Public school,' he reflected. 'Best six-cylinder model. Lord, how I love the product and dislike the type! But fortunately the type is pretty rare.'

CHAPTER 12

The Street of the White Peacock

Jaikie rubbed the dust from his eyes, for he had landed in a heap of debris, and looked round for Newsom. Newsom was at his elbow, having exhibited an unexpected agility. He was still a little puzzled to learn how Newsom came to be with him. After his business with the Countess he had found him waiting with the car, stubbornly refusing to move till he had the word from his master. He had despatched him with a message to Randal Glynde and the man had returned unbidden. 'Boss' orders,' he had explained. 'The boss says I'm to stick to you, sir, till he tells me to quit.' And when in the evening the expeditionary force left the camp Newsom had begged for a place in it, had indeed insisted on being with Jaikie in whatever part the latter was cast for. It was not 'boss' orders' this time, but the plea of a sportsman to have a hand in the game, and Jaikie, looking at the man's athletic figure and remembering that he was English, had a little doubtfully consented. Now he was more comfortable about that consent. At any rate Newsom was an adept at climbing walls.

The Countess had allowed him to pick six Greenshirts, herself showing a most eager interest in their selection. They were all young townsmen, for this was not a job for the woodlander or mountaineer, and four of them could speak English. All were equipped with pistols, electric torches, and the string-soled shoes of the country. As reserves he had twenty of a different type, men picked for their physique and fighting value. He thought of them as respectively his scouts and his shock troops. He had made his dispositions pretty much in the void, but he reasoned that he wanted light men for his first reconnaissance, and something heavier if it came to a scrap. His judgment had been sound, for when in the evening the party, by devious ways and in small groups, concentrated at the Cirque Doré encampment, he found that Randal Glynde had had the same notion.

Randal, having had the house in the Street of the White Peacock for some time under observation, and knowing a good deal about its antecedents, had come to certain conclusions. The place was large and rambling, and probably contained cellars extending to the river, for in old days it had been the dwelling of a great merchant of Krovolin. There was no entrance from the street, the old doorway having been built up, and coming and going was all by the courtyard at the back. The prisoners might be anywhere inside a thousand square yards of masonry, but the odds were that they were lodged, as Jaikie had been, in rooms facing the street. The first thing was to get rid of the watchers there, and this was the immediate task of the six Greenshirts. But it must be done quickly and circumspectly so as not to alarm the inmates. There were five watchers by day and three by night, the latter taking up duty at sundown. If a part of the Cirque passed through the street in the first hours of the dark, it would provide excellent cover for scragging the three guards, and unobtrusively packing them into one of the vans. The street must be in their hands, for it was by the street front that escape must be made. Randal, who had become a very grave person, was insistent upon the need for speed and for keeping the business with his watchers secret from Mastrovin. Mastrovin must not be alarmed, for, like Jaikie, he feared that, if he were cornered too soon, he would have recourse to some desperate brutality.

It was Jaikie's business to get inside the house, and the only way was by the courtyard at the back. Randal had had this carefully reconnoitred, and his report was that, while the gate was kept locked and guarded, the wall could be climbed by an active man. It was impossible to do more than make a rudimentary plan, which was briefly this. Jaikie was to get into the courtyard, using any method he pleased, and to overpower, gag, and bind the guard. Randal had ascertained that there was never more than a single guard. For this purpose he must have a companion, since his fighting weight was small. His hour of entrance must be 10 p.m., at which time the Six were to deal with the watchmen in the street. Their success was to be notified to Jaikie by Luigi's playing of Dvořák's *Humoresque* on his fiddle, which in that still quarter at that hour of night would carry far.

Then there was to be an allowance of one hour while the Six kept watch in the street, and Jaikie, having entered the house, discovered where the prisoners were kept. After that came the point of uncertainty. It might be possible to get the prisoners off as inconspicuously as Jaikie himself had made his departure. On the other hand, it might not, and force might have to be used against desperate men. At all costs the crisis, if it came, was to be postponed till eleven o'clock, at which time the reserves, the Twenty, would arrive in the courtyard. It was assumed that Jaikie would have got the gates open so that they could enter. He must also have opened the house door. Two blasts on his whistle would bring the rescuers inside the house, and then God prosper the right!

That last sentence had been the parting words of Randal, who had no part allotted him, being, as he said, an ageing man and no fighter. Jaikie remembered them as he crouched in the dust of the courtyard and peered into the gloom. So far his job had been simple. A way up the wall had been found in a corner where an adjacent building slightly abutted and the stones were loose or broken. He had lain on the top and examined the courtyard in the dying light, and he had listened intently, but there had been no sight or sound of the watchman. Then, followed by Newsom, he had dropped on to soft rubble, and lain still and listened, but there was no evidence of human presence. The place was empty. Satisfied about this, he had examined the gate. He had been given some elementary instruction in lock-picking that evening at the Cirque, and had brought with him the necessary tools. But to his surprise they were not needed. The gate was open.

A brief reconnaissance showed him that the courtyard was different from what it had been on his arrival two days ago. The medley of motor cars had gone. The place was bare, except for the heaps of stone and lime in the corner where someone seemed to have been excavating... Jaikie did his best to think. What was the meaning of the unlocked gate? Someone must be coming there that night and coming in a hurry. Or someone must be leaving in a hurry. Why had Mastrovin suddenly opened his defences? The horrid thought came to him that Mastrovin might be gone, and have taken Alison and the others with him. Was he too late? The mass of the house rose like a cliff, and in that yard he seemed to be in a suffocating cave. Far above him he saw dimly clouds chasing each other in the heavens, but there was no movement of air where he sat. The place was so silent and lifeless that his heart sank. Childe Roland had come to the Dark Tower, but the Dark Tower was empty.

And then he saw far up on its facade a light prick out. His momentary despair was changed to a furious anxiety. There was life in the place, and he felt that the life was evil and menacing. The great blank shell held a brood of cockatrices, and among them was what he loved best in the world. Hitherto the necessity for difficult action had kept his mind from brooding too much on awful presentiments. He had had to take one step at a time and keep his thoughts on the leash. There had been moments when his former insouciance had returned to him and he had thought only of the game and not of the consequences... Indeed, in the early evening, as he approached Krovolin, he had had one instant of the old thrill. Far over the great plain of the Rave, from the direction of the capital, had come the sound of distant music and dancing bells. He had known what that meant. Mr Dickson McCunn was entering his loyal city of Melina.

But now he knew only consuming anxiety and something not far from terror. He must get inside the house at once and find Alison. If she had gone, he must follow. He had a horrid certainty that she was in extreme peril, and that he alone was to blame for it... He got to his feet and was about to attempt the door, when something halted him.

It was the sound of a fiddle, blanketed by the great house, but dropping faint liquid notes in the still air. It held him like a spell, for it seemed a message of hope and comfort. One part of the adventure at any rate had succeeded, and the Six were in occupation of the Street of the White Peacock. It did more, for it linked up this dark world with the light and with his friends. He listened, he could not choose but listen, till the music died away.

It was well that he did so, for Newsom's hand pulled him down again. 'There's someone at the gate,' he whispered. The two crouched deeper into the shadows.

The gate was pushed open, and a man entered the courtyard. He had an electric torch which he flashed for a moment, but rather as if he wanted to see that the torch was in working order than to examine the place. That flash was enough to reveal the burly form of Mastrovin. He shut the gate behind him, but he did not lock it. Evidently he expected someone else to follow him. Then he walked straight to the excavation, and, after moving some boards aside, he disappeared into it.

The sight of Mastrovin switched Jaikie from despondency into vigorous action. 'After him,' he whispered to Newsom. Clambering over the rubble they looked down a steep inclined passage, where a man might walk if he crouched, and saw ahead of them the light of Mastrovin's torch. It vanished as he turned a corner.

The two followed at once, Newsom hitting his head hard on the roof. Jaikie did not dare to use his own torch, but felt his way by the wall, till he came to a passage debouching to the right. That was the way Mastrovin had gone, but there was no sign of his light. Jaikie felt that he could safely look about him.

They were in a circular space whence several passages radiated. That by which they had come was new work, with the marks of pick and shovel still on it. But the other passages were of ancient brick, with stone roofs which might have been new two centuries ago. Yet in all of them was the mark of recent labour, a couple of picks propped up against a wall, and spilt lime and rubble on the floor. Jaikie deduced that the passage from the upper air was not the only task that Mastrovin's men had been engaged in; they had been excavating also at the far ends of some of the other passages.

He did not stop, for their quarry must not be lost track of. He turned up the alley Mastrovin had taken, feeling his way by the wall.

'There's wiring here,' he whispered to Newsom.

'I spotted that,' was the answer. 'Someone's up to no good.'

Presently they reached a dead end, and Jaikie thought it safe to use his torch. This revealed a steep flight of steps on the left. It was a spiral staircase, for after two turnings they had a glimpse of light above them. Mastrovin was very near. Moreover, he was speaking to someone. The voice was quite distinct, for the funnel of the staircase magnified it, but the words were Evallonian, which Jaikie did not understand.

But Newsom did. He clutched Jaikie's arm, and with every sentence of Mastrovin's that clutch tightened. Then some command seemed to be issued above, and they heard the reply of Mastrovin's interlocutor. The light wavered and moved, and presently disappeared, for Mastrovin had gone on. But there came the sound of feet on the stairs growing louder. The other man was descending – in the dark.

It was a tense moment in Jaikie's life. He took desperate hold of his wits, and reasoned swiftly that the man descending in the dark would almost certainly hug the outer wall, the right-hand wall of the spiral, where the steps were broader. Therefore he and Newsom must plaster themselves against the other wall. The staircase was wide enough to let two men pass abreast without touching. If they were detected he would go for the stranger's throat, and he thought he could trust Newsom to do the same.

The two held their breath while the man came down the stairs. Jaikie, sensitive as a wild animal, realised that his guess had been right – the man was feeling his way by the outer wall. Newsom's shoulder was touching his, and he felt it shiver. Another thing he realised – the stranger was in a hurry. That was to the good, for he would not be so likely to get any subconscious warning of their presence.

For one second the man was abreast of them. There was a waft of some coarse scent, as if he were a vulgar dandy. Then he was past them, and they heard him at the foot of the stairs groping for the passage.

Jaikie sat down on a step to let his stifled breath grow normal. But Newsom was whispering something in his ear.

'I heard their talk,' he gasped. 'I've got their plan… They are going to let the Countess occupy the town… She must cross the river to get to Melina… They've got the bridge mined, and will blow it up at the right moment…and half the place besides… God, what swine!'

To Jaikie the news was a relief. That could only be for the morrow, and in the meantime Mastrovin would lie quiet. That meant that his prisoners would be in the house. The cockatrices – and the others – were still in their den.

But Newsom had more to say.

'There are people coming here – more people. That fellow has gone to fetch them.'

Jaikie, squatted in the darkness, hammered at his wits, but they would not respond. What could these newcomers mean? What was there to do in the house that had not been done? Mastrovin had the bridge mined, and half the town as well, and could make havoc by pressing a button. He had his cellars wired, and new passages dug. All that was clear enough. But why was he assembling a posse tonight?...

Then an idea struck him. If the gates were open to let people in, they were open to the let the same people out. And they might take others with them... He had it. The prisoners were to be removed that night, and used in Mastrovin's further plans. When he had struck his blow at Juventus they might come in handy as hostages. Or in the last resort as victims.

From the moment that he realised this possibility came a radical change in Jaikie's outlook. The torments of anxious love were still deep in his soul, but overlying them was a solid crust of hate. His slow temper was being kindled into a white flame of anger.

He looked at his watch. It was one minute after half past ten. The Twenty would not arrive till eleven.

'I must go on,' he whispered. 'I must find what that brute is after and where he keeps my friends... You must go back and wait in the yard. Please Heaven our fellows are here before the others. If they are, bring them up here – I'll find some way of joining up with you... If the others come first, God help us all. I leave it to you.'

As he spoke he realised sharply the futility of asking a cockney chauffeur to hold at bay an unknown number of the toughest miscreants in Evallonia. But Newsom seemed to take it calmly. His voice was steady.

'I'll do my best, sir,' he said. 'I'm armed, and I used to be a fair shot. Have you a pair of clippers in that packet of tools you brought?'

Jaikie dived into his pocket and handed over the desired article.

'Good,' said Newsom. 'I think I'll do a spot of wire-cutting.' And without another word he began to feel his way down.

Jaikie crept upward till the stairs ended in a door. This was unlocked, as he had expected, for Mastrovin was leaving his communications open behind him. Inside all was black, so he cautiously flashed his torch. The place was dusty and unclean, a passage with rotting boards on the floor and discoloured paper dropping from the walls. He tiptoed along it till it gave on to a small landing from which another staircase descended. Here there were two doors and he cautiously tried the handles. One was locked, but the other opened. It was dark inside, but at the far end there was a thin crack of light on the floor. There must be a room there which at any rate was inhabited.

The first thing he did, for he had put out his torch, was to fall with a great clatter over some obstacle. He lay still with his heart in his mouth, waiting for the far door to be thrown open. But nothing happened, so he carefully picked himself up and continued with extreme circumspection. There were chairs and tables in this place, a ridiculous number of chairs, as if it had been used as a depository for lumber, or perhaps as a council chamber. He had no further mishap, and reached the streak of light safely… There were people in that farther room; he could hear a voice speaking, and it sounded like Mastrovin's.

Another thing he noticed, and that was the same odd smell of coarse scent which he had sniffed as the man passed him on the stairs. The odour was like a third-rate barber's shop, and it came through the door.

He could hear Mastrovin talking, rather loud and very distinct, like a schoolmaster to stupid pupils. He was speaking English too.

'You are going away,' he was saying. 'Do you understand? I will soon visit you – perhaps in a day or two. I do not think you will try to escape, but if you do, I warn you that I have a long arm and will pluck you back. And I will punish you for it.'

The voice was slow and patient as if addressed to backward children. And there was no answer. Mastrovin must be speaking to his prisoners, but they did not reply, and that was so unlike Sir Archie that a sudden horrid fear shot into Jaikie's mind. Were they dying, or sick or wounded? Was Alison?…

He waited no longer. Had the door been triple-barred he felt that he had the strength to break it down. But it opened easily.

He found himself in a small, square, and very high room, wholly without windows, for the air entered by a grating near the ceiling. It smelt stuffy and heavily scented. Mastrovin sat in an armchair, with behind him a queer-looking board studded with numbered buttons. There was a clock fixed on the wall above it which had a loud solemn tick.

The three prisoners sat behind a little table. Archie looked as if he had been in the wars, for he had one arm in a sling, and there was a blood stained bandage round his head. He sat stiffly upright, staring straight in front of him. So did Janet, a pale unfamiliar Janet, with her hair in disorder and a long rent in one sleeve. Like her husband, she was looking at Mastrovin with blank unseeing eyes. Alison sat a little apart with her arms on the table and her head on her arms. He saw only her mop of gold hair. She seemed to be asleep.

All that Jaikie took in at his first glance was the three prisoners. What devilry had befallen them? He had it. They had been drugged. They were now blind and apathetic, mindless perhaps, baggage which Mastrovin could cart about as he chose. There had evidently been a row, and Archie had suffered in it, but now he was out of action. It was the sight of Alison's drooped head that made him desperate, and also perfectly cool. He had not much hope, but at any rate he was with his friends again.

This reconnaissance took a fraction of a second. He heard Mastrovin bark, 'Hands up!' and up shot his arms.

There were two others in the room, Dedekind with his red pointed beard, and a sallow squat man, whom he remembered in the Canonry. What was his name? Rosenbaum?

It was the last who searched him, plucking the pistol from his breeches pocket. Jaikie did not mind that, for he had never been much good with a gun. For the first time he saw the clock on the wall, and noted that it stood at a quarter to eleven. If he could spin out that quarter of an hour there was just the faintest chance, always provided that Mastrovin's reinforcements did not arrive too soon.

'I have come back,' he said sweetly. 'I really had to get some decent clothes, for I was in rags.'

'You have come back,' Mastrovin repeated. 'Why?'

'Because I liked your face, Mr Mastrovin. I have the pleasantest recollection of you, you know, ever since we met two years ago at Portaway. Do you remember the Hydropathic there and the little Glasgow journalist that you cross-examined? Drunken little beast he was, and you tried to make him drunker. Have you been up to the same game with my friends?'

He glanced at Archie, trying to avoid the sight of Alison's bowed head. To his surprise he seemed to detect a slight droop of that gentleman's left eye. Was it possible that the doping had failed, and that the victims were only shamming?... The clock was at thirteen minutes to eleven.

Mastrovin was looking at him fixedly, as if he were busy reconstructing the past to which he had alluded.

'So,' he said. 'I have more against you than I imagined.'

'You have nothing against me,' said Jaikie briskly. 'I might say I had a lot against you – kidnapping, imprisonment, no food or drink, filthy lodgings, and so forth. But I'm not complaining. I forgive you for the sake of your face. You wanted me to tell you something, but I couldn't for I didn't know. Well, I know now, and I've come back to do you a good turn. You would like to know where Prince John is. I can tell you.'

Jaikie stopped. His business was to spin out this dialogue.

'Go on,' said Mastrovin grimly. He was clearly in two minds whether or not this youth was mad.

'He is with the Countess Troyos. I know, for I saw him there this morning.'

'That is a lie.'

'All right. Have it your own way. But when you blow up the bridge here tomorrow you had better find out whether I am speaking the truth, unless you want to kill the Prince. Perhaps you do. Perhaps you'd like to add him to the bag. It's all the same to me, only I thought I'd warn you.'

He was allowed to finish this audacious speech, because Mastrovin was for once in his masterful life fairly stupefied. Jaikie's purpose was to anger him so that he might lay violent hands on him. He thought that, unless they took to shooting, he could give them a proof of the eel-like agility of the Gorbals Diehards, not to speak of the most famous three-quarter back in Britain. He did not think they would shoot him, for they were sure to want to discover where he had got his knowledge.

He certainly succeeded in his purpose. Mastrovin's face flushed to an ugly purple, and both Dedekind and Rosenbaum grew a little paler. The last-named said something in Evallonian, and the three talked excitedly in that language. This was precisely what Jaikie wanted. He observed that the clock was now at eight minutes to the hour. He also noted that Alison, though her head was still on the table, was looking sideways at him through her fingers, and that her eyes had an alertness unusual in the doped.

Suddenly he heard a shot, muffled as if very far off. This room was in the heart of the house, and noises from the outer world would come faintly to it, if at all. But he had quick ears, and he knew that he could not be mistaken. Was the faithful Newsom holding the bridge alone like Horatius? He could not hold it long, and there were still five deadly minutes to go before the Twenty could be looked for...

Yet it would take more than five minutes to get the prisoners out of the house and the gate. That danger at any rate had gone. What remained was the same peril which had brooded over the library at Castle Gay, before Dickson McCunn like a north wind had dispersed it. These wild beasts of the jungle, if cornered, might make a great destruction. Here in this place they were all on the thin crust of a volcano. He did not like that board with studs and numbers behind Mastrovin's head.

Again came the faint echo of shots. This time Mastrovin heard it. He said something to Dedekind, who hurried from the room. Rosenbaum would have followed, but a word detained him.

Mastrovin sat crouching like an angry lion, waiting to spring, but not yet quite certain of his quarry.

'Stand still,' he told Jaikie, who had edged nearer Alison. 'If you move I will kill you. In a moment my friend will return, and then you will go – ah, where will you go?'

He sucked his lips, and grinned like a great cat.

There were no more shots, and silence fell on the place, broken only by the ticking of the clock. Jaikie did not dare to look at the prisoners, for the slightest movement on his part might release the fury of the wild beast in front of him. He kept his eyes on that face which had now become gnarled like a knot in an oak stump, an intense concentration of anxiety, fury and animal power. It fascinated Jaikie, but it did not terrify him, for it was like a monstrous gargoyle, an expression of some ancient lust which was long dead. He had the impression that the man was somehow dead and awaited burial, and might therefore be disregarded.

He strove to stir his inertia to life, but he seemed to have become boneless. 'It's you that will be dead in a minute or two,' he told himself, but apathetically, as if he were merely correcting a misstatement. Anger had gone out of him, and had taken fear with it, and only apathy remained. He felt Mastrovin's eyes beginning to dominate and steal his senses like an anaesthetic. That scared him, and he shifted his gaze to the board on the wall, and the clock. The clock was at three minutes after eleven, but he had forgotten his former feverish calculation of time.

The door opened. Out of a corner of his eye he saw that Dedekind had returned. He noted his red beard.

Jaikie was pulled out of his languor by the behaviour of Mastrovin, who from a lion couchant became a lion rampant. He could not have believed that a heavy man well on in years could show such nimbleness. Mastrovin was on his feet, shouting something to Rosenbaum, and pointing at the newcomer the pistol with which he had threatened Jaikie.

The voice that spoke from the door was not Dedekind's.

'Suppose we lower our guns, Mr Mastrovin?' it said. 'You might kill me – but I think you know that I can certainly kill you. Is it a bargain?'

The voice was pleasant and low with a touch of drawl in it. Jaikie, in a wild whirling survey of the room, saw that it had fetched Alison's head off her hands. It woke Janet and Archie, too, out of their doll-like stare. It seemed to cut into the stuffiness like a frosty wind, and it left Jaikie in deep bewilderment, but – for the first time that night – with a lively hope.

Mr Glynde sniffed the air.

'At the old dodge, I see,' he said. 'You once tried it on me, you remember. You seem to have struck rather tough subjects this time.' He nodded to the Roylances and smiled on Alison.

'What do you want?' The words seemed to be squeezed out of Mastrovin, and came thick and husky.

'A deal,' said Randal cheerfully. 'The game is against you this time. We've got your little lot trussed up below – also my old friend, Mr Dedekind.'

'That is a lie.'

Randal shrugged his shoulders.

'You are a monotonous controversialist. I assure you it is true. There was a bit of a tussle at first before our people arrived, and I'm afraid two of yours were killed. Then the rest surrendered to superior numbers. All is now quiet on that front.'

'If I believe you, what is your deal?'

'Most generous. That you should get yourself out of here in ten minutes and out of the country in ten hours. We will look after your transport. The fact is, Mr Mastrovin, we don't want you – Evallonia doesn't want you – nobody wants you. You and your bravos are back numbers. Properly speaking, we should string you up, but we don't wish to spoil a good show with ugly episodes.'

Randal spoke lightly, so that there was no melodrama in his words, only a plain and rather casual statement of fact. But in that place such lightness was the cruellest satire. And it was belied by Randal's eyes, which were as sharp as a hawk's. They never left Mastrovin's pistol hand and the studded board behind his head.

Mastrovin's face was a mask, but his eyes too were wary. He seemed about to speak, but what he meant to say will never be known. For suddenly many things happened at once.

There was the sound of a high imperious voice at the door. It opened and the Countess Araminta entered, and close behind her a wild figure of a man, dusty, bleeding, with a coat nearly ripped from his back.

The sight of the Countess stung Mastrovin into furious life. A sense of death and fatality filled the room like a fog. Jaikie sprang to get in front of Alison, and Archie with his unwounded arm thrust Janet behind him. In that breathless second Jaikie was conscious only of two things. Mastrovin had fired, and then swung round to the numbered board; but, even as his finger reached it he clutched at the air and fell backward over the arm of his chair. There was a sudden silence, and a click came from the board as if a small clock were running down.

Then Jaikie's eyes cleared. He saw a pallid Rosenbaum crouching on the floor. He saw Randal lower his pistol, and touch the body of Mastrovin. 'Dead,' he heard him say, 'stone dead. Just as well perhaps.'

But that spectacle was eclipsed by other extraordinary things. The Countess Araminta was behaving oddly – she seemed to be inclined to sob. Around his own neck were Alison's arms, and her cheek was on his, and the thrill of it almost choked him with joy. He wanted to weep too, and he would have wept had not the figure of the man who had entered with the Countess taken away what breath was left in him.

It was Newsom the chauffeur, transfigured beyond belief. He had become a younger man, for exertion had coloured his pallid skin, his whiskers had disappeared, and his tousled hair had lost its touch of grey. He held the Countess with one arm and looked ruefully at his right shoulder.

'Close shave,' he said. 'The second time tonight too. First casualty in the Revolution.' Then he smiled on the company. 'Lucky I cut the wires, or our friend would have dispersed us among the planets.'

The Countess had both hands on his arm, and was looking at him with misty eyes.

'You saved my life,' she cried. 'The shot was meant for me. You are a hero. Oh, tell me your name.'

He turned, took her hand, bent over it and kissed it.

'I am Prince John,' he said, 'and I think that you are going to be kind enough to help me to a throne.'

She drew back a step, looked for a second in his face, and then curtseyed low.

'My king,' she said.

Her bosom heaved under her tunic, and she was no more the Praefectus but a most emotional young woman... She looked at Randal and Jaikie, and at Janet and Archie, as if she were struggling for something to relieve her feelings. Then she saw Alison, and in two steps was beside her and had her in her arms.

'My dear,' she said, 'you have a very brave lover.'

CHAPTER 13

The March on Melina

In Krovolin's best hotel, the Three Kings of the East, Jaikie enjoyed the novel blessings of comfort and consideration. By the Countess' edict Alison, the Roylances and he were at once conducted there, and the mandate of Juventus secured them the distinguished attentions of the management. The released prisoners were little the worse, for they had not been starved as Jaikie had been, and the only casualty was Archie, who had been overpowered in a desperate effort the previous morning to get into the Street of the White Peacock. The doping had been clumsily managed, for some hours before Jaikie's arrival the three had been given a meal quite different from the coarse fare to which they had been hitherto treated. They were offered with it a red wine, which Archie at his first sip pronounced to be corked. Alison had tasted it, and, detecting something sweet and sickly in its flavour, had suspected a drug, whereupon Janet filled their glasses and emptied them in a corner. 'Look like sick owls,' she advised, when they were taken to Mastrovin's sanctum, where the overpowering scent was clearly part of the treatment. Mastrovin's behaviour showed that her inspiration had been right, for he had spoken to them as if they were somnambulists or halfwits...

On the following morning Jaikie, feeling clean and refreshed for the first time for a week, descended late to the pleasant restaurant which overlooked the milky waters of the Rave. The little city sparkled in the sunlight, and the odour and bustle of a summer morning came as freshly to his nose and ears as if he had just risen from a sickbed. He realised how heavy his heart had been for days, and the release sent his spirits soaring... But his happiness was more than the absence of care, for last night had been an epoch in his life, like that evening two years before when, on the Canonry moor, Alison had waved him goodbye. For the first time he had held Alison in his arms and felt her lips on his cheek. That delirious experience had almost blotted out from his memory the other elements in the scene. As he dwelt on it he did not see the dead Mastrovin, and the crouched figure of Rosenbaum, and the Countess Araminta on the verge of tears, or hear the ticking of the clock, and the pistol shot which ended the drama; he saw only Alison's pale face and her gold hair like a cloud on his shoulder, and heard that in her strained voice which he had never heard before... Jaikie felt the solemn rapture of some hungry, humble saint who finds his pulse changed miraculously into the ambrosia of Paradise.

A waiter brought him the morning paper. He could not read it, but he could guess at the headlines. Something tremendous seemed to he happening in Melina. There was a portrait of the Archduke Hadrian, edged with laurels and roses, and from it stared the familiar face of Mr McCunn. There was a photograph of a street scene in which motor cars and an escort of soldiers moved between serried ranks of presumably shouting citizens. In one, next to a splendid figure in a cocked hat, could be discerned the homely features of Dickson.

He dropped the paper, for Alison had appeared, Alison, fresh as a flower, with the colour back in her cheeks. Only her eyes were still a little tired. She came straight to him, put her hands on his shoulders, and kissed him. 'Darling,' she said.

'Oh, Alison,' he stammered. 'Then it's all right, isn't it?'

She laughed merrily and drew him to a breakfast table in the window. 'Foolish Jaikie! As if it would ever have been anything else!'

There was another voice behind him, and Jaikie found another fair head beside his.

'I shall kiss you too,' said Janet Roylance, 'for we're going to be cousins, you know. Allie, I wish you joy. Jaikie, I love you. Archie? Oh, he has to stay in bed for a little – the doctor has just seen him. He's all right, but his arm wants a rest, and he got quite a nasty smack on the head... Let's have breakfast. I don't suppose there's any hope of kippers.'

As they sat down at a table in the window Alison picked up the newspaper. She frowned at the pictures from Melina. Her coffee grew cold as she puzzled over the headlines.

'I wish I could read this stuff,' she said. 'Everything seems to have gone according to plan, but the question is, what is the next step? You realise, don't you, that we've still a nasty fence to leap. We've got over the worst, for the Blood-red Rook has taken Prince John to her bosom. She'll probably insist on marrying him, for she believes he saved her life, and I doubt if he is man enough to escape her. Perhaps he won't want to, for she's a glorious creature, but – Jaikie, I think you are lucky to have found a homely person like me. Being married to her would be rather like domesticating a Valkyrie. You managed that business pretty well, you know.'

'I don't deserve much credit, for I was only fumbling in the dark... Mr Glynde was the real genius. Do you think he arranged for the Countess to turn up, or was it an unrehearsed effect? If he arranged it he took a pretty big risk.'

'I believe she took the bit in her teeth. Couldn't bear to be left out of anything. But what about Cousin Ran? He has disappeared over the skyline, and the only message he left was that we were to go back to Tarta and await developments. I'm worried about those developments, for we don't know what may happen. Everything has gone smoothly – except of course our trouble with Mastrovin – but I'm afraid there may be an ugly snag at the end.'

'You mean Mr McCunn?'

'I mean the Archduke Hadrian, who is now in the royal palace at Melina wishing to goodness that he was safe home at Blaweary.'

'I trust him to pull it off,' said Jaikie.

'But it's no good trusting Dickson unless other people play up. Just consider what we've done. We've worked a huge practical joke on Juventus, and if Juventus ever came to know about it everything would be in the soup. Here you have the youth of Evallonia, burning with enthusiasm and rejoicing in their young prince, whom they mean to make king instead of an elderly dotard. What is Juventus going to say if they discover that the whole thing has been a plant to which their young prince has been a consenting party? Prince John's stock would fall pretty fast. You've wallowed in *super cherie* from your cradle, Jaikie dear, so you don't realise how it upsets ordinary people, especially if they are young and earnest.'

Jaikie laughed. 'I believe you are right. Everybody's got their own *panache*, and the public-school notion of good form isn't really very different from what in foreigners we call melodrama. I mean, it's just as artificial.'

'Anyhow, there's not a scrap of humour in it,' said Alison. 'The one thing the Rook won't stand is to be made ridiculous. No more will Juventus. So it's desperately important that Dickson should disappear into the night and leave no traces. How many people are in the plot?'

Jaikie as usual counted on his fingers.

'There's we three – and Sir Archie – and Ashie – and Prince John – and Prince Odalchini – and I suppose Count Casimir and maybe one or two other Monarchists. Not more than that, and it's everybody's interest to keep it deadly secret.'

'That's all right if we can be certain about Dickson getting quietly away in time. But supposing Juventus catches him. Then it's bound to come out. I don't mean that they'll do him any harm beyond slinging him across the frontier. But he'll look a fool and we'll look fools and, much more important, Prince John will look a fool and a bit of a knave – and the Monarchist leaders, who Ran says are the only people that can help Juventus to make a success of the Government... We must get busy at once. Since that ruffian Ran has vanished, we must get hold of Prince John.'

But it was not the Prince who chose to visit them as they were finishing breakfast, but the Countess Araminta. Jaikie had seen her in camp as Praefectus, and was prepared to some extent for her air of command, but the others only knew her as the exotic figure of London and Geneva, and as the excited girl whose nerves the night before had been stretched to breaking point. Now she seemed the incarnation of youthful vigour. The door was respectfully held open by an aide-de-camp, and she made an entrance like a tragedy queen. She wore the uniform of Juventus, but her favourite colour glowed in a cap which hung over one shoulder. There was colour too in her cheeks, and her fine eyes had lost their sullenness. Everything about her, her trim form, the tilt of her head, the alert grace of her carriage, spoke of confidence and power. Jaikie gasped, for he had never seen anything quite like her. '*Incessu patuit dea*,' he thought, out of a vague classical reminiscence.

They all stood up to greet her.

'My friends, my good friends,' she cried. She put a hand on Jaikie's shoulder, and for one awestricken moment he thought she was going to kiss him.

She smiled upon them in turn. 'Your husband is almost well,' she told Janet. 'I have seen the doctor... What do you wish to do, for it is for you to choose? I must go back to my camp, for here in Krovolin during the next few days the whole forces of Juventus will concentrate. I shall be very busy, but I will instruct others to attend to you. What are your wishes? You have marched some distance with Juventus – do you care to finish the course, and enter Melina with us? You have earned the right to that.'

'You are very kind,' said Janet. 'But if you don't mind, I believe we ought to go home. You see, my husband should be in Geneva and I'm responsible for my cousin Alison... I think if Archie were here he would agree with me. Would it be possible for us to go back to Tarta and rest there for a day or two? We don't want to leave Evallonia till we know that you have won, but – you won't misunderstand me – I don't think we should take any part in the rest of the show. You see, we are foreigners, and it is important that everybody should realise that this is your business and nobody else's. My husband is a member of our Parliament, and there might be some criticism if he were mixed up in it – not so much criticism of him as of you. So I think we had better go to Tarta.'

Janet spoke diffidently, for she did not know how Juventus might regard the House of the Four Winds and its owner. But to her surprise the Countess made no objection.

'You shall do as you wish,' she said. 'Perhaps you are right and it would be wise to have no foreign names mentioned. But you must not think that we shall be opposed and must take Melina by storm. We shall enter the city with all the bells ringing.'

She saw Janet's glance fall on the newspaper on the floor.

'You think there is a rival king? Ah, but he will not remain. He will not want to remain. The people will not want him. Trust me, he will yield at once to the desire of his country.'

'What will you do with the Archduke?' Alison asked.

'We will treat him with distinguished respect,' was the answer. 'Is he not the brother of our late king and the uncle of him who is to be our king? If his health permits, he will be the right-hand counsellor of the Throne, for he is old and very wise. At the Coronation he will carry the Sacred Lamp and the Mantle of St Sylvester, and deliver with his own voice the solemn charge given to all Evallonia's sovereigns.'

Alison groaned inwardly, having a vision of Dickson in this august role.

'I must leave you,' said the Countess. 'You have done great service to my country's cause, for which from my heart I thank you. An evil thing has been destroyed, which could not indeed have defeated Juventus but which might have been a thorn in its side.'

'Have you got rid of Mastrovin's gang?' Jaikie asked.

She looked down on him smiling, her hand still on his shoulder.

'They are being rounded up,' she replied; 'but indeed they count for nothing since he is dead. Mastrovin is not of great importance – not now, though once he was Evallonia's evil genius. At the worst he was capable of murder in the dark. He was a survivor of old black days that the world is forgetting. He was a prophet of foolish crooked things that soon all men will loath.'

Her voice had risen, her face had flushed, she drew herself up to her slim height, and in that room, amid the debris of breakfast and with the sun through the long windows making a dazzle of light around her, the Countess Araminta became for a moment her ancestress who had ridden with John Sobieski against the Turk. To three deeply impressed listeners she expounded her creed.

'Mastrovin is dead,' she said; 'but that is no matter, for he and his kind were dead long ago. They were *revenants*, ghosts, hideous futile ghosts. They lived by hate, hating what they did not understand. They were full of little vanities and fears, and were fit for nothing but to destroy. Back numbers you call them in England – I call them shadows of the dark which vanish when the light comes. We of Juventus do not hate, we love, but in our love we are implacable. We love everything in our land, all that is old in it and all that is new, and we love all our people, from the greatest to the humblest. We have given back to Evallonia her soul, and once again we shall make her a great nation. But it

will be a new nation, for everyone will share in its government.'
She paused. 'All will be sovereigns, because all will be subjects.'

She was a true actress, for she knew how to make the proper
exit. Her rapt face softened. With one hand still on Jaikie's
shoulder she laid the other on Alison's head and stroked her hair.

'Will you lend me your lover, my dear?' she said. 'Only for a
little – since he will join you at Tarta. I think he may be useful as
a liaison between Juventus and those who doubtless mean well
but have been badly advised.'

Then she was gone, and all the colour and half the light
seemed to have left the room.

'Gosh!' Jaikie exclaimed, when they were alone. 'It looks as if
I were for it.' He remembered the phrase about subjects and
sovereigns as coming from a philosopher on whom at Cambridge
he had once written an essay. No doubt she had got it from Dr
Jagon, and he had qualms as to what might happen if the public-
school code got mixed up with philosophy.

Janet looked grave.

'What a woman!' she said. 'I like her, but I'm scared by her.
The Blood-red Rook is not the name – she's the genuine eagle.
I'm more anxious than ever about Mr McCunn. Juventus is a
marvellous thing, but she said herself that it was implacable.
There's nothing in the world so implacable as the poet if you
attempt to guy his poetry, and that's what we've been doing.
There's going to be a terrible mix-up unless Dickson can
disappear in about two days and leave no traces behind him; and
I don't see how that's to be managed now that he is planted in
a palace in the middle of an excited city.'

To three anxious consultants there entered Prince John.
Somehow or other he had got in touch with his kit, for he was
smartly dressed in a suit of light flannels, with a rose in his
buttonhole.

'I'm supposed to be still incognito,' he explained, 'and I have
to lurk here till the concentration of Juventus is complete. That
should be sometime tomorrow. Sir Archie is all right. I've just

seen him, and he is to be allowed to get up after luncheon. I hope you can control him, Lady Roylance, for I can't. He is determined to be in at the finish, he says, and was simply blasphemous when I told him that he was an alien and must keep out of it. It won't do, you know. You must all go back to Tarta at once. He doesn't quite appreciate the delicacy of the situation or what compromising people you are.'

'We do,' said Janet. 'We've just had a discourse from the Countess. You won't find it easy to live up to that young woman, sir.'

Prince John laughed.

'I think I can manage Mintha. She is disposed to be very humble and respectful with me, for she has always been a staunch royalist. Saved her life, too, she thinks though I don't believe Mastrovin meant his shot for her – I believe he spotted me, and he always wanted to do me in. She's by way of being our prophetess, but she is no fool, and, besides, there's any number of sober-minded people to keep her straight. What I have to live up to is Juventus itself, and that will take some doing. It's a tremendous thing, you know, far bigger and finer than any of us thought, and it's going to be the salvation of Evallonia. Perhaps more than that. What was it your Pitt said – "Save its country by its efforts and Europe by its example"? But it's youth, and youth takes itself seriously, and if anybody laughs at it or tries to play tricks with it he'll get hurt. That's where we are rather on the knife-edge.

'My dear Uncle Hadrian,' he went on, 'is in bed at home in France and reported to be sinking. That is Odalchini's last word, and Odalchini has the affair well in hand. My uncle's secretary is under his orders, and not a scrap of news is allowed to leave the chateau.'

'The Countess seems to be better disposed to Prince Odalchini,' said Janet.

'She is. Odalchini has opened negotiations with Juventus. He has let it be known that he and his friends will not contest my right to the throne, and that the Archduke has bowed to this view and proposes to leave the country. Of course he speaks for Casimir and the rest. That is all according to plan. Presently His Royal Highness will issue a proclamation resigning all claims. But in the meantime our unhappy Scotch friend is masquerading in the palace of Melina – in deep seclusion, of course, for the Archduke is an old and frail man, and is seeing no one as yet – but still there, with the whole capital agog for a sight of him. You will say, smuggle him out and away with him across the frontier. But Juventus has other ideas – Mintha has other ideas. There is to be a spectacular meeting between uncle and nephew – a noble renunciation – a tender reconciliation – and the two surviving males of the Evallonian royal house are to play a joint part in the restoration of the monarchy. Juventus has the good sense to understand that it needs Casimir and his lot to help it to get the land straight, and it thinks that that will be best managed by having its claimant and their claimant working in double harness, I say "Juventus thinks", but it's that hussy Mintha who does the thinking, and the others accept it. That's the curse of a romantic girl in politics... So there's the tangle we're in. There will be the devil to pay if the Archduke isn't out of the country within three days without anyone setting eyes on him, and that's going to be a large-size job for somebody.'

'For whom?' Jaikie asked.

'Principally for you,' was the answer. 'You seem to get all the worst jobs in this business. You're young, you see – you're our Juventus.'

'She says I have to go with her.'

'You have to stay here. I asked for you. Thank Heaven she has taken an enormous fancy to you. Miss Alison needn't be jealous, for Mintha has about as much sex as a walking-stick. I dare say she would insist on marrying me, if she thought the country needed it, but I shall take jolly good care to avoid that. No warrior queen for me... All of you except Jaikie go back to Tarta this afternoon, and there Odalchini will keep you advised about what is happening. Jaikie stays here, and as soon as possible he goes to Melina. Don't look so doleful, my son. You won't be alone there. Randal Glynde, to the best of my belief, is by this time in the palace.'

Late that afternoon Janet and Alison, accompanied by a bitterly protesting Archie, left Krovolin for the House of the Four Winds. Next day there began for Jaikie two crowded days filled with a manifold of new experiences. The wings of Juventus, hitherto on the periphery of Evallonia, drew towards the centre. The whole business was a masterpiece of organisation, and profoundly impressed him with the fact that this was no flutter of youth, but a miraculous union of youth and experience. Three-fourths of the higher officers were mature men, some of them indeed old soldiers of Evallonia in the Great War. The discipline was military, and the movements had full military precision, but it was clear that this was a civilian army, with every form of expert knowledge in it, and trained more for civil reconstruction than for war.

Dr Jagon, who embraced him publicly, enlarged on its novel character. 'It is triumphant democracy,' he declared, 'purged of the demagogue. Its root is not emotion but reason – sentiment, indeed, of the purest, but sentiment rationalised. It is the State disciplined and enlightened. It is an example to all the world, the pioneer of marching humanity. God be praised that I have lived to see this day.'

Prince John's presence was formally made known, and at a review of the wings he took his place, in the uniform of Juventus, as Commander-in-Chief. The newspapers published his appeal to the nation, in which he had judiciously toned down Dr Jagon's philosophy and the Countess' heroics. Presently, too, they issued another document, the submission of the Monarchist leaders. City and camp were kindled to a fervour of patriotism, and addresses poured in from every corner of the land.

On the afternoon of the second day Jaikie was summoned to the Prince's quarters, where the Countess and the other wing commanders were present. There he was given his instructions. 'You will proceed at once to Melina, Mr Galt,' said the Prince, 'and confer with Count Casimir Muresco, with whom I believe you are already acquainted. Tomorrow we advance to the capital, of whose submission we have been already assured. We desire that His Royal Highness the Archduke should be associated with our reception, and we have prepared a programme for the approval of His Royal Highness and his advisers. On our behalf and on behalf of Juventus you will see that this programme is carried out. I think that I am expressing the wishes of my headquarters staff.'

The wing commanders bowed gravely, and the Countess favoured Jaikie with an encouraging smile. He thought that he detected in Prince John's eye the faintest suspicion of a wink. As he was getting into his car, with an aide-de-camp and an orderly to attend him, Ashie appeared and drew him aside.

'For God's sake,' he whispered, 'get your old man out of the way. Shoot him and bury him if necessary.'

'I'd sooner shoot the lot of you,' said Jaikie.

'Well, if you don't you'd better shoot yourself. And me, too, for I won't survive a fiasco. Mintha has got off on her high horse, and Juventus is following her. She has drawn up a programme of ceremonies a yard long, in which your old fellow is cast for a principal part. There'll be bloody murder if they find themselves let down. They're a great lot, and my own lot, but they won't stand for ragging.'

II

Dickson, enveloped in a military greatcoat and muffled up about the neck because of his advanced age and indifferent health, enjoyed his journey in the late afternoon from Krovolin to Melina. He sat beside Prince Odalchini on the back seat of a large Daimler, with Count Casimir opposite him. There were police cars in front and behind, and a jingling escort of National Guards who made their progress slow. The movement, the mellow air, the rich and sunlit champaign raised his spirits and dispelled his nervousness. His roving eye scanned the landscape and noted with pleasure the expectant villagers and the cheering group of countrymen. On the outskirts of the capital a second troop of Guards awaited them, and as they entered by the ancient River Port there was a salute of guns from the citadel and every bell in every steeple broke into music. It had been arranged, in deference to His Royal Highness' frailty, that there should be no municipal reception, but the streets were thronged with vociferous citizens and the click of cameras was like the rattle of machine-guns.

The cars swung through what looked like a Roman triumphal arch into a great courtyard, on three sides of which rose the huge baroque Palace. At this point Dickson's impressions became a little confused. He was aware that troops lined the courtyard – he heard a word of command and saw rifles presented at the salute. He was conscious of being tenderly assisted from his car, and conducted between bowing servants through a high doorway and across endless marble pavements. Then came a shallow staircase, and a corridor lined with tall portraits. He came to anchor at last in what seemed to be a bedroom, though it was as big as a church. The evening was warm, but there were fires lit in two fireplaces. As he got out of his greatcoat he realised that he was alone with Prince Odalchini and Count Casimir, each of whom helped himself to a stiff whisky and soda from a side table.

'Thank Heaven that is over,' cried the latter. 'Well over, too. Your Royal Highness will keep your chamber tonight, and you will be valeted by my own man. Do not utter one word, and for God's sake try to look as frail as possible. You are a sick man, you understand, which is the reason for this privacy. Tomorrow you will have to show yourself from one of the balconies to the people of Melina. Tomorrow, too, I hope that your own equerry will arrive. It is better that you should be alone tonight. You realise, I think, how delicate the position is? Silence and great bodily weakness – these are your trump cards. It may be a little lonely for you, but that is inevitable.'

Dickson looked round the immense room, which was hung with tapestries depicting the doings in battle of the sixteenth-century King John of Evallonia. From the windows there was a wide view over the glades of the park with a shining river at the end. The two fires burned brightly, and on a bed like a field he observed his humble pyjamas. His spirits were high.

'Ugh,' he said, 'I'll do fine. This is a cheery place. I'll not utter a cheep, and I'll behave as if I was a hundred years old. I hope they'll send me up a good dinner, for I'm mortal hungry.'

Dickson spent a strange but not unpleasant evening. Count Casimir's valet proved to be an elderly Frenchman whose reverence for royalty was such that he kept his eyes downcast and uttered no word except '*Altesse*', and that in a tone of profound humility. Dickson was conducted to an adjoining bathroom, where he bathed in pale-blue scented water. In the bathroom he nearly drowned himself by turning on all the taps at once, but he enjoyed himself hugely splashing the water about and watching it running in marble grooves to an exit. After that he was enveloped in a wonderful silk dressing-gown, which hid the humbleness of his pyjamas – pyjamas from which he observed that the name-tag had been removed.

The dinner served in his bedroom was all that his heart would wish, and its only blemish was that, from a choice of wines offered him, he selected a Tokay which tasted unpleasantly like a medicine of his boyhood, so that he was forced to relapse upon a whisky and soda. 'Even in a palace life may be lived well,' he quoted to himself from a favourite poet. After dinner he was put to bed between sheets as fine as satin, and left with a reading lamp on his beside table surrounded by a selection of fruit and biscuits. He turned out the lamp, and lay for some time watching the glow of the fire and the amber twilight in the uncurtained windows. Outside he could hear the tramp of the sentries and far off the rumour of crowded streets. At first he was too excited to be drowsy, for the strangeness of his position came over him in gusts, and his chuckles were mingled with an unpleasant trepidation. 'You'll need to say your prayers, Dickson my man,' he told himself, 'for you're in for a desperate business. It's the kind of thing you read about in books.' But the long day had wearied him, and he had dined abundantly, so before long he fell asleep.

He woke to a bright morning and a sense of extreme bodily well-being. He drank his tea avidly; he ran off the hot bath which had been prepared for him, and had a cold one instead. He took ten minutes instead of five over his exercises, and two instead of five over his prayers. He put on his best blue suit – he was thankful he had brought it from Rosensee – and a white shirt and a sober tie, for he felt that this was no occasion for flamboyance in dress. From all his garments he noted with interest that the marks of identification had been removed. As he examined his face in the glass he decided that he did not look the age of the Archduke and that he was far too healthily coloured for a sick man, so he rubbed some of the powder which Count Casimir had given him over his cheeks and well into his thinning hair. The result rather scared him, for he now looked a cross between a consumptive and a badly made-up actor. At breakfast he was compelled to exercise self-denial. He could have eaten anything provided, but he dared not repeat his performance at dinner the night before, so he contented himself with three cups of coffee, a peach, and the contents of the toast rack. The servants who cleared away saw an old man resting on a couch with closed eyes, the very image of a valetudinarian.

After that time hung heavy on his hands. It was a fine morning and he felt that he could walk twenty miles. The sound of the bustle of an awaking city, and the view from the windows of miles of sunburnt grass and boats on the distant river, made him profoundly restless. His great bedroom was furnished like a room in a public building, handsomely but dully; there was nothing in it to interest him, and the only book he had brought was Sir Thomas Browne, an author for whom at the moment he did not feel inclined. Urn-burial and a doctor's religion were clean out of the picture. A sheaf of morning papers had been provided, but he could not read them, though he observed with interest the pictures of his entry into Melina. He prowled about miserably, taking exercise as a man does in the confined space of a ship's deck.

Then it occurred to him that he might extend his walk and do a little exploration. He cautiously opened the door and looked into a deserted corridor. The place was as empty and as silent as a tomb, so there could be no risk in venturing a little way down it. He tried one or two doors which were locked. One opened into a vast chamber where the furniture was all in dust sheets. Then he came to a circular gallery around a subsidiary staircase, and he was just considering whether he might venture down it when he heard voices and the sound of footsteps on the marble. He skipped back the road he had come, and for an awful minute was uncertain of his room. One door which he tried refused to open, and the voices were coming nearer. Happily the next door on which he hurled himself was the right one, and he dropped panting into an armchair.

This adventure shook him out of all his morning placidity. 'I won't be able to stand this place very long,' he reflected. 'I can't behave like a cripple, when I'm fair bursting with health. It's worse than being in jyle.' And then an uglier thought came to him. 'I've got in here easy enough, but how on earth am I going to get out? I must abdicate, and that's simple, but what's to become of me after that? How can I disappear, when there will be about a million folk wanting a sight of me?'

He spent a dismal forenoon. He longed for some familiar face, even Peter Wappit, who had been sent back to Tarta. He longed especially for Jaikie, and he indulged in some melancholy speculations as to that unfortunate's fate. 'He had to face the daft Countess,' he thought, 'and Jaikie was always terribly nervous with women.' Then he began to be exasperated with Count Casimir and Prince Odalchini, who had left him in this anxious solitude. And Prince John. It was for Prince John's sake that he had come here, and unless he presently got some enlightenment he would go out and look for it.

He was slightly pacified by the arrival of both the Count and Prince Odalchini about midday, for both were in high spirits. Luncheon was served to the three in his bedroom, a light meal at which no servants were present and they waited on themselves. They had news of high importance for him. Prince John was with Juventus – had been accepted with acclamation by Juventus and not least by the Countess Araminta. Juventus was in a friendly mood and appeared willing to accept the overtures of the Monarchists, who had already informed it that the Archduke would not resist what was plainly the desire of the people, but would relinquish all claims to the throne. 'We must prepare your abdication,' said Count Casimir. 'It should be in the papers tomorrow, or the day after at the latest. For the day after tomorrow Juventus will reach Melina.'

'Thank God for that,' said Dickson. 'I'll abdicate like a shot, but what I want to know is, how I'm going to get away. I must be off long before they arrive, for yon Countess will be wanting my blood.'

'I hope not,' said the Count. 'Juventus will have too much on its hands to trouble about a harmless old gentleman.'

'I'm not worrying about Juventus,' said Dickson gloomily. 'It's the woman I'm thinking about, and from all I've heard I wouldn't put it past her.'

'One of your difficulties will be the Press,' Prince Odalchini said. 'Correspondents are arriving here from all quarters of Europe – mostly by the air, since the frontiers are closed.'

'Here! This is awful,' cried the alarmed Dickson. 'I know the breed, and they'll be inside this place and interviewing me, and where will we all be then?'

'I think not. You are well guarded. But there's one man I'm uncertain about. He flew here this morning from Vienna, and I don't quite know what to do about him. He's not a correspondent, you see, but the representative of the English Press group that has always been our chief ally.'

'What's his name?' Dickson asked with a sudden hope.

The Prince drew a card from his pocket.

'Crombie,' he read. 'The right-hand man of the great Craw. I haven't seen him, but he has written to me. I felt that I was bound to treat him with some consideration, so he is coming here at three o'clock.'

'You'll bring him to me at once,' said Dickson joyfully. 'Man, you know him – you saw him in the Canonry – a lad with a red head and a dour face. It's my old friend Dougal, and you can trust him to the other side of Tophet. You'll bring him straight up, and you'll never let on it's me. He'll get the surprise of his life.'

Mr McCunn was not disappointed. Dougal at three o'clock was duly ushered into the room by Count Casimir. 'Your Royal Highness, I have to present Mr Crombie of the Craw Press,' he said, and bowed himself out.

Dougal made an awkward obeisance and advanced three steps. Then he stopped in his tracks and gaped.

'It's you!' he stammered.

'Ay, it's me,' said Dickson cheerfully. 'You didn't know what you were doing when you whippit me out of Rosensee and sent me on my travels. This was my own notion, and I'm sort of proud of it. I got it by minding what happened when Jimmy Turnbull was running for Lord Provost of Glasgow, and his backers put up David Duthie so that the other and stronger lot could run Jimmy. You'll mind that?'

'I mind it,' said Dougal hoarsely, sinking into a chair.

'And by the mercy of Providence it turned out that I was the living image of the old Archduke. It has answered fine. Here I am as His Royal Highness, the brother of his late Majesty, and Juventus has gone daft about Prince John, and I'm about to abdicate, and in two – three days Prince John will be King of Evallonia and not a dog will bark. I think I've done well by that young man.'

'Ay, maybe you have,' said Dougal grimly. 'But the question is, what is to become of you? This is not the Glasgow Town Council, and Evallonia is not Scotland. How are you going to get out of this?'

'Fine,' Dickson replied, but less confidently, for Dougal's solemn face disquieted him. 'There's not a soul knows about it, except two or three whose interest it is to keep quiet. When I've abdicated I'll just slip cannily away, and be over the border before Juventus gets here.'

'You think that will be easy? I only arrived this morning, but I've seen enough to know that the whole of Melina is sitting round the palace like hens round a baikie. They're for you and they're for Prince John, and they want to see the two of you make it up. And half the papers in Europe have sent their correspondents here, and I know too much about my own trade to take that lightly. To get you safely out of the country will be a heavy job, I can tell you.'

'I'll trust my luck,' said Dickson stoutly, but his eyes were a little anxious. 'Thank God you're here, Dougal.'

'Yes, thank God I'm here. The trouble with you is you're too brave. You don't stop to think of risks. Suppose you're found out. Juventus is a big thing, a bigger thing than the world knows, but it's desperate serious, and it won't understand pranks. Won't understand, and won't forgive. At present it's inclined to be friendly with the Monarchists, and use them, for it badly needs them. But if it had a suspicion of this game, Count Casimir and Prince Odalchini and the rest would be in the dock for high treason. And yourself! Well, I'm not sure what would happen to you, but it wouldn't be pleasant.'

'You're a Job's comforter, Dougal. Anyway, it's a great thing to have you here. I wish I had Jaikie too. You'll come and bide here, for I'll want you near me?'

'Yes, I'd better move in. I'll see the Count about it at once. Some of us will have to do some pretty solid thinking in the next twenty-four hours.'

Dougal found Count Casimir in a good humour, for he had further news from Krovolin. It appeared that Juventus not only forgave the putting forward of the Archduke, but applauded it as a chance of making the monarchical restoration impressive by enlisting both the surviving males of the royal house. The Countess Araminta was especially enthusiastic, and an elaborate programme had been drawn up – first the meeting of Prince John and his uncle – then the presentation to Melina of the young man by the old – and last, the ceremonial functioning of the Archduke at the Coronation.

'The wheel has come full circle,' said the Count. 'Now all the land is royalist. But it is the more incumbent upon us to proceed with caution, for a slip now would mean a dreadful fall. We must get our friend away very soon.'

At this conference a third person was present – Randal Glynde, so very point-device that his own employees would scarcely have recognised in him the scarecrow of the Cirque Doré. His hair and beard were trimly barbered, the latter having been given a naval cut, and his morning suit was as exquisite a thing as the clothes he had worn at the Lamanchas' party. 'I am His Royal Highness' chief equerry,' he told Dougal, 'just arrived from France. The news will be in the evening papers. Since I speak Evallonian I can make life a little easier for him.'

Dougal had listened gloomily to Count Casimir's exposition of the spectacular duties which Juventus proposed for the Archduke.

'You haven't told Mr McCunn that?' he demanded anxiously, and was informed that the Count had only just heard it himself.

'Well, you mustn't breathe a word of it to him. Not on your life. He's an extraordinary man, and though I've studied him for years, I haven't got near the bottom of him. He's what you might call a desperate character. What other man would have taken on a job like this – for fun? For fun, remember. He has always been like that. He thinks it was his promise to Prince John, but that was only a small bit of it. The big thing for him was that he was living up to a notion he has of himself, and that notion won't let him shirk anything, however daft, if it appeals to his imagination. He's the eternal adventurer, the only one I've ever met – the kind of fellow Ulysses must have been – the heart of a boy and the head of an old serpent. I've been trying to solemnise him by telling him what a needle point he's standing on – how hard it will be for him to get away, and what a devil's own mess there'll be if he doesn't. He was impressed, and a little bit frightened – I could see that – but in a queer way he was pleased too. He'll go into it with a white face and his knees trembling, but he'll go through with it, and by the mercy of God he'll get away with it. But just let him know what Juventus proposes and he won't budge one step. The idea of a Coronation and his carrying the Sacred Lamp and all the rest of it would fair go to his head. He would be determined to have a shot at it and trust to luck to carry him through. Oh, I know it's sheer mania, but that's Mr McCunn, and when he sticks his hoofs into the ground traction engines wouldn't shift him... You've got that clear? I want you to arrange for me to move in here, for I ought to be near him.'

Count Casimir bowed. 'I accept your reading of him,' he said, 'and I shall act on it.' Then he added, rather to Randal than to Dougal, 'I believe he was originally a Glasgow grocer. The provision trade in Scotland must be a remarkable profession.'

Dickson had on the whole a pleasant evening. In the first place he had Mr Glynde, an exquisite velvet-footed attendant, whose presence made other servants needless except for the mere business of fetching and carrying. Then he enjoyed the business of writing his abdication. The draft was prepared by Count Casimir, but he took pains to amend the style, assisted by Randal, in whom he discovered a literary connoisseur of a high order. I am afraid that the resulting document was a rather precious composition, full of Stevensonian cadences and with more than a hint of the prophet Isaiah. Happily Count Casimir was there to turn it into robust Evallonian prose.

Dickson and Randal dined alone together, and the former heard with excitement of the doings in the Street of the White Peacock. The peril of Alison and the Roylances, not to speak of Jaikie, made him catch his breath, and the manner of Mastrovin's end gave him deep satisfaction.

'I'm glad yon one is out of the world,' he said. 'He was a cankered body. It was your shot that did it? What does it feel like to kill a man?'

'In Mastrovin's case rather like breaking the back of a stoat that is after your chickens. Have you ever been the death of anyone, Mr McCunn?'

'I once had a try,' said Dickson modestly. Then his thoughts fastened on Jaikie.

'You tell me he's safe and well? And he gets on fine with the Countess?'

'He promises to be her white-headed boy. She is a lady of violent likes and dislikes, and she seems to have fallen completely for Master Jaikie. Prince John, of course, is deep in his debt. I think that if he wants it he might have considerable purchase at the new Court of Evallonia.'

'Do you say so? That would be a queer profession for a laddie that came out of the Gorbals. There's another thing.' Dickson hesitated. 'I think Jaikie is terrible fond of Miss Alison.'

Randal smiled. 'I believe that affair is going well. Last night, I fancy, clinched it. They clung together like two lovers.'

Dickson's eyes became misty.

'Well – well. It's a grand thing to be young. That reminds me of something where I want you to help me, Mr Glynde. My will was made years ago, and is deposited with Paton and Linklater in Glasgow. I haven't forgot Jaikie, but I think I must make further and better provision for him, as the lawyers say. I've prepared a codicil, and I want it signed and witnessed the morn. I've determined that Jaikie shall be well-tochered, and if Miss Alison has the beauty and the blood he at any rate will have the siller. No man knows what'll happen to me in the next day or two, and I'd be easier in my mind if I got this settled.'

'Tomorrow you must stay in bed,' said Randal, as he said good night. 'You must profess to be exceedingly unwell.'

Dickson grinned. 'And me feeling like a he-goat on the mountains!'

III

Next day an unwilling Dickson kept his bed. He had the codicil of his will signed and witnessed, which gave him some satisfaction. Randal translated for him the comments of the Evallonian Press on his abdication, and he was gratified to learn that he had behaved with a royal dignity and the self-abnegation of a patriot. But after that he grew more restless with every hour.

'What for am I lying here?' he asked repeatedly. 'I should be up and off or I'll be grippit.'

'Juventus works to a schedule,' Randal explained, 'and its formal entry into Melina is timed for tomorrow. The Press announces today that you are seriously indisposed, and therefore you cannot appear in public before the people, which is what Melina is clamouring for. News of your being confined to bed this morning has already been issued, and a bulletin about your health will be published at midday. You appreciate the position, Mr McCunn?'

'Fine,' said Dickson.

'It is altogether necessary that you get away in good time, but it is also necessary that you have a good reason for your going – an excuse for Melina, and especially for Juventus. They are not people whose plans can be lightly disregarded. If there is to be peace in Evallonia, Count Casimir and his friends must be in favour with Juventus, and that will not happen if we begin by offending it. We must get a belief in your critical state of health firm in the minds of the people, and our excuse for your going must be that any further excitement would endanger your life. So we must move carefully and not too fast. Our plan is to get you out of here tonight very secretly, and the fact that you did not leave till the question of your health became urgent will, we hope, convince Juventus of our good intentions.'

'That's maybe right enough,' said Dickson doubtfully, 'but it's a poor job for me. I have to lie here on my back, and I've nothing to read except Sir Thomas Browne, and I can't keep my mind on him. I'm getting as nervous as a peesweep.'

Luncheon saw an anxious company round his bed, Prince Odalchini, Count Casimir, Dougal and Mr Glynde. They had ominous news. The advanced troops of Juventus had arrived, a picked body who had been instructed to take over the duty of palace guards. They had accordingly replaced the detachment of National Guards, which had been sent to occupy the approaches to the city. There had been no difficulty about the transference, but it appeared that there was going to be extreme difficulty with the palace's new defenders. For these Juventus shock troops had strict orders, and a strict notion of fulfilling them. No movement out of the city was permitted for the next twenty-four hours. No movement out of the Palace was permitted for the same period. Count Casimir had interviewed the officer commanding and had found him respectful but rigid. If any member of the Archduke's entourage wished to leave it would be necessary to get permission by telephone from headquarters at Krovolin.

'I do not think that Juventus is suspicious,' said the Count. 'It is only its way of doing business. It has youth's passion for meticulous detail.'

'That puts the lid on it for us,' said Dougal. 'We can't ask permission for Mr McCunn to leave, for Juventus would be here in no time making inquiries for itself. And it will be an awful business to smuggle him out. I can tell you these lads know their work. They have sentries at every approach, and they are patrolling every yard of the back parts and the park side. Besides, once he was out of here, what better would he be? He would have still to get out of the city, and the whole countryside between here and Tarta is policed by Juventus. They are taking no chances.'

There were poor appetites at luncheon. Five reasonably intelligent men sat in a stupor of impotence, repeating wearily the essentials of a problem which they could not solve. They must get Dickson away within not more than twenty hours, and they must get him off in such a manner that they would have a convincing story to tell Juventus. Dickson sat up in his bed in extreme discomposure, Dougal had his head in his hands, Count Casimir strode up and down the room, and even Randal Glynde seemed shaken out of his customary insouciance. Prince Odalchini had left them on some errand of his own.

The last-named returned about three o'clock with a tragic face.

'I have just had a cipher telegram,' he said. 'I have my own means of getting them through. The Archduke Hadrian died this morning at eleven o'clock. His death will not be announced till I give the word, but the announcement cannot be delayed more than two days – three at the most. Therefore we must act at once. There is not an hour to waste.'

'There is not an hour to waste,' Casimir cried, 'but we are an eternity off having any plan.'

'I'm dead,' said Dickson. 'At least the man I'm pretending to be is dead. Well, I'll maybe soon be dead myself.' His tone was almost cheerful, as if the masterful comedy of events had obliterated his own cares.

'There is nothing to do but to risk it,' said Prince Odalchini. 'We must go on with our plan for tonight, and pray that Juventus may be obtuse. The odds I admit are about a thousand to one.'

'And on these crazy odds depends the fate of a nation,' said Casimir bitterly.

To this miserable conclave entered Jaikie – Jaikie, trim, brisk and purposeful. He wore the uniform of a Juventus staff officer, and on his right arm was the Headquarters brassard. To Dickson's anxious eyes he was a different being from the shabby youth he had last seen at Tarta. This new Jaikie was a powerful creature, vigorous and confident, the master, not the plaything, of Fate. He remembered too that this was Alison's accepted lover. At the sight of him all his fears vanished.

'Man Jaikie, but I'm glad to see you,' he cried. 'You've just come in time to put us right.'

'I hope so,' was the answer. 'Anyway, I've come to represent Juventus Headquarters here till they take over tomorrow.'

He looked round the company, and his inquiring eye induced Casimir to repeat his mournful tale. Jaikie listened with a puckered brow.

'It's going to be a near thing,' he said at last. 'And we must take some risks... Still, I believe it can be done. Listen. I've brought a Headquarters car with the Headquarters flag on the bonnet. Also I have a pass which enables me and the car and anyone I send in the car to go anywhere in Evallonia. I insisted on that, for I expected that there might be some trouble. That is our trump card. I can send Mr McCunn off in it, and that will give us a story for Juventus tomorrow... But on the other hand there is nothing to prevent the Juventus sentries from looking inside, and if they see Mr McCunn – well, his face is unfortunately too well known from their infernal papers, and they have their orders, and they're certain to insist on telephoning to Krovolin for directions, and that would put the fat in the fire. We must get them into a frame of mind when they won't want to look too closely. Let me think.'

'Ay, Jaikie, think,' said Dickson, almost jovially. 'It must never be said that a Gorbals Die-hard was beat by a small thing like that.'

After a little Jaikie raised his head.

'This is the best I can do. Mr McCunn must show himself to Melina. In spite of his feebleness and the announcement in the Press today, he must make an effort to have one look at his affectionate people. Ring up the newspaper offices, and get it into the stop press of the evening papers that at seven o'clock the Archduke will appear on the palace balcony. You've got that? Then at a quarter past seven my car must be ready to start. You must go with it, Prince. Have you a man of your own that you can trust to drive, for I daren't risk the Juventus chauffeur.'

Prince Odalchini nodded. 'I have such a man.'

'What I hope for is this,' Jaikie went on. 'The Juventus guards, having seen the Archduke on the balcony a few minutes before, and having observed a tottering old man who has just risen from a sickbed, won't expect him to be in the car. I'll have a word with their commandant and explain that you are taking two of your servants to Tarta, and that you have my permission, as representing the Headquarters staff.'

He stopped.

'But there is a risk, all the same. If they catch a glimpse of Mr McCunn they will insist on ringing up Krovolin. I know what conscientious beggars they are, and I'm only a staff officer, not their commander. Couldn't we do something to distract their attention at the critical moment?' He looked towards Randal with a sudden inspiration.

Mr Glynde smiled.

'I think I can manage that,' he said. 'If I may be excused, I will go off and see about it.'

As the hour of seven chimed from the three and thirty towers of Melina, there was an unusual bustle in the great front courtyard of the Palace. The evening papers had done their work, rumour with swift foot had sped through the city, and the Juventus sentries had permitted the entrance of a crowd which the Press next day estimated as not less than twenty thousand. On the balcony above the main portico, flanked by a row of palace officials, stood a little group of men. Some wore the uniform of the old Evallonian Court, and Jaikie alone had the Juventus green. They made a passage, in which appeared Count Casimir and Prince Odalchini, both showing the famous riband and star of the White Falcon. Between them they supported a frail figure which wore a purple velvet dressing-gown and a skull-cap, so that it looked like some very ancient Prince of the Church. It was an old man, with a deathly white face, who blinked his eyes wearily, smiled wanly, and bowed as with a great effort to the cheering crowds. There was a dignity in him which impressed the most heedless, the dignity of an earlier age, and an extreme fragility which caught at the heart. The guards saluted, every hat was raised, but there was some constraint in the plaudits. The citizens of Melina felt that they were in the presence of one who had but a slender hold on life.

Dickson was stirred to his depths. The sea of upturned faces moved him strangely, for he had never before stood on a pinnacle above his fellow men. He did not need to act his part, for in that moment he felt himself the authentic Archduke, an exile returning only to die. He was wearing a dead man's shoes. Next day the papers were to comment upon the pathetic spectacle of this old man bidding *Ave atque vale* to the people he loved.

The car was waiting in a small inner courtyard. It was a big limousine with the blinds drawn on one side, so that the interior was but dimly seen. Dickson entered and sat himself in the duskiest corner, wearing the military overcoat in which he had arrived, with the collar turned up and a thick muffler. Dougal took the seat by the driver. The car moved through the inner

way and came into the outer court, which was the private
ance to the Palace. At the other end the court opened into
famous thoroughfare known as the Avenue of the Kings, and
e stood the Juventus sentries.

he Headquarters flag fluttered at the car's bonnet, and
ce Odalchini's hand through the open window displayed the
liar green and white Headquarters pass. The sentries saluted,
their officer, whom Jaikie had already interviewed, nodded
took a step towards the car. It may have been his intention
to examine the interior, but that will never be known, for his
activities were suddenly compelled to take a different form.

In the Avenue was a great crowd streaming away from the
ceremony in the main palace courtyard. The place was broad
enough for thousands, and the sounding of the car's horn had
halted the press and made a means of egress. But coming from
the opposite direction was a circus procession, which, keeping its
proper side of the road, had got very close to the palace wall. It
had heard the horn of the car and would have stopped, but for
the extraordinary behaviour of an elephant. The driver of the
animal, a ridiculous figure of a man in flapping nankeen trousers,
an old tunic of horizon blue and a scarlet cummerbund,
apparently tried to check it, but at the very moment that the car
was about to pass the gate it backed into the archway, scattering
the Juventus guards.

There was just room for the car to slip through, and, as it
swung into the avenue, Dickson, through a crack in the blind,
saw with delight that his retreat was securely covered by the
immense rump of Aurunculeia.

IV

The last guns of the royal salute had fired, and the cheering of
the crowds had become like the murmur of a distant
groundswell. The entrance hall of the Palace was lined with the
tall Juventus guards, and up the alley between them came the

new King-designate of Evallonia. There was now nothing of McTavish and less of Newsom about Prince John. The Juventus uniform well became his stalwart figure, and he was no more the wandering royalty who for some years had been the sport of fortune, but a man who had found again his land and his people. Yet in all the group, in the Prince and his staff and in the wing commanders, there was a touch of hesitation, almost of shyness, like schoolboys who had been catapulted suddenly into an embarrassing glory. The progress from Krovolin to Melina had been one long blaze of triumph, for again and again the lines of the escort had been broken by men and women who kissed the Prince's stirrup, and it had rained garlands of flowers. The welcome of Melina had been more ceremonial, but not less rapturous, and they had listened to that roar of many thousands, which, whether it be meant in love or in hate, must make the heart stand still. All the group, even the Countess Araminta, had eyes unnaturally bright and faces a little pale.

At the foot of the grand staircase stood Count Casimir and Jaikie. Ashie translated for the latter the speeches that followed. The Count dropped on his knee.

'Sire,' he said, 'as the Chamberlain of the king your father I welcome you home.'

Prince John raised him and embraced him.

'But where,' he asked, 'is my beloved uncle? I had hoped to be welcomed by him above all others.' His eye caught Jaikie's for a moment, and what the latter read in it was profound relief.

'Alas, Sire,' said the Count, 'His Royal Highness' health has failed him. Being an old man, the excitement of the last days was too much for him. A little more and your Majesty's joyful restoration would have been clouded by tragedy. The one hope was that he should leave at once for the peace of his home. He crossed the frontier last night, and will complete his journey to France by air. He left with profound unwillingness, and he charged me to convey to Your Majesty his sorrow that his age and the frailty of his body should have prevented him from offering you in person his assurances of eternal loyalty and affection.'

The Countess' face had lost its pallor. Once again she was the Blood-red Rook, and it was on Jaikie that her eyes fell, eyes questioning, commanding, suspicious. It was to her rather than to Prince John that he spoke, having imitated the Count and clumsily dropped on one knee.

'I was faithful to your instructions, Sire,' he said, 'but a higher Power has made them impossible. I was assured that you would not wish this happy occasion to be saddened by your kinsman's death.'

He saw the Countess' lips compressed as if she checked with difficulty some impetuous speech. 'True public school,' thought Jaikie. 'She would like to make a scene, but she won't.'

Prince John saw it too, and his manner dropped from the high ceremonial to the familiar.

'You have done right,' he said aloud in English. 'Man proposeth and God disposeth. Dear Uncle Hadrian – Heaven bless him wherever he is! And now, my lord Chamberlain, I hope you can give us something to eat.'

ENVOI

Down in the deep-cut glen it had been almost dark, for the wooded hills rose steeply above the track. But when the horses had struggled up the last stony patch of moraine and reached the open uplands the riders found a clear amber twilight. And when they had passed the cleft called the Wolf's Throat, they saw a great prospect to the west of forest and mountain with the sun setting between two peaks, a landscape still alight with delicate, fading colours. Overhead the evening star twinkled in a sky of palest amethyst. Involuntarily they halted.

Alison pointed to lights a mile down the farther slope.

'There are the cars with the baggage,' she said, 'and the grooms to take the horses back. We can get to our inn in an hour. You are safe, Dickson, for we are across the frontier. Let's stop here for supper, and have our last look at Evallonia.'

Mr McCunn descended heavily from his horse.

'Ay, I'm safe,' he said. 'And tomorrow there will be a telegram from France saying I'm dead. Well, that's the end of an auld song.' He kicked vigorously to ease his cramped legs, and while Dougal and Sir Archie took the food from the saddlebags and the two women spread a tablecloth on a flat rock, he looked down the ravine to the dim purple hollow which was the country they had left.

Jaikie's last word to Dougal at Melina had been an injunction to make the end crown the work. 'Be sure and have a proper finish,' he had told him. 'You know what he is. Let him think he's in desperate danger till he's over the border. He would break his heart if he thought that he was out of the game too soon.' So Dougal had been insistent with Prince Odalchini. 'You owe Mr McCunn more than you can ever repay, and it isn't much that I ask. He must believe that Juventus is after him to bring him back. Get him off tonight, and keep up the pretence that it's deadly secret. Horses – that's the thing that will please his romantic soul.'

So Dickson had all day been secluded in the House of the Four Winds, his meals had been brought him by Dougal, and Peter Wappit had stood sentry outside his chamber door. As the afternoon wore on his earlier composure had been shot with restlessness, and he watched the sun decline with an anxious eye. But his spirits had recovered when he found himself hoisted upon an aged mare of Prince Odalchini's, which was warranted quiet, and saw the others hooted and spurred. He had felt himself living a moment of high drama, and to be embraced and kissed on both cheeks by Prince Odalchini had seemed the right kind of farewell. The ride through secluded forest paths had been unpleasant, for he had only once been on a horse in his life before, and Archie bustled them along to keep up the illusion of a perilous flight. Dougal, no horseman himself, could do nothing to help him, but Alison rode by his side, and now and again led his beast when he found it necessary to cling with both hands to the saddle.

But once they were in the mountain cleft comfort had returned, for now the pace was easy and he had leisure for his thoughts. He realised that for days he had been living with fear. 'You're not a brave man,' he told himself. 'The thing about you is that you're too much of a coward to admit that you're afraid. You let yourself in for daft things because your imagination carries you away, and then for weeks on end your knees knock together... But it's worth it – you know it's worth it, you old epicurean,' he added, 'for the sake of the relief when it's over.' He realised that he was about to enjoy the peace of soul which he had known long ago at Huntingtower on the morning after the fight.

But this time there was more than peace. He cast an eye over his shoulder down the wooded gorge – all was quiet – he had escaped from his pursuers. The great adventure had succeeded. Far ahead beyond the tree-tops he saw the cleft of the Wolf's Throat sharp against the sunset. In half an hour the frontier would be passed. His spirit was exalted. He remembered something he had read – in Stevenson, he thought – where a sedentary man had been ravished by a dream of galloping through a midnight pass at the head of cavalry with a burning valley behind him. Well, he was a sedentary man, and he was not dreaming an adventure, but in the heart of one. Never had his wildest fancies envisaged anything like this. He had been a king, acclaimed by shouting mobs. He had kept a throne warm for a friend, and now he was vanishing into the darkness, an honourable fugitive, a willing exile. He was the first grocer in all history that had been a Pretender to a Crown. The clack of hooves on stone, the jingling of bits, the echo of falling water were like strong wine. He did not sing aloud, for he was afraid of alarming his horse, but he crooned to himself snatches of spirited songs. 'March, march, Ettrick and Teviotdale' was one, and 'Jock o' Hazeldean' was another.

Even on that hilltop the summer night was mild, and the fern was warm, baked by long hours of sun. The little company felt the spell of the mountain quiet after a week of alarums, and ate their supper in silence. Dickson munched a sandwich with his face turned east. He was the first to speak.

'Jaikie's down there,' he said. 'I wonder what will become of Jaikie? He's a quiet laddie, but he's the dour one when he's made up his mind. Then he's like a stone loosed from a catapult. But I've no fear for Jaikie now he has you to look after him.' He turned to beam upon Alison and stroked her arm.

'He doesn't know what to do,' said the girl. 'We talked a lot about it in the summer. He went on a walking tour to think things out and discover what he wanted most.'

'Well, he has found that out,' said Dickson genially. 'It's you, Miss Alison. Jaikie's my bairn, and now I've got another in yourself. I'm proud of my family. Dougal there is already a force for mischief in Europe.'

Dougal grinned. 'I wonder what Mr Craw will say about all this. He'll be over the moon about it, and he'll think that he and his papers are chiefly responsible. Humbug! There are whiles when I'm sick of my job. They talk about the power of the Press, and it is powerful enough in ordinary times. The same with big finance. But let a thing like Juventus come along, and the Press and the stock exchange are no more than penny whistles. It's the Idea that wins every time – the Idea with brains and guts behind it.'

'Youth,' said Janet. 'Yes, youth is the force in the world today, for it isn't tired and it can hope. But you have forgotten Mr McCunn. He made the success of Juventus possible, for he found it its leader. It's a pity the story can't be told, for he deserves a statue in Melina as the Great Peacemaker.'

'It's the same thing,' said Dougal. 'He's youth.'

'In two months' time I'll be sixty-three,' said Dickson.

'What does that matter? I tell you you're young. Compared to you Jaikie and I are old, done men. And you're the most formidable kind of youth, for you've humour, and that's what youth never has. Jaikie has a little maybe, but nothing to you, and I haven't a scrap myself. I'll be a bigger man than Craw ever was, for I haven't his failings. And Jaikie will be a big man, too, though I'm not just sure in what way. But though I become a multimillionaire and Jaikie a prime minister, we will neither of us ever be half the man that Mr McCunn is. It was a blessed day for me when I first fell in with him.'

'Deary me,' said Dickson. 'That's a grand testimonial, but I don't deserve it. I have a fair business mind, and I try to apply it

– that's all. It was the Gorbals Die-hards that made me. Eight years ago I retired from the shop, and I was a timid elderly body. The Die-hards learned me not to be afraid.'

'You don't know what fear is,' said Dougal.

'And they made me feel young again.'

'You could never be anything but young.'

'You're wrong. I'm both timid and old – the best you can say of me is that, though I'm afraid, I'm never black afraid, and though I'm old, I'm not dead old.'

'That's the best that could be said about any mortal man,' said Archie solemnly. 'What are you going to do now? After this game of king-making, won't Carrick be a bit dull?'

'I'm going back to Blaweary,' said Dickson, 'to count my mercies, for I'm a well man again. I'm going to catch a wheen salmon, and potter about my bits of fields, and read my books, and sit by my fireside. And to the last day of my life I'll be happy, thinking of the grand things I've seen and the grand places I've been in. Ay, and the grand friends I've known – the best of all.'

'I think you are chiefly a poet,' said Alison.

Dickson did not reply for a moment. He looked at her tenderly and seemed to be pondering a new truth.

'Me!' he said. 'I wish I was, but I could never string two verses together.'

233

John Buchan

The Courts of the Morning

South America is the setting for this adventure from the author of *The Thirty-nine Steps*. When Archie and Janet Roylance decide to travel to the Gran Seco to see its copper mines they find themselves caught up in dreadful danger; rebels have seized the city. Janet is taken hostage in the middle of the night and it is up to the dashing Don Luis de Marzaniga to aid her rescue.

Greenmantle

Sequel to *The Thirty-nine Steps*, this classic adventure is set in war-torn Europe. Richard Hannay, South African mining engineer and hero, is sent on a top-secret mission across German-occupied Europe. The result could alter the outcome of World War I. Other well-known characters make a reappearance here: Sandy, Blenkiron and Peter Pienaar.

John Buchan

Grey Weather

Grey Weather is the first collection of sketches from John Buchan, author of *The Thirty-nine Steps*. The subtitle, *Moorland Tales of My Own People*, sets the theme of these fourteen stories. Shepherds, farmers, herdsmen and poachers are Buchan's subjects and his love for the hills and the lochs shines through.

The Long Traverse

This enchanting adventure tells the story of Donald, a boy spending his summer holidays in the Canadian countryside. John Buchan knew that some Indians were said to have the power of projecting happenings of long ago onto a piece of calm water.

In this tale he chooses Negog, the Native American Indian, as Donald's companion and guide. Negog conjures up a strange mist from a magic fire and brings to life visions from the past. Through these boyish adventures peopled with Vikings, gold prospectors, Indians and Eskimos, Donald learns more about history than school has taught him.

John Buchan

Sick Heart River

Lawyer and MP Sir Edward Leithen is given a year to live. Fearing he will die unfulfilled, he devotes his last months to seeking out and restoring to health Galliard, a young Canadian banker. Galliard is in remotest Canada searching for the River of the Sick Heart. Braving an Arctic winter, Leithen finds the banker. Leithen's health returns, but only one of the men will return to civilization.

The Thirty-nine Steps

John Buchan's most famous and dramatic novel presents spy-catcher Richard Hannay. Hannay is in London when he suddenly finds himself caught up in a dangerous situation and the main suspect for a murder committed in his own flat. He is forced to go on the run to his native Scotland.